TRUTH IS...

MICHELLE MITCHELL

ISBN: 978-1539902072

Manufactured and Printed in the United States of America

Acknowledgements

First, can I take a moment and say look at God! Of all the dreams that I had growing up, who knew but God, that I would one day I'd call myself a published author. Thank You for the opportunity to release this title, Truth is… and thank you in advance for the future titles. Thank you for this craft; use me as you please.

To Jacquelin Thomas, thank you for believing in my work and giving me guidance and encouragement through this process, and providing me with the tools to share my voice with the world. Thank you for challenging me to grow as a writer. You are a never-ending inspiration. I started as a fan of your work, and now I'm so blessed to have you as a mentor and a friend. I'm forever grateful.

To my parents, Lenton and Miriam Mitchell, thank you for my family, my education, the roof you put over my head, and the art of storytelling. I believe my roots and upbringing helped me find that creativity within and it doesn't hurt that my father is artistic too. I share my love of fiction with my mother, and it's exciting to me to know that I'll now be on her bookshelf among the other titles that we've read together. I love you both.

To my sisters, Shaniqua and Elisha, thanks for your support and sisterly love throughout the process. Thank you both for giving me a childhood that was never dull and full of imagination, I also credit my creativity to you. From creating forts to finding an excuse to why we were up when we should have been asleep—you two are everything to me. I love you both.

To my loving fiancé, Albert Goines Jr, thanks for trying to push me out of my comfort zone in every way possible. Thank you for loving me and telling me to write on those nights when I just wanted to talk to you on the phone. We've come a long way, and I'm happy to have you in my life. I love you. Oh, and thanks for sharing me with my laptop.

And to the rest of my loving family, thank you for the continued entertainment and support—my brother-in-law's: Michael Lovejoy and Keith Martin; my nieces and nephews: Tiara Lovejoy, Michael Lovejoy Jr, Israel Waldon, Marc Touissaint, Faith Lovejoy, Destinee Lovejoy, Keith Martin Jr, Keilynn and Kanaan Martin; my godchildren Jada, Jaden, and Shaniya; my aunts and uncles and my long list of cousins, which I fear naming because I have so many that I might miss one—thank you for supporting my dream. Thanks also to my future in-laws: Marilyn Goines (mother-in-law), Albert Goines Sr. (father-in-law and wife Eleanor), Larissa Reed (sister-in-law); and all of my new extended family, thank you for your support and kind words.

To my friends and peers: Erin Whitlock Brown, Trina Mason, Nikyia Bell, Tiffany Wallace North, Shanda DuBose, Melanie Deck, Miki Peterson, Lisa Conley, Dwight Baker, Vernon Davis—thank you for supporting the work, being a listening ear, giving me feedback, being a reader, and most importantly a friend. Thank you for keeping me positive and patience as I waited for this day. You all are amazing!

To LaChelle Weaver, thank you for listening and offering your advice, your feedback, your positivity—and your friendship. I'm so thankful to have met you and have you in my life. You my Sister Scribe are such a phenomenal author and I can't wait to see what you bring next. And thank you for introducing me to the phenomenal, Rebecca Pau.

To Rebecca Pau, thank you for capturing the essence of this Truth Is… and giving it the feel that I need to tell this story. You are amazing at what you do, and I can't wait to work with you again in the future. Thank you for designing this amazing cover.

To the Malachi Bailey and Briana Whitaker, I'm glad I had you both in the beginning stages reviewing my work and providing me with your feedback, and continuing to be there cheering me on.

Thank you to Lasheera Lee, LaShaunda Hoffman at SORMAG, the Literary Guru Yolanda Gore, Michael and Joi in the Morning, Barnes and Noble Cumberland, LaToya Murchison, Jamantha Williams Watson of Urban Image Magazine, Mike Jordan of Lit Atlanta—for providing an outlet for me to share my work with you and your audience. I'm forever grateful.

Thank you to Brown Girls Books for giving me the opportunity to work on The Ex Chronicles and Single Mama Dating Drama, and giving me an extended family through the works we've done together and the times we've spent together. And a huge thank you to The Victorious Ladies Reading Book Club, you all have rallied behind me from the beginning and I'm blessed to have your belief and support in my project. I can't wait to read your collection of stories and the individual projects that you all have in the works. You all are beyond extraordinary.

To Kimberla Lawson Roby, Sistah Souljah, Rhonda McKnight, Eric Jerome Dickey, Omar Tyree, Lolita Files,

Victoria Christopher Murray, Reshonda Tate Billingsley, Carl Weber, Brenda Jackson and there's so many more that I could name but—thank you for showing me 'us' in literature. Thank you for changing the way that I read. Thank you for being game-changers and paving the way for African-American authors.

To all of my coworker friends, current and former, thank you for helping get out the word about my book and promoting amongst your family and friends. Thank you for sharing in this dream and always telling me how proud you are—it means more than you think.

And to all of my Acworth Elementary School, Awtrey Middle School, North Cobb High School, Georgia Southern University alumni, Facebook and Instagram friends, thank you for hyping me up and telling me that you were ready for this moment. As you are reading this, I thank you again for your support and I hope you'll enjoy.

To my Pilgrim Baptist Church family, thank you for harassing me about this project and sticking around to see it come to fruition.

And to you, the person reading this book that I haven't met yet, you are appreciated.

Email: authormichellemitchell@yahoo.com
Facebook: www.facebook.com/AuthorMichelleMitchell
Twitter: https://twitter.com/expbutterflies
Instagram: www.instagram.com/authormichellemitchell

Dedicated to the truth seekers and truth tellers,
my mother and grandmothers

Miriam Mitchell
Liza Mitchell
Lillie Holliman (1937-2006)

Prologue

Ansley stared over at her laptop, wringing her hands together; her curiosity nagging at her. Could everything she ever wanted to know about a guy be right at her finger tips?

She rose from the sofa and walked over to the makeshift office she created in her condo by the window. Lowering herself in the chair, she left clicked on the mouse to bring her purveyor of the truth to life. Or at least she aspired to find some hidden truths.

The cat and mouse game she was playing in her head right now was borderline manic. She wasn't sure if she should research Davis. After all, she wouldn't want him Googling her, but then again she had nothing to hide. And in reality, researching a potential love interest was a given now-a-days when it came to meeting someone new.

As far as Ansley was concerned, Davis had led her down this road of suspicion. Besides, if he wasn't so obscure, she wouldn't have to play catfish detective.

Guilt began to settle in. This wasn't right. Or was it?

"Okay enough back and forth, it's go time," she said aloud. She took a deep breath and keyed in the link for Don't Date Him Girl.com.

Ansley felt a twinge of sadness consume her. This was disappointing to her that dating now required a keen sense of snooping or a thorough background check.

She located the search bar on her screen, and entered

the name Davis Montclair. She was impressed at how thorough the site seemed to be—it was her very own Angela Lansbury.

As she watched the waiting wheel spinning, letting her know that her laptop was searching for information, Ansley got up from her chair and walked over to the refrigerator.

"I don't know why I was planning to do this without wine. Sleuthing deserves at least a glass," she said to herself.

Pouring her merlot to the rim, Ansley took a quick sip and turned back towards her desk. She held her glass as if it was her life source, gripping the stem a little tighter than required. Ansley took another sip, which turned into a gulp. With a slight turn of her body, Ansley reached over and grabbed the wine bottle from the island.

Who knows what was waiting for her on that screen.

Returning to her seat, Ansley took a deep breath before hitting the space key to wake her laptop from its quick siesta. She shuddered inward at the numerous entries awaiting her. She wasn't sure if any or all would share a tale about the man attempting to woo her, but she wasn't leaving this screen until she got some answers.

She scrolled and scrolled until she found one submission that listed Davis Montclair, but as an alias and the frequented cities of Atlanta and Chicago.

This got her attention.

No turning back now, Ansley thought as she clicked on the link.

Her eyes shifted from one horrific line to the next. She didn't want to believe it was him, but once she got to the last section her heart dropped.

There right in front of her, was a photo of Davis Montclair with the woman who claimed he scorned her. She read over the entry again, just as stunned as she was upon reading it the first time.

She was confused and hurt. This man described here was not the man she was getting to know—the man who initially stood a great chance of winning her heart.

As a single tear escaped her, Ansley was left sitting with unanswered questions. She whispered, "Who are you?"

Chapter 1

"Ansley, I'm sorry but we're going to have to let you go," said Robin Barnett, the Editor-in-Chief of New Breed Publishing and the grim reaper of Ansley's livelihood. Sitting in Robin's office, she tried to maintain her composure. Her foot tapped against the plush carpet, unbeknownst to the self-absorbed, narcissist sitting across from her. "You really don't have the…voice... that appeals to our readers."

New Breed Publishing produced Atlanta Urbane, one of the hottest e-magazines in the city, spotlighting young entrepreneurs, entertainers, authors and the Who's who of Atlanta. Ansley was fortunate enough to become a feature writer, getting into the industry straight out of college.

Ansley thought the concept for the e-magazine was edgy and progressive; it was the voice of her generation. Unfortunately, she joined the team during the midst of the Robin era. Quincy Barnett left the company in his daughter's incapable hands while trying to expand the brand to other cities.

In Ansley's opinion, Robin was driving the company into the ground. It would not surprise her if the publication shut down before she made it to the unemployment office. Robin was a wanna-be-fashionista who seriously needed a class on how to dress when coming to work. Her provocative attire always screamed happy hour. Ansley recalled one of Robin's most infamous outfits, a sheer white top with a lacy bra and some barely there shorts. It was not a surprise to anyone though, workplace rules never applied to Robin. She did as she pleased.

"I understand. It's business—not personal, right?" Ansley said, leaning back against in her seat, her stance becoming more defensive by thc minute. She knew Robin was not very fond of her. Not that she would say that to her directly.

Robin took a breath and batted her poorly applied eyelash extensions. "The department is going in another direction, and... if I'm being honest, I don't see how you fit in... I'm just not a fan. Do you have any questions?"

She stood up and shook her head at Robin's curt response. "No, I think I'm all set here."

Robin gave her a fake smile. "Well, take care...oh and if I don't see you, happy New Year."

Ansley sent a sharp glare in Robin's direction before walking out of the office. Just as she got to the doorway, she heard the witch utter, "And that's how it's done."

"Girl, you are brutal. I couldn't work for you," Ansley heard another voice say.

"Umm—excuse me, did you have a third party in our conversation?" Ansley stepped back into the office and toward Robin's desk. Noticing that the phone was on speaker, she stood with her hands planted on her hips as she waited for a response.

"It's very rude to eavesdrop. Besides it's only my girl, Roxy."

"Roxy, as in Roxanne the office gossip in marketing? Wow," Ansley took a calming breath. "You know what? I'm not even gonna let you take me there."

She took the phone off speaker and disconnected the

call.

Robin gasped. "Excuse me…"

"I wish I could …"

Robin lifted her right hand and shooed Ansley out the door.

Robin had been anti-Ansley from the start and it was all because Robin's father, Quincy had been her biggest supporter. He was a visionary and tried to help everyone find that best version of him or herself. After observing her work ethic, he offered to become her mentor. She felt that Robin was jealous early on and knew that she would take the first opportunity to cut her loose.

Ansley reminded herself that her dreams were greater than this company, but with less than a year as an established journalist, she would have to rejoin the large number of nameless writers in the industry unknown—faceless and voiceless.

While Ansley was grateful to have gotten the opportunity, she couldn't stop thinking on how she had sacrificed love for a limited position that did not escalate her career to the height she desired. If she knew then what she was learning now, she would have focused more in the direction of her relationship with Ryan, but she was afraid to put all of herself into that relationship when she still had dreams unfulfilled. Not willing to go all in…at least not the way Ryan described, she let him go. Now she was left with regret, wishing she had him to lean on.

She went to her cubicle, gathered her personal belongings and walked toward the exit. There was nothing left for her here, but there was much to anticipate in the city. At least she hoped so.

Fired from a job the day before New Year's Eve was not

anything she anticipated happening. She certainly had not planned to spend the coming year looking for a job. Ansley wanted to be the bigger person—she wanted to feel gratitude that they waited until the end of December to let her go, but her mind could only process the negative.

Once she settled inside her car, she pulled out her phone to call Simeon, one of her best friends.

"Simeon Harris speaking," she said in her heavy Southern drawl.

Ansley could hear the click of Simeon's nails against the keyboard. Simeon was a Marketing Executive with the Bloomquist Corporation. "Hey lady. What you got going for the rest of the day? I need to grab lunch, and by lunch…I mean I need a drink."

"Oh goodness," Simeon said. "What did she do?"

"You know how Robin makes it her business to belittle my work daily. Trying to tell me that I can't relate to our African American readership…well, she finally decided to stop toying with me and executed the final blow."

Robin's words were a slap in the face to Ansley, as she was African American, and very in touch with the community as compared to Robin, who would only take a stand for a sale at Saks.

Simeon's sigh was audible. "I'm so sorry, girl. Where do you want to meet?"

"The usual spot is fine… I'll be two drinks ahead of you," Ansley said.

One hour later, Ansley waved to Simeon when she spotted her sashay through the doors of Tin Lizzy's. The stares of admiration and lust by the male patrons didn't cause Simeon to react at all. She was accustomed to being the focal point of every man in the room. Simeon wore her raven black hair in a long, layered bob, which complemented her deep mocha complexion. She was beautiful, intelligent, and possessed an extremely fit physique. She had even tried to help Ansley get a more sculpted body, but her friend did not want to be bound to a meal plan. Ansley complained that it felt unnatural.

"Okay sweetie. Let's snap you out of this emotional pothole. I could see that frown clear across the room," Simeon said, as she sat down across from Ansley. "Have you had a chance to think about what you would want to do next?"

"Right before they dropped the bomb on me, I had just enrolled in an online master's degree program," Ansley stated. "I'm debating on whether or not I should move forward."

"Think about it before you make an impulsive decision," Simeon advised. "What about your manuscript? Didn't you say you had started working on a project?"

Ansley frowned. "I haven't touched that thing in years."

"Well, just sit down and let the characters tell you the story. It'll come to you, or so they say," Simeon responded, repeating something she'd probably heard an author say at a book signing.

Ansley shrugged off Simeon's sentiments. Every dream that Ansley had for her life after college included writing. She wanted to be a feature writer for the Atlanta Journal Constitution, and release some reference books for journalism students on how to find internships and plot out a career path. That was her passion. She attempted to write fiction as well, but that project was now collecting dust with the rest of her textbooks.

"Hey, it was just a suggestion. As far as the job is concerned, I have some contacts, so I'll make a few calls and see if I can generate some leads for you."

"Thanks girl," Ansley responded. "I won't turn down your offer. I know you have connections." She paused a moment before saying, "What's going on with you? Give me somc good news."

"Work has been crazy these past few weeks," Simeon responded. "But the New Year's Eve party tomorrow night will be the perfect way to close out the week. Oh, and don't forget you're my plus one. I'll understand if you want to back out, but I hope you won't because we've had this planned for a while now. And I'm not trying to hear that, I don't have anything to wear mess either."

Simeon settled back against the cushion of her seat.

Ansley could tell by her friend's body language that she was mentally preparing for a letdown. The raised brow and crossed arms were a big clue of Simeon's current disposition.

"I'm not really in the mood to party, but I did promise that I'd go. I'm not sure how much fun I'm going to be though."

"We're going to have a great time. This is exactly what you need to lift your spirits, trust. It's going to be all the way turnt up."

As if on cue, Levon, their favorite waiter came to the table with their usual order. "Okay dolls, I have a pitcher of Peach Patron Margaritas and the barbecue chicken and goat cheese quesadillas for two," he said.

Ansley and Simeon were regulars at Tin Lizzy's. It was their safe haven and the place where they first met. It was just three months ago that the two of them met at the bar while sitting and complaining about their horrible bosses.

They became fast friends after bonding over margaritas and the Tex-Mex cuisine. They went from grabbing an occasional drink for networking purposes to dining there two to three times a week, it was like their own version of the television show, Cheers. Everyone knew their names and on occasion, they would get the royal treatment, which meant the manager comped meals for them.

"These drinks are everything to me right now," Ansley said with a little too much enthusiasm.

Simeon took a sip. "Their drinks stay on point."

Ansley nodded and sighed. Even her favorite drink wasn't giving her the instant boost she needed. Simeon noticed and patted Ansley's hand.

"It will all work out. Now eat your half. I can't promise that I won't try to put my fork on your side."

They continued to chat for a while as they ate their meal, but Ansley was getting tired of faking it. All she wanted to do was go home, take a warm bath, and get in the bed.

"Thanks for coming out. I really appreciate you being there for me."

"You would do the same for me. It's not a problem."

"I hate to eat and run, but I think I'm going to go ahead and make my way to the house."

Ansley rose and Simeon stood as well to say goodbye.

"Let me know when you get home. I'm gonna finish our drinks." Simeon's smile was full of mischief.

"Levon," Ansley called. "Make sure she's not stumbling out of here." Once he gave her a thumbs up, Ansley was on her way out the door.

Outside, Ansley fumbled around in her purse searching for her keys as she walked. She was not paying attention to where she was going, which caused her to literally fall into a pair of masculine arms.

"Excuse me, I'm so sorry," she said, looking up at the man.

As he helped steady her, Ansley casted her eyes away from him, unable to hide her emotions. After all these years, seeing him still made her heart beat overtime.

She found her voice. "Oh wow… Ryan." She allowed herself to sneak another glimpse at him. How he managed to become even more handsome after all these years, she shook her head. "You look—amazing."

Ryan Bennett was her college sweetheart. He had always been attractive and adulthood really agreed with him. He was tall, 6 feet and 5 inches of solid, sexy caramel, built, well-groomed and full of never-ending, glory-halle-stupid, fine. His brown sugar sprinkled eyes were always warm and welcoming, and he had the longest eyelashes that Maybelline Cosmetics would no doubt want to bottle up and sell. She could kick herself for giving up their relationship.

He looked at her and smiled briefly.

"Hey Ans…" he said. "You're just as beautiful as ever."

Ansley blushed and mouthed, "Thank you."

"Is everything okay? Based on our collision, I can only assume you were a little distracted."

She felt a little gratification that he was taking the time to check on her. Up until that moment, Ansley had barely acknowledged the woman hovering to Ryan's right. She seemed all too bothered about this unanticipated reunion.

"Oh, that," she chuckled. "I was trying to find my keys when I ran into you. I'm okay though. Just got some disappointing news, but other than that I'm doing okay."

"So what's the bad news? Do you want to talk about it?

I can give you a call later if you want."

"Well... um, it's nothing major. I just need to get home, take a long shower, and relax to some jazz or something. Look, I don't want to hold you up...so," she said, looking at his date, who was now tapping her foot.

"Oh! My bad... sorry about that. Ansley, this is my friend from work... umm..."

"Nina. My name is Nina."

"Just like in *Love Jones*. Nice to meet you," Ansley greeted. "That was one of our favorite movies in college. Right, Ryan?"

"Oh yeah," Ryan chuckled. "I didn't even think about that. I use to love me some Nia Long, still do—a blues for Nina." Ryan shook his head. "Anyway, Nina, this is my Ansley... I mean this is Ansley," he said with a nervous laugh.

Nina sneered at Ansley.

"Ryan... can we go somewhere else to eat? It looks too crowded and a little low brow here," she said, rolling her eyes in Ansley's direction.

Ansley laughed and shook her head. The way his cowworker was acting—she must have thought she and Ryan were on a date. Whatever the case, she didn't intend to get into an altercation with this woman over her ex. It just didn't make sense to go there.

"Ansley, give me a call if you want to talk about whatever is bothering you... or if you just want to catch up," he said before walking away. Ansley wondered how he managed to walk with Nina so close alongside him as if they were participating in a three-legged race.

As she stood there watching them disappear around the corner, she recalled a time when it was her and Ryan that were inseparable. They walked to class together. They always made time for each other—or at least until she started to lose sight of their relationship. She thought about the night that changed everything.

Ansley and Ryan sat on the floor of his apartment, eating pizza and watching Love Jones. It was their movie.

Ansley reached over to grab some popcorn, and noticed that Ryan was watching her and not the movie. She smiled. "I see someone is not watching the movie. What's on your mind?

Ryan grabbed the remote from behind him on the sofa, and pressed the pause button. He turned his head in Ansley's direction.

"Ansley, we are about to graduate in a few months. Can you believe it's already been four years?"

"I know right. I was looking through photos from freshman year the other day, and just seeing how much I've changed. You too," she reached over and patted Ryan's evidence of the freshman fifteen.

"Oh you trying to be funny. That's alright though, you don't have to love my something extra," he said before reaching over to caress her thick thighs. "I love my baby's curves and lady lumps. You still freshman year sexy. I'll give it to you."

They laughed together. As Ryan turned the rest of his body in her direction, Ansley also adjusted her body so that she could face him.

She smiled at him. Ansley loved Ryan. She never thought that she could love someone they way that she loved him. She noticed the shift in his mood, and braced herself.

"I've been waiting until we got together tonight to

share something with you," he said fiddling with the edges of the pizza box that rest between them.

Ansley wanted to interject and make him rush the information, but she remained quiet and waited to see what he would say next.

"I wanted to let you know that I got offered a position as a Financial Analyst with American Express."

"Oh my gosh. Ryan, that's incredible. So where will your office be? I hope they put you in the Atlanta office, the commute to Lawrenceville would tack on some extra miles for you. Give me a kiss, a hug or something. We need to celebrate."

She crawled across the floor to get closer to him. They shared a kiss, a lackluster kiss if Ansley was to tell it.

"Ryan baby, that kiss was a little bland. Are you nervous? You have a while before you start, or are they starting you early?"

"It's in New York. I'll be moving up north and I want you to join me. Ansley Renee Wright, I can't imagine starting this journey without you. I know I don't have a ring right now, but will you marry me?"

Relocating with him meant giving up her dream to write for the Atlanta Journal Constitution. However, Ryan just didn't understand why she didn't want to work for the Wall Street Journal or New York Times, which frustrated her. Now here she stood, jobless and nowhere near getting a call from the AJC. Every submission she submitted had been declined or unanswered.

Coming back to present, Ansley wished she had a do over, she would be his wife and she would've found her way into the industry, or freelanced, but she would have made it happen. Back then, she failed to realize that her passion wasn't based on her home address, it was based on where it lived inside of her.

No job. Seeing an ex and he looks to be winning. Yet he still showed concern for her—when reality checked in, it was prompt and painful.

It was official. Today totally sucked.

Simeon ran her fingers through her hair; the ends always seemed to get a little tangled when she did wand curls. She refreshed her lip-gloss, and gazed around the restaurant as she waited to settle her bill. When Levon returned to the table with her debit card, he also brought her a message.

"Miss Simeon, the gentleman at the bar has taken care of your bill." Levon pointed. "The one in the tweed blazer, and wearing those anointed, take-me-to-the-king pants. Yes, yes, honey. Don't keep him waiting."

Simeon burst out laughing. "You know you need to cut it out."

She adjusted her body to get a better look. Liking what she saw, she smiled and allowed her tongue to tease the corner of her mouth as she recalled the last time she laid eyes on this fine specimen at the bar.

She returned her card to the clutch she carried, and walked over towards the bar to extend her thanks. By the way he leaned back against the bar drinking in her frame, Simeon could tell the energy that she felt upon sight was mutual.

"Montgomery, well isn't this a pleasant surprise. What are you doing in Georgia?"

As he reached around her waist, pulling her close for a hug, Simeon's body temperature elevated, right along with her desire for him. They had history; one that she hoped they could rekindle and put on repeat forever.

She met him a few months ago while attending a conference in Chicago on marketing and social media. He was attending a conference in the same hotel. They struck up a conversation over drinks in the restaurant's bar lounge area. As far as Simeon was concerned, their business was far from over.

She inhaled his scent, the familiarity of lavender and oak enticed her senses. She had instant recall of this fragrance, but couldn't recall the name of the cologne. Simeon was so consumed with remembering the name, she almost missed his response to her query.

"I came to Georgia to help my cousin with some projects and decided to take on a contract position while I'm down here."

"Wait, are you saying you quit your job in Chicago?" Simeon inquired.

"No. Not yet. I'm just down here to test the waters. You know I never got your number. You were a hard woman to track down."

Simeon tilted her head and smiled. "Not buying into that real estate of lies. I gave you a card."

He shook his head and shrugged. "I got a lot of cards at that conference. I couldn't recall your name—I never said I was Colombo, but I'm here now, so why don't you have another drink with me. Maybe we can pick up where we left off?"

He grazed her breast with his hand.

"Seriously? That's the best you can come up with?"

Simeon turned away, and began to walk towards the exit. She wasn't about the let him treat her like some tramp. She deserved better.

Her face flush, and jaws clenched. She attempted to calm her nerves by inhaling and exhaling out her negative thoughts, but with each step she could not fight how she felt—she was simmering hot. She couldn't believe that he had hope to run into her, but only for a quickie. They shared a romantic evening, albeit a one night stand, but this was not normally her style. It also bothered her that he never called after that night. She didn't even get a Facebook request. However, she never bothered to reach out to him either.

"Simeon wait," he said, walking briskly to catch up with her. "I'm sorry. You're a beautiful woman and that night, wow—it was special to me, too. At the time though, as you may recall I was going through some things with my ex-girlfriend. As soon as I came to town, I decided to look you up. I remembered you talking about this place so I chanced it. It's fate."

"So you're telling me that this is not just an attempt to get me back into bed." Lowering her voice, Simeon stated, "I'm nobody's jump-off."

"I know that. Look, I think we should get to know one another better. We can start by having lunch later this week."

Simeon's eyes lit up and she clapped her hands. "I'd love it."

She wanted him as much as he wanted her. The night they spent together had been spectacular. It had been automatic, explosions of desire. Her body gave a tiny shudder just at the memory of what they had shared.

Simeon began to dance in place humming the song *Automatic* by The Pointer Sisters. She noticed that Montgomery was giving her a peculiar look, and noted that she needed to not scare him away. She needed to welcome him back to the comfort zone that she had established in Chicago.

She winked at him, turning to walk back toward the exit. Stealing a peek over her shoulder, Simeon asked, "Aren't you coming?"

He smiled as she took his hand leading the way, as Simeon continued to hum The Pointer's Sister song, *Automatic* in her head.

Chapter 2

Ansley woke up with a slight headache. She did not think three margaritas would make her to feel so lousy. However, the two additional glasses of wine she had at home should've been an indication of what was sure to come. She was an intermediate level drinker with advance level tendencies—which is why she kept a hang-over toolkit fully equipped with Goodie powders for such occasions.

Ansley stretched out her body in bed, before sitting up and planting her feet on the cool, hardwood floors. She sat on the edge of the mattress for a second before attempting to make her way to the master bathroom.

She paused in front of her dresser mirror, shaking her head at her reflection. She looked like a makeover before picture. Her shoulder-length, jet black hair was tangled, damp, and dangling against her back. She took the hair tie from her wrist, and pulled her hair atop her head in a messy bun. Ansley kept a ponytail holder nearby at all times, she loved her long tresses but in the event of extreme heat, humidity, or any number of hair fail catastrophe scenarios, she had to be prepared.

Ansley rubbed her hand across her face. Her toffee complexion was flushed, with the exception of the earth tone hues attempting to hide her faint freckles. She had fallen asleep with her makeup on. Now her mascara looked like war paint smudged across her eyes and face. Ansley looked exactly like she felt; beat down and in need of rest.

She glanced over her shoulder to look at the clock on her nightstand. Ansley huffed when she recalled that she did not have anywhere to be until way later. The realization deflated her and she shuffled into the bathroom, turning on the shower.

Minutes later, she stepped beneath the hot water until she was fully submerged. She washed stale makeup and her worries down the drain.

Feeling rejuvenated after her shower, Ansley towel dried her body, and then wrapped her hair in a separate towel. She grabbed the floral silk robe hanging on the bathroom door and slipped it on, not bothering to tie the sash as she padded barefoot into her room to check her cellphone for messages.

She had a voicemail message from Simeon.

"Hey Ans, it's Simeon. You never called to say that you made it home. I hope you're feeling better..."

She knew the next message on her phone must be from Simeon since the call was disconnected mid-message.

"Hey sweetie. The call disconnected. Anyway, I emailed you several contacts this morning; hopefully one of them can help you find something. You deserve a little pampering after yesterday, so I scheduled you an appointment at the spa and with your hair stylist so you could tighten up those edges. See you tonight. Love ya."

Ansley gave a little smile. Simeon was always full of surprises, and this was by far one of the best, and it was definitely right on time.

* * *

Ansley pulled her black-on-black Range Rover into the valet parking at Spa Sydell in Buckhead. With her hair freshly pressed and styled, she was now prepped and ready to be immersed in a state of relaxation.

She could not wait to unzip and unsnap all of the restrictive clothes that were holding her hostage. Women wore some of the most uncomfortable clothing, but nothing could compare to the universal sigh of relief heard around the country when a woman had the chance to take off her bra.

Instant relaxation.

"Hello and welcome to Spa Sydell. Do you have an appointment with us today?" the receptionist asked.

"Yes, it should be under Ansley Wright," she confirmed.

"Ah, I see you are getting the hot stone treatment. You're going to love it."

Simeon knows me so well. She loved this particular treatment.

Ansley walked back to the locker room to get undressed and slip into a terry-cloth robe. She retreated to the lounge to sip on a cool glass of cucumber water and await her masseur. Ansley could not wait to lay across that massage table, she had not been to the spa in a while.

Just as she was getting comfortable in her chair, her name was called.

"Ansley Wright...," he said.

"Yes. I'm ready," she said with a smile. She rose and followed her massage therapist into the hallway.

As they continued down the hall, her heart rate increased when she passed by one of the most attractive men she had seen in a while. Well, with the exception of Ryan, this guy could definitely take her mind in another direction. When they made eye contact, Ansley felt a wave of desire flow through her.

His smooth, dark chocolate skin was glowing against the white terry-cloth robe. His chest was giving a peek-a-boo show and she was his captive audience. She was so engrossed she didn't realize that her masseur had stopped walking. She ran smack into him.

"Oh my goodness. Excuse me, I was a little distracted," she stammered.

"I could tell," he said, not withholding his chuckle at her expense.

Ansley didn't know what it was about that man, but she was curious about him. As she removed her robe and lay across the massage table, she began to play out scenarios in which to strike up a conversation with him, just in case she ran into him afterward. Flirting was an art form that she had yet to master.

The massage therapist entered the room putting an end to her daydream, and inciting the real thing as she drifted off with the glide of his strong hands and thumbs kneading away the stress in her body. As his hands worked out her kinks, she felt an intense feeling of euphoria. *Do work with those magic hands.*

She closed her eyes and imagined the hands on her lower back belonged to man from the hallway. Ansley smiled at the thought.

Chapter 3

Once Ansley left the spa, she drove over to her friend Lanae's house to pick-up the knee-length, midnight blue cocktail dress that she loaned her a few months ago. She planned to wear it to-night for the New Year's Eve party that Simeon's company was hosting. Ansley sat across from her friend, Lanae, telling her about the beautiful man she encountered. She had hoped to get another glimpse of him, but that opportunity never came.

Ansley was running slightly behind in getting ready for the event, but she wanted to spend some time with her friend and fill her in on everything going on in her life. While she was fumbling through love and life, Lanae was living Ansley's dream.

Lanae Moses married her college sweetheart, and was the mother to a very inquisitive four-year-old daughter. She worked as a home-based blogger for Atlanta Motherhood. Lanae's life seemed so balanced and tranquil—something that Ansley wanted for herself.

"Wait—so y'all didn't even speak to each other and he's got you planning your wedding already?" Lanae clowned.

Ansley flushed in embarrassment. "Whatever. It's not that deep, but there was just this energy between us." She stood and walked around the island in the kitchen to stand next to Lanae, who was preparing dinner. She picked up a knife to help Lanae chop up the vegetables for the soup she was making.

"Was it like déjà vu? Do you think you have met him before?"

"I wish I understood how to describe the feeling. My body has never reacted that way at first glance."

"Who knows, maybe fate will allow you to cross paths again, but in the meantime please put those veggies in the pot and stop assaulting them. I think they're pretty much dead at this point."

They shared a laugh.

"Okay, okay. New topic, how is my goddaughter doing?" Ansley said.

"Kennedy's doing fine. She's over at her grandmother's today."

"She's such a beautiful little girl," Ansley gushed.

"That she is. Now back to this man, did you guys exchange information?"

"No. I wish that's how it went down. That was a flirt and run. Better yet, it was a drive-by."

Lanae laughed. "What do you mean?"

"By the time I realized he was fine I was being escorted into the room and he was going around the corner."

"Oh well," Lanae said with her hands raised. "I know that's not your main focus anyway, how are you feeling about the job situation? Are you still going to school in the January?"

Nodding, Ansley, said, "Well, I decided that I'm going to go ahead and work on my master's degree in Journalism. I put out a few feelers with a some of Simeon's contacts and people I have met in the industry, but I don't expect to hear anything until after the New Year."

"Good. Praise God. Glad to see that you're not wallowing in self-pity," Lanae responded with a smile. "And promise me that you won't allow whatever new job you're blessed with to interrupt school."

"Umm... yes, mom?" Ansley said with a side-eye glance at her friend. "Where is Jacob?" she asked referring to Lanae's husband of eight years.

"At his second home," she said with a hint of sarcasm. "He's at the office meeting with distributors. The publication is expanding and will now be available on the West coast."

"That's awesome. Now don't tell me that he's going to have to relocate and you're going with him," Ansley said half-joking.

"If God leads us to leave, then I'll call you from Los Angeles."

Ansley rolled her eyes and smiled.

Lanae scrunched up her face.

"Anyway, how's Simeon doing?" Lanae asked with a smirk on her face.

Ansley laughed. Lanae and Simeon were like oil and water. Simeon was the friend Ansley went to when she wanted to unwind and have fun without worrying about what anyone thought. Lanae, in comparison, had been there for Ansley for the past five years and was often Ansley's sounding board. Lanae was the one that could get Ansley back to a peaceful state when she let her emotions shift from cruise control to unregulated.

"She's doing Simeon as usual—I'm actually going to be her plus one for a New Year's Eve party tonight," she said.

"Oh—that's why you're picking up the dress. I'm connecting the dots," she stated. "Have fun tonight and worry about tomorrow, *tomorrow*."

"That's the plan. Let the turn-up begin," Ansley said as she began dancing in her seat.

Ansley walked into the Mardi Gras themed party after choosing one of the beautifully decorated masks that were on display for guests to select. She chose the black and crème mask with lace detailing because it complemented her dress perfectly.

Flame-eaters, jugglers, and fortune-tellers were sprinkled throughout the room. The servers walked around with a variety of hors d'oeuvres and champagne flowed from every direction of the venue. Ansley was most excited to see they had a live band, adding to the New Orleans vibe.

"It's about time," Simeon stated. "I thought you stood me up."

They embraced before admiring each other's outfits.

"Girl, that dress is hot. Is it new?" Ansley asked.

Simeon wore a strapless, red cocktail dress that hugged her figure.

"New to you, but not to me. I've had it for a while now. The last time I wore it, it brought me some good luck. I'm hoping the same thing happens again tonight."

"I'm sure whoever you're looking to impress is probably planning their approach."

"We shall see," she said with a determined smile. "Okay go mingle and enjoy. I'll catch up with you. The boss wants us to make sure our clients are enjoying themselves."

Ansley lifted a champagne flute from a passing server carrying a tray. She canvased the room, walking up to a few familiar faces and exchanging information. Might as well make the most of the night and network, she thought.

The deejay was playing some up-tempo jazz, but it was not what she would call party music. As if on cue, he switched it up and played *Let the Beat Hit'Em* by Lisa Lisa and Cult Jam.

She hadn't heard that song in forever. It was one of her favorites.

Ansley swayed in place and watched as couples and groups of friends swarmed to the middle of the floor. When she looked around and didn't spot Simeon, she opted to go solo out on the dance floor.

She merged into the crowded dance floor and joined a group that was busting out all of their best moves from the 80s and 90s.

Ansley was doing her best cabbage patch moves when she locked eyes with a masked gentleman across the room. Chills ran through her body, it was him. Although she couldn't see his face, she would recognize that body anywhere.

Their eyes remained locked as he walked towards her. She noticed that he shifted his eyes to her swaying hips on occasion, but the goal was to keep her eyes trained on him.

The music faded into the background as their bodies merged at the hip. He pulled her into him as if this was how it should be.

Ansley didn't flinch at his touch. The interaction, in her mind, was the type of affection she expected between a man and a woman. She knew it was premature to be thinking of him in a romantic way, but the draw that he had on her was stronger than the concept of reason.

Her breath caught as he leaned down to talk into her

ear.

"Hello again," he whispered. Her body trembled and he pulled her closer.

"Hi. How did you know?"

"That you were the woman from the spa," he said completing her thought.

Ansley nodded.

"I felt your presence. I was talking to someone and the urge to turn around led me back to those gorgeous eyes of yours. It's like they can see straight through to my soul. Sorry, I know that makes no sense."

Ansley smiled. "Trust me. I get it more than you think."

As an intimate silence enclosed them, she lowered her head onto his chest, allowing him to pull her in closer.

Their heartbeats matched the tempo of the music playing in the background. The deejay was now playing *Stairway to Heaven* and she felt that it was a sign of things to come. They glided across the floor, moving in perfect symmetry. It was as if they were attending a private party where they were the only invited guest.

After the song ended, they walked hand-in-hand over to the bar. Nothing about the exchange felt odd to her. As they stood there ordering drinks, they just stared into each other's eyes.

Ansley ended the silence when she broke into laughter.

"I'm so sorry," she told him. "This is so unexpected. A pleasant, unexpected twist to the evening, but I'm surprised to see you… what is your name?"

He began to laugh as well. "My name is Davis. Davis Montclair. And while I can continue to just call you gorgeous in my head, what is your name?"

"Ansley Wright. Davis, you have an amazing smile,"

she said, no longer able to hide her attraction. No need to play games when the heat was escalating between them. She felt it and she knew he did too.

"Thank you, and you're just indescribably beautiful. There are truly no words that I can say that can describe your beauty."

Ansley blushed.

As she attempted to figure out what to say next, Davis leaned down close to her and with everyone else chanted, "5-4-3-2-1... Happy New Year."

There it was.

Confirmation that there was indeed a spark igniting between them.

His kiss started out gentle, and then became more intense as he sucked on her bottom lip before releasing her back to reality.

He took a step back, giving her some space.

Ansley exhaled.

"I'm sorry, but I heard everyone counting and just couldn't resist kissing you any longer," he told her, his tone was unapologetic.

Ansley filled the space between them, placing her arm behind his back.

"Well, by all means, please continue... it was just starting to get good."

As he lowered his head and continued to kiss her, she reached up and touched his face. Her hand grazed the mask partially covering his face, but he took her hand and stopped her.

"Phew," Davis uttered. "We should probably slow down. At least, allow me to take you on a proper date. That's what you deserve. While this has been magical, I want a chance to woo you."

Ansley smiled. "I couldn't think of a better way to start this year. You've actually given me something to look forward to—thank you."

Davis retrieved a business card from his blazer. "Here's my contact information. Call me this week… preferably when you get home."

Ansley took the business card, tracing it with her fingers as he kissed her on the forehead and backed away.

Happy New Year to me, she thought.

Simeon was livid.

She had deliberately worn a dress, which clearly made a take-me home statement in hopes that Montgomery would arrive and have the same reaction that he had on the night when they first met. She wanted to see the same desire glowing in his gaze, but he was nowhere to be found. After the countdown, she was left smooch-less and sulking at the bar alone.

Simeon checked her phone again, hoping to find that he had at least sent a text message, but that was a fruitless wish.

She inhaled deeply and exhaled slowly.

She grabbed another glass of champagne. In her heart, she knew she needed to let this go and move on, but her pride would not allow her to release the notion that he should have been begging to share this night with her.

What could have been more important than being with me?

Earlier in the week, they enjoyed an intimate night together, and had spoken almost every day after that. The majority of the communication was via text, because he rarely answered her calls. That said, they still had pretty constant communication.

Simeon pasted on a smile as she struggled to hide her growing displeasure. The last thing she wanted now, was for her boss to see her frowning when she was supposed to be mingling and entertaining.

She glanced around the room and noticed Ansley kissing someone near the bar on the opposite side of the room. *That should be me and Montgomery.*

Simeon was jealous.

She did not want to be, but from the day the two met, it seemed that Ansley always ended up winning despite the odds that were stacked against her. While Simeon did not really want to see Ansley crumble, she wanted to win. She was nobody's runner-up. Holding up her half empty glass of champagne, she said, "Cheers to you, Ansley… as usual."

Chapter 4

"Thank you for your time, Mr. Wilson," Ansley said.

This was her third rejection. Finding a new gig was a job in itself. She had been unemployed for almost a month, and was beginning to feel deflated. January was well on its way out, and Ansley felt she had not gotten anywhere.

She decided to remain in school, but her focus was to secure a full-time job. Ansley had done some freelance writing for a few online magazines and Atlanta-based publications, but it was not the same as being on staff. There was no job security.

Ansley sat down to work on an assignment for school that would be due soon. As she located the file to start on her paper, she stopped when she saw her manuscript. It was still there on the drive and based on the last modified date, she had not even opened the file since around her junior year in college. If she were honest, she hadn't been inspired to work on it since she called it quits with Ryan.

Maybe in some ways he was her muse. She chose being a goal digger in Atlanta over trying to have it all with him in New York. At that time, she just could not see her dreams in any other hue than the colors she chose for herself. That's what made the most sense to her back then.

She shook off the thought and started on her assignment for her Media Law class, when her phone rang. When she saw Davis' number on the screen she beamed.

"Good morning, handsome."

"Hey, beautiful. I know you said you would be doing homework today. How's it going?"

Ansley and Davis had been speaking on the regular since they met at the office party. They had attempted to meet up a few times, but had yet to have the date he proposed.

"Eh," she murmured, her tone void of enthusiasm. "It's coming along I guess. I haven't made as much progress as I would like. I'm a little distracted."

"Maybe you need a change of scenery. Have you eaten yet?" Davis asked.

"Not yet. I was trying to make some leeway with this paper first and then I was going to try to squeeze in a late lunch in maybe an hour or so."

"I have a better idea," Davis said. "Why don't you grab your things and meet me at the Smyrna Public Library? Do you know where that is?"

While the invite would have been perfect any other time, she could not entertain his offer. "Thank you for the offer, but I really don't have time," she said. "Besides the library won't allow you to bring food in there."

Ansley sat listening to silence awaiting his response. She hoped he did not think she was trying to dodge his offer. She just really wanted to stay focused.

"I'll give you some time to get ready and I'll see you at two. Meet you at the front entrance," he said before hanging up the phone.

"Hello?" Ansley took the phone away from her ear and looked to see if the call was still connected.

He hung up, guess I'm taking my butt to the library.

Ansley looked down at her heather gray Falcons sweatshirt with the hole on the upper right sleeve. Her tortoise shell glasses had slid to the tip of her nose, and her long black hair was pulled into a messy bun.

She contemplated on calling back to cancel, but in reality she was not getting much done here. It would not hurt to see if changing her environment would help her with moving forward with this project.

Ansley got up from her desk and walked into her bedroom. She went to her closet and pulled out a pair of jeans and a rust-colored, cable-knit sweater. She held the garments against her body as she looked in the mirror. *He should have given me more time to get ready.*

It was already half past noon, and she needed to shower and change and that did not include the amount of time it would take to drive across town to the library. Ansley had to admit it though, Davis was taking control of the situation and making demands of her time—she thought it was sexy.

Ansley reached into the top of her closet to locate her chocolate booties, then grabbed a leather jacket of the same color. She thought about taking her hair down, but decided she would just freshen up her bun. Though she wanted to look good for him, she didn't want to appear as if she went out of her way to impress him.

She walked into her bathroom and over to the shower to turn the water on. She waited until she saw steam before undressing and stepping inside.

I'm only going because I'm hungry. Ansley snickered. She wasn't fooling anyone. She was going because she was into Davis and could not wait to find out more about him. The universe was drawing them into each other but she was still waiting for the reveal. Maybe today would give her a glimpse of what the future held.

Ansley sat in her car in the library parking lot, contemplating on whether to get out. She chatted with Lanae the entire ride over. Of course she had questions like 'who is he' and 'where did he come from' and demanded that Ansley call her once it was over. Several scenarios played out in Ansley's mind, the main one being, what if he did not show up? She did not even know what kind of car he drove to identify him. Ansley wondered if he was already inside waiting on her.

Getting antsy, she decided to get out of the car, find a quiet spot, and start working on her paper. She turned off the ignition and then sat for a second before turning it back on. Ansley unlocked her phone and typed Davis' name into Google. She scrolled and selected a few Facebook and LinkedIn profiles that popped up in her search, but none of them belonged to the man she sought.

She gave a slight start at the tapping on her passenger side window.

It was Davis.

Ansley took a moment to put her rattled nerves in check before rolling the window down. "Seriously? That was a mean thing to do. Not cool."

She wished he was not so cute because she really would not have minded reenacting David and Goliath and flinging a rock at his head right about now.

Davis guffawed. "You should pay attention to your surroundings." He attempted to control his laughter. "Can I carry those things for you?"

"Yeah okay," she said, rolling her eyes at him. "Thank you for the gesture, but this doesn't excuse your behavior or your tardiness."

Ansley had always been a stickler for being on time. From kindergarten through her college years, she was always on time and if she knew she would be late she made sure to let someone know.

"You look nice today."

"Thank you," she said, realizing that he wasn't going to respond to her attitude. *Don't sweat the minor moments, dwell in those major moments Ansley. It was just a joke.*

Davis offered his free hand to help her out of the car.

"Thank you," she said as she took his hand gingerly and stepped down from her truck.

He never let go of her hand.

"What made you choose this location anyway? Is this your local library or something?" she asked, while attempting to ignore the heat radiating throughout her from his touch.

"I actually live downtown, but you mentioned that you lived near Cumberland Mall, so here we are." He opened the door letting her into the library.

She was a true Charlotte York Goldenblatt, from the hit series *Sex and the City*, when it came to romance and any possible sign of chivalry from a man made her biological clock go into warp speed. Ansley could not wait to see if he had what it took to make her swoon.

She was preparing to settle into a spot near the computer lab, but noticed that Davis kept walking toward one of the meeting rooms. Usually those rooms booked early and walk-ins did not have a chance at getting a space. Realization set in and she realized that she owed him an apology for assuming that he was late. It was clear that he had gotten there ahead of time.

Ansley walked in behind him as he put her things down on the table. She grinned and mouthed "thank you" as he pulled out her chair.

"Okay, my lady, I have a turkey Swiss sandwich and a chicken salad sandwich. Which one would you like?"

Ansley couldn't help but giggle like a teenager. Sneaking in food reminded her of her high school days, when she and her friends would go to the library during lunch and smuggled in snacks. "This is so wrong, but I'll take the chicken salad sandwich, please and thank you."

He passed her the sandwich, grazing her hand with his own. His touch ignited a sensation deep inside of her. Try as she might to ignore it, those darn toes of hers were always a clear sign of surrender, she was helpless in this moment and while she was not sure how she would feel—she was not afraid of what this could lead to with Davis.

She watched Davis as he prepared a place for their meal. He set everything up for her before biting into his own sandwich.

"How are you doing in school overall?" he asked in between bites.

"It's going great," Ansley said, not looking up from her laptop. "I didn't really think I could do the online classroom format, but it's been working out well."

She did not want to make eye contact—the eyes always told the real story and her story had them becoming much closer. She had to pace things out, even though their spark was brighter than fireworks on the Fourth of July, Ansley did not want to take the dive just yet.

"Good, good...glad to hear it," he said. "I won't be disturbing you again. Go ahead and enjoy your sandwich. Let me know if I need to get anything for you."

"Davis, I have to say thank you. I honestly think I needed this."

He exposed a dimple in his left cheek. As if he wasn't sexy enough. She loved a man with dimples, but just the one would do just fine.

"I'm going to read my book and you just work on your paper."

"Don't you have to get back to work?" Ansley asked.

"I'm a contractor," he replied. "I don't have any jobs today, but I do have a full load the rest of this week. Right now I'm exactly where I need to be, so don't worry about me."

She lifted her eyes in his direction. *Is he for real?*

With that, Ansley nodded and went back to her paper. She enjoyed how Davis just wanted to be there for her. They had not known each other long, but she felt a sincere connection to him, and wondered if he felt the same way. Ansley decided not to put too much thought into it—she would enjoy the moment and her time with Davis. Time would reveal the next page in this budding romance.

Davis pretended to be enthralled in his book, but he sat at the table observing Ansley using as much discretion as possible. It was hard for him because he wanted to just look at her and study the freckles that accessorized her eyes and accented her narrow nose. He loved how her deep brown eyes shined when her mouth curled upward. He loved the way her lips were slightly thin at the top, but plump at the bottom.

She was a beautiful puzzle that he could not wait to put together. He had always loved a challenge, and would stop at nothing to win her over. He could tell she was holding back, but he saw everything he needed to see on New Year's Eve. The way their connection was unspoken, but so clear to them both—she was into him too.

Davis hoped that this mini date would give her a glimpse into what it would be like to be his woman. He was convinced that by the time Ansley left the library, the walls around her heart would start to crumble. He felt certain that she would be his woman—if she would just give him a chance.

Davis had every confidence that he would have Ansley wrapped around his finger in no time. He had not met a woman who was immune to him. Davis thought about the other women he was entertaining, but they weren't like Ansley—she was special and he was not willing to risk his potential relationship with her. *This time I think I'll choose pleasure before business...the others will have to wait.*

Ansley could not believe that Davis sat with her for two hours while she did homework. The entire time he read his book, and catered to her every need from running to get coffee to providing light conversation when she needed a break away from staring at the screen.

As they walked out of the library, Davis escorted her to her vehicle and placed all of her things in the back of her truck. He surprised her when he wrapped his arms around her in a tight embrace. *He must have read my mind.*

"Thank you for doing this, Davis," Ansley stated. "This is exactly what I needed."

He did not say anything, everything he wanted to communicate was narrated by his eyes. "I guess I'd better let you go, but I hope to see you again."

She blushed. "It's a strong possibility."

"I'll call you."

Ansley loved how Davis waited until she was safe in her car before walking away.

As she pulled out of the parking lot, she saw him walk over and sit on the bench at the bus stop. He was from Chicago and told her that most people used public transportation in the city. She also learned that part of the reason he lived downtown was because he preferred easy access to the eateries, events and shopping by foot or transit. She was not that surprised that he didn't ask for a ride home. He had made it clear that this day was all about her, and he only wanted her to focus on what she needed to complete.

Ansley decided to treat herself to a manicure and pedicure before heading home. She had an interview tomorrow and her nails looked terrible.

The nail salon was super busy, so she went and signed in with the receptionist. They were playing one of the local radio stations and the host Mocha Love was talking about dating in the city. She loved this show.

"What's up Atlanta? It's your girl, Mocha Love and we

have a hot one for you today. Ladies, I have to know, do you really know your man? If not, please turn your ears on to our special guest, founder of "Don't Date Him, Girl," a website dedicated to exposing the men that all women probably need to avoid. You don't want to miss this one, ladies."

Ansley laughed. This is why she planned to take things nice and slow with Davis, no matter what her biological clock was telling her. There were a lot of men out there with nothing but a calling card of drama. At this point in her life, Ansley wanted to stay focused finishing her master's degree program and building a successful career.

Love could wait.

Simeon heard a knock at her front door. She was not expecting anyone. Opening the door to see Montgomery standing there, caused her to suck her teeth.

She stood with her arms folded across her chest. "Why are you here?"

"Whoa, I was hoping for a more enthusiastic greeting like happy New Year or heck… even a good morning. You haven't even invited me in."

Simeon cocked her head to the side. "You have some nerve. You stood me up and I haven't heard or even received a text message to say that you're sorry. It's been almost a month."

"You're right. I had a family emergency, but that's no reason not to follow up with you. Do you forgive me?"

Simeon tapped her foot. Her patience with him was

minimal, but it was Montgomery and he had left a mark on her that she wasn't ready to erase. "You still haven't told me why you're here. Am I only good enough for you to sleep with… is that it? You come to my door wanting to be invited in, yet when I invite you to be my date—you don't bother to show up." Deep down, Simeon knew that Monty liked her. He could easily have disappeared at this point, but he was standing here trying to apologize.

Montgomery ran his hand across his face. "Listen, do you want me to leave? I'm here now. So what's up? You gonna let me in or not?"

Simeon took a deep breath. She could tell he wasn't willing to discuss his absence from the party any further, but she wanted to know why he left her dateless at her office's New Year's Eve party. As it stood, it seemed as if his feelings did not run as deep as hers flowed for him.

"Fine. Bring your gorgeous behind on in here." Her smile was flirtatious. She grabbed the center of his shirt and pulled him inside her home.

Simeon had a hunch that if she turned him away—there were plenty of others waiting for his attention. Therefore, she decided to drop the subject for now, but he was going to have to step things up if he planned to keep coming around.

"Hold on," she said, stopping him with her hand. "I need you to know that I'm not trying to chase after you. So you need to make up your mind…either be here or be there, but not in between."

Simeon began unbuttoning her blouse.

He shook his head and approached her. Putting his hands around her waist and dipping his head so that their lips could connect for a kiss.

"You're wild. You know that, right?" he whispered in her ear after allowing her lips a break from the workout.

"Monty, you have no idea just how wild I can be, but you will before the night is over."

He began kissing her again.

This timc when thcy connected, it was more intense, but lacked the passion and heartfelt emotions she craved. Simeon wanted more from him, and she was determined to keep him around. No matter what it took, she planned to become the main attraction in his life.

Chapter 5

Ansley had been fussing over her outfit all morning. This crazy February weather had her torn between business classics or the option of mixing in a sweater. She decided on a black pantsuit with a crisp white button down blouse for the tenth interview she'd have since New Breed fired her.

She was relieved to find out that Robin had not torched her name around Atlanta, but she was finding it a challenge to land a job where the industry wanted far more experience than she had.

Ansley had less than a year of practicing her craft post-college. Being the editor of a collegiate newspaper and magazine did not have as much influence as she had thought it would. She reached out to a few contacts by phone and email, hoping they had some more leads, but thus far she had not made any leeway. With the exception of Simeon, she had arranged for Ansley to have a meeting with Jason Moretti of Grind House Media. There were no guarantees, but she was glad for the prospect.

Putting the finishing touches to her outfit, Ansley accented her look with simple pearl earrings that her mother had given her after she graduated college and a pair of black pumps. Then, she grabbed her wool pea coat and headed to the elevators. Ansley felt confident and ready to start a new day.

On the way to the job interview, Ansley gave Simeon a

call at her office.

"Simeon Harris speaking."

"Hey, how are you, love?" Ansley said.

"I'm good. I can only chat for a second—headed to a meeting. Perfect timing, though; I got an email from Jason over at Grind House. He's really excited to speak with you today."

"That's good to hear because I'm ready to meet him. I'm actually on the way there now," she said. "I just wanted to call and say thanks again and don't forget to say a prayer for me."

Simeon chuckled sarcastically. "Will do. Meet up later at Tin Lizzy?

Ansley squinted her eyes and scrunched her nose. *Umm...somebody is feeling some type of way today.*

"If you say so," Ansley replied. "Is everything okay?"

"I told you I was about to run to a meeting. Everything is fine this way," Simeon responded, her tone nonchalant.

Ansley twisted her lips and considered Simeon's tone again. Something was off with her, but she would address it later when they were at the restaurant.

"Okay, well I'll see you after work.

"Sounds like a plan," Simeon said. "Talk to you later."

Ansley reasoned that her friend must have been stressing over her meeting. Or perhaps it's because they had not spoken very much since the holiday party. Ansley had gotten busy with job hunting and getting to know Davis. She had yet to share any details about him with Simeon or Lanae because she wanted to get to know him better.

The more Ansley thought about it, that's probably the reason Simeon was dry with her. The past few conversations they had were about her job hunt and they had not spoken to just catch up. She hadn't been a very good friend. She would have to make up for that over dinner and drinks. But first, she had to go slay her interview.

"Ansley Wright is here to see you," the receptionist said through the intercom. She then looked up at her. "Please have a seat. He'll be right out to see you."

Ansley scoped out the room to find a place to get her nerves aligned. The waiting area was a great space for the creative thinker, but was not doing much to assist in putting her mind at ease.

The office was very upscale and industrial. The ceiling had exposed beams and eccentric lighting, the floor was a black lacquer and the armchairs in the lobby were a heather gray accompanied by vibrant accessories, adding splashes of white, lemon, and teal throughout the room. The walls displayed framed issues of the past years and awards.

Grind House was very similar to New Breed Publishing, except they had a human resources department and a company that was managed by people with experience over hiring based on one's bloodline. New Breed presented the illusion of sophistication, but Grind House exhibited a body of work that could support the claim.

"Ansley Wright? I'm Jason Moretti," he said, extending his hand. "Welcome to Grind House. It is nice to finally meet you. Simeon has said great things about you," he said. "Come on back to my office."

Ansley shook his hand. She could not help but notice

how attractive he was. Jason Moretti was tall and lean. His thick, coffee brown hair, cleft chin, olive complexion and round, green eyes—he was red carpet ready. Ansley admired his sense of style as well. From his faded blue distressed jeans, brown chucks, and buttoned down flannel. It was casual but he made it work.

She was feeling like a college senior all over again. Excited for the moment, but nervous about what was to come.

Once inside his office, she started to feel a little more at ease. Ansley attributed her shift in mood to the calming earth tones throughout the room, which was a major contrast to the vivid appeal of the reception area. Much like Jason, the office had a subtle charm.

"So Ansley, I'm going to cut straight to the chase," Jason said. "We want to hire you as a contributing writer for Grind House. As a contributor, you'll have full use of the office—pretty much the same access as a regular staff writer. If all goes well, perhaps we can move you into a staff position. What do you say to that?"

Ansley sat stunned for a second. She had not even spoken or shown him any of her clips. Of course, she knew it was quite possible that he had a chance to read some of the articles that she had written while working at New Breed Publishing, but considering that Robin's goal was to discredit Ansley's writing ability—she thought he'd at least want to review her work.

"Oh wow, this went smoothly," she said trying to add humor to an awkward situation. She was flabbergasted. Most people would accept the job and dash out of the door before he changed his mind. Ansley wanted to make sure Jason knew that she planned to provide quality work and was not just planning to use her connections as a free ride.

"I have to be honest and tell you that I called Robin over at New Breed," he said.

"Do you mind sharing what was said?" Ansley asked.

"Well, Robin said that she thought your writing was mediocre at best, but her father saw something special in you. I reached out to Quincy and he told me I would be crazy not to hire you. Considering his years of history in this business, I took him at his word and decided that I could not let you slip through the cracks."

"I respect Quincy immensely and his vision. He gave me a chance and I'll forever be grateful."

Jason did not respond right away. She was not sure how to take this all in, but she knew she should speak. "I'm very familiar with your publication and would love to join the Grind House family," she said. "I take it that you're familiar with my writing style?"

He nodded. "You have a voice that our readership can relate to and I'm happy to have you join our team."

Jason had no idea how much his endorsement meant to her. "Thank you for the opportunity. I do have a question. What is the salary?"

"We are able to offer you a fifteen percent increase above what you were making before," he said before passing her the official offer letter.

Ansley broke into a smile. "Jason, where do I sit and when do I start?"

They shook hands.

As he gave her a tour of the building, Ansley observed the other Grind House employees working. She felt right at home in the midst of phone interviews, keys tap dancing, interview tapes being played for transcription, and people making plans.

Being back in the print world—it was her heartbeat. Ansley was eager to begin this new chapter. She was going to be making more money and she had the option of working from home—things were looking up.

She had a new job and Ansley couldn't wait to tell her girls about it. Her future was already looking brighter.

Ansley pulled up to Tin Lizzy's excited to share her news with Simeon. She walked into the restaurant and saw that Simeon had yet to arrive.

She walked over to their usual booth and sat down. Ansley pulled out her cell phone to call Lanae. She updated her and promised to drop by after her dinner with Simeon.

Ansley removed her laptop from her tote. While she was waiting on her friend, she decided to get started on a project for her new job. She already had a few ideas to pitch to Jason and didn't want to delay in getting them in front of him.

After jotting down a few notes, she looked over the syllabus for the week; she had a paper due on Monday. *There goes my weekend for sure.*

"Hey, pretty girl," Levon greeted. "You want to wait on Simeon or do you want me to start you off with a glass of white?"

She looked up. "Hey you. No, I will go ahead and have a glass of wine. How have you been?"

"Honey, this place is driving me crazy…you hear. I'm still waiting for my special someone to come and take me away from this life." Grinning, Levon added, "I'm trying to be a kept man, honey."

"You are too funny." Ansley laughed, although she knew he was not joking at all.

"Some might say in more ways than one," he said with a wink. "I'll be right back with your drink."

Levon was always good for a laugh.

"Mind if I join you?"

She looked up into the warm brown eyes of Davis. Even in casual clothing—he oozed sex appeal. He wore a teal, half-zip Polo sweater with a pair of khaki slacks. The fit of his clothing highlighted his efforts in the gym each day. The first time she met him he was in a suit and then at the spa, he was in a white terry cloth robe. He wore his clothes well…they did not wear him.

"Hey you," she greeted him. "I'm waiting on my friend, but I'm sure she won't mind. Have a seat."

Davis slid into the booth. "So what has you beaming?" Davis inquired. "I noticed the way your eyes were sparkling when you came through the door."

Ansley smirked. "I just landed a job with Grind House."

His eyes grew large. "Oh word? That's great!"

"Thank you. I think so, too." Ansley craned her neck and looked towards the window facing the parking lot.

"Is everything okay? You see a better option outside?" Davis joked.

Ansley giggled. "Sorry about that. I see my girl, Simeon pulling up outside. That's her in the silver Mercedes. I guess I can introduce you two."

Davis turned around to get a look. "You said her name is Simeon. That's a unique name."

Ansley noted the shift in his body language. He

slumped down in the chair and avoided eye contact. She reached across the table and touched his hand.

"Hey. I'm not saying that you have to leave or anything. I'm just saying that she's here now, but you don't have to leave."

"Oh no, it's not a problem at all. I need to get going anyway." He leaned over and kissed her on the cheek, and then slid out of the booth. "I'll give you a call later."

"Uh. Okay. Don't you want to wait and meet Simeon?"

"No. I mean I just want to leave on this high of getting a glimpse of you. I have plenty of time to meet your friends. Talk to you later."

Ansley watched as he strolled through the patio exit, disappearing into the parking lot. *That man is fine.*

As Ansley turned her attention back toward the front of the room, Simeon came waltzing through the door. Her long layered bob looked freshly pressed and her mint colored pant-suit complimented her deep brown complexion.

"Hey sis. You wearing that suit."

"Thanks. Who was that?" Simeon didn't waste any time inquiring.

The corner of Ansley's mouth went up, and her eyes twinkled. "Oh, that was just Davis. I'll tell you about him later. What's up, hon?"

Simeon raised her left brow and frowned. "Ut-uh, nah. Who is Davis? Is that Mr. New Year's Eve?"

Ansley bit her bottom lip. "You saw that, huh? Yes, I met him at the office party. Do you know him from work?"

Simeon frowned and rolled her eyes. "Nope. I don't know him from work. Honestly, I've only seen the back of his head. So anyway, how did the interview go?"

Ansley's smile evaporated. "Don't you want to explain

this little twinge of an attitude I just peeped? I could have sworn I just saw your eyes roll up and to the side."

Simeon tossed her hand to her chest. "Girl, I'm happy for you, but I'm having some guy troubles. You would've known this if you hadn't been so caught up lately."

Ansley cringed inwardly. It was true. She hadn't been much of a friend but for good reason. She cleared her throat. "Guilty, but the majority of the time was spent with me looking for jobs and doing homework assignments. I promise." She placed her hand across her heart as if she was swearing her truth.

"Yeah okay. I guess you can slide," Simeon replied. "Are y'all supposed to be a couple now?" She began humming the melody to *You Got It Bad* by Usher.

"Ha... Ha... real cute."

Simeon crinkled her nose. "What? Don't give me the stink eye because you're smitten. I see we need to talk about this guy before things get too deep."

"What do you mean by that?" Ansley raised a brow. "What is there to discuss?"

Levon walked back to the table with their usual orders, and Ansley could tell by the mischievous grin on his face that he wanted to gossip.

"Okay girl, spill it. What's the tea?" he asked. "I know I did not just see that fineness drinking you up with his eyes and now he's gone. Why are you still sitting here? I would've been hot on his trail. Trust and believe that honey. Simeon, get your girl."

Ansley and Simeon both laughed so hard that tears formed in their eyes.

Levon shook his head in disappointment and walked away.

Ansley grabbed one of the plates that he brought over and served herself. She eyed the cheese pulling away as she placed the triangular goodness in front of her. "Levon is a mess, but his timing is perfect. I'm starving. I was dreaming about these quesadillas on the way over here."

"Yeah he's a fool, but back to my question—who is the guy?" Simeon asked as she picked up a plate.

"His name is Davis and I really like him."

"So are you two a couple now?"

"No we haven't gotten to that point. It's only been about a month since I laid eyes on the man." Ansley gushed, "He did the sweetest thing the other day." She went on to fill Simeon in on her library date with Davis. "It's the little things like that I want in a relationship."

Simeon stared down at her nails in between checking her text messages. This was not the reaction that Ansley was expecting. She thought her friend would be happy for her. "Sorry, didn't mean to bore you."

Simeon looked up. Her eyes squinted. "That was nice, but … just don't get too excited about this mystery man. I mean how much could you know about him in a month?"

Ansley slipped a curious glance at Simeon. "Where is all of this negative energy coming from?"

"Did you miss my saying that I'm having man problems or you just can't be bothered to care about what's going on outside of yourself?" Simeon snarled.

Ansley studied Simeon's contorted face as she continued her rant.

"I've never been disregarded like that. For me to be stood up, and you somehow managed to walk out with a new love interest...well, I'm sorry, but that just doesn't sit well with me."

Ansley sat stunned. "Sweetie, I understand how you must be feeling. What he did was horrible and I hope you called him out, but you need to redirect your anger. I'm not the one who made you feel that way."

She tossed her head back in laughter. "He? Ansley do you even know my guys name? All you cared about was that I help you find a job. You don't care about what's going on in my life."

Ansley's forehead creased with worry. She moved Simeon's plate of untouched quesadillas to the side. "Listen, if I did something to upset you, I apologize but as I'm trying to recollect what I could have done—I'm bankrupt on that one. Did something happen?"

"Of course, you don't get it. It's only fitting that you can't grasp what's going on outside of yourself. You can be so self-absorbed. Please excuse my interruption of the Ansley show. Well let's get back to talking about you and the job that I got you. Congrats by the way."

"Whoa. What's gotten into you? This is not who you are or who we are as friends? Talk to me."

Simeon snatched her purse off the seat, shaking her head in disgust. "Don't even bother. I have to get going. I have a presentation in the morning. We can finish this another time, okay?" She slid out of the booth to leave.

Ansley stood as well. "Simeon, we should talk about whatever is bothering you. It's clear that you're hurt. C'mon, have a seat."

Simeon looked heavenward. "We're cool. I just have to get home and finish this presentation. We'll talk later."

She started back toward the exit.

Ansley kept up the pace with her, matching her step for step. "Simeon wait—don't walk out like this."

She grabbed Simeon's arm.

Simeon spun around and pushed her into a nearby table. "Get your hands off me."

Ansley caught herself on the edge of the table with her right hand before falling to the floor. She looked around, embarrassed at the scene they were making. She braced herself as Simeon approached.

"I—I'm sorry," Simeon stammered. "I didn't mean to do that. Let me help you."

"It's fine. Just go." She rose and smoothed out her clothes.

Simeon muttered a curse as she dashed across the room and out the front exit.

"Chile—what was that about?" Levon asked, while trying to clear the mess Simeon created.

"I wish I could tell you," Ansley murmured. "Something's definitely up with her, but she's not telling me anything."

"Well, you better keep an eye on her."

Ansley stood there confused. She had never seen Simeon act this way and didn't understand what had just happened. At any rate, she would be giving her friend some space, she had other things to focus on, which didn't involve drama.

Simeon rushed to her car, not wanting to run into any of the other patrons in the restaurant. As she pulled out her keys, she looked across the street to see Montgomery getting on the bus. She rushed in his direction to let off some steam. Her pace slowed and her breath caught when she realized he was wearing the same outfit that Ansley's friend Davis had on.

She closed her eyes hoping that she was seeing a mirage, but as they locked eyes through the window as the bus pulled away, she knew that she was not seeing anything but the ugly truth. Her lip quivered and her hands tightened into fists. *You'll pay for playing with my heart. Just you wait and see.*

Chapter 6

Hours later, Ansley sat in her living room while finishing up discussion questions in the virtual classroom.

Once she hit submit, Ansley made a beeline straight to her bedroom. Kicking off her shoes and unsnapping her womanly constraints, she navigated to the bathroom and turned on the shower. She loved taking showers; this is where she did most of her thinking. This was the place where she felt most at peace.

As she worked shampoo into her hair creating a lather, she just couldn't wash out the thoughts of what went down earlier that day. Simeon's behavior didn't make sense to her. The only gripe Simeon seemed to express was that she got stood up so Ansley assumed that perhaps her anger was just misplaced. She shook her head. Her behavior wasn't acceptable. Ansley knew she had to call her and let her know that if they were going to continue to be friends, she was going to have to address her actions today.

Moments later, she stepped out feeling better and towel dried her body. Ansley was in no mood to tame her long tresses just, she allowed them to air dry. She smoothed lotion over her body, and then exchanged her towel for her favorite white terry-cloth robe. She walked over to her nightstand and grabbed her phone to check her messages. She anticipated that Simeon would take the first step and ask to talk about what happened, but since she hadn't Ansley was not planning to let it go without finding out what she was thinking.

The phone rang several times before Simeon answered.

"Ansley if you're calling to talk to me about today, I already apologized and there's nothing more to discuss—just back off."

Ansley pulled her phone back from her ear in disbelief. "Uh, no ma'am. You don't get to jump onto the call and dismiss me. If you want us to continue to be friends, then I suggest you start talking quick."

Simeon groaned. "Ansley—I'm sorry okay. I don't know what else you want from me."

"I want you to tell me about what time you lost your mind and thought it was okay to put your hands on me? We have never handled our problems this way, and since when do we even have a problem?"

Simeon responded with silence.

"Ansley, you wouldn't understand what goes on in my head on a daily so again, I'm asking you to drop it."

Ansley sucked her teeth. "Nope. You embarrassed me and I need you to talk about it or tell me goodbye. The only options you have now or whether we will talk in-person or over the phone?"

Simeon sighed. "I guess I'll come there. When?"

"I'm planning a dinner party, and you can come early so we can lay this all out. Alright?"

Click. Simeon hung up without another word. Ansley shook her head and put her phone in the pocket of her robe. She walked into the living room and turned on the television to see what she could indulge in, but before she could decide on a show, her phone rang.

"Hello," she answered.

"Hey, pretty girl. How you doing?" Davis asked.

Her skin flushed. "I'm doing okay. Just relaxing and watching some television."

"Oh okay. Would you like some company?"

Ansley briefly entertained the idea. It was kind of early to invite him over to her home, but she was game to step out and meet him if that's what he was suggesting.

"Over the phone or are you talking about in person?"

"Come on now, Ansley—of course, I mean in person. I can tell that you're not into that idea," he said.

By the way his tone faded she could tell his mood had plummeted. Trying to change the tone of the conversation, Ansley said, "I would love to see you. There's a cute coffee shop that has great coffee, pastries and live music tonight. We can go there."

"Sounds like a plan to me. What's the address?"

The next morning, joy bubbled up in Ansley as she thought about her evening with Davis. Laying there in her bed, she allowed her mind to reflect back to that night.

Davis had been amazing. They'd met at the Café Au Latte, which was a block from her house. Since she planned to walk, she decided to be casual. She wore a pair of light wash, denim jeans and a burgundy and black, fitted sweater. She wanted her look to be effortless. Ansley didn't want Davis to think she was trying too hard.

She arrived ten minutes early, and found a nice corner booth, sat down, and waited for Davis to arrive. She loved this place. The aroma of fresh coffee and cookies baking met her at the door. The mood was contemporary and cozy. The setting of the café consisted of dimmed lighting, and there was an array of art pieces on the wall that were done by local artist. Ansley had been frequenting even more as of late, since she was always in need of late night brew as she worked.

There wasn't a huge crowd tonight so she wasn't concerned with Davis spotting her. Moments later, he strolled in canvassing the room. Ansley knew he had spotted her when Davis lifted his chin in her direction. The sight of him made her knees wobble under the table. She waved him over to the table where she sat sipping on a Chamomile Tea.

"Hey you," she stood to greet him. Wrapping her arms around his neck and leaning in close to him. She allowed her hand to graze his ebony skin down along his soft, curly beard. Ansley hoped that he never shaved. Lord knows that she loved a bearded man.

Davis pulled away from her embrace and stared into her eyes. "Now that's what I'm talking about. You making a brother feel real missed right now."

Once she sat, he slid in behind her.

"That would be a true statement. I won't even deny it," Ansley beamed.

Happiness coursed through her. He was right, she did miss him. She hadn't realized just how much she would miss being around him. The day they met at the library, she did not have the chance to engage him, but this time there was no work to be done and she could focus on learning him.

"So what made you pick this place? I've never been here before. It's nice," he said while looking around.

Her eyes brightened. "I love the food, beverages, music, and the overall feel of this place. It's another place where I'm a regular. Maybe after tonight you'll be a regular too."

"A place to call ours? That would be nice."

He took her hand in his.

It felt nice to her. Comfortable even. As they stared into each other's eyes, she could feel her face heating up as he slowly leaned in closer gently pecking her on the lips. It was soft, sweet, and innocent.

Her mouth tingled. She noticed her hands were shaking and her palms felt damp. It had been a minute since she had a kiss that encompassed all of her senses. Ansley felt as if her body was in sensory overload.

As their lips parted, she could see the desire filling his eyes. She touched her lips.

"I think we are getting more attention than the band," she said noticing a few onlookers.

Davis whispered. "No offense to the band, but that was something to see…care to show it to me again?"

Heat curled up her spine. She rubbed the side of his face. "How about… we just say to be continued for now. Our season has just begun, we have plenty of time for that."

She could tell he was pleased with her response by the way he consumed her with his eyes. Her breath caught when he took her hands into his and kissed the palm of her left hand.

"I'm really digging you."

Ansley heard his sincerity and it warmed her heart. "I like you too Davis."

Davis' brows shot up and the corners of his mouth curled upward too. "I'm glad to hear you say that because I'm interested in seeing where this could go. If you're willing...."

Ansley would have never anticipated meeting someone and connecting with them so quickly but with Davis the transition felt natural.

"So what are you saying? I'm just trying to be clear on if you are talking about dating exclusively?" she asked, wanting to make sure she understood exactly what he was proposing.

Before he could respond, the waitress came over to check on them.

"Is everything okay here? The café bar will be closing soon."

"Actually, I would love to get some of the assorted fruit and whatever pastry the lady might like."

"Hmm, you know what, the fruit will be fine and another latte please."

"I'll be right back with those items."

As the waitress set out to fill their order, Davis resumed his mission.

"Now back to your question... yes, exclusivity is what I want. I think we should take advantage of the situation."

He took Ansley's hands into his and peered deeply into her eyes. "When we first met, you must admit it felt like we were two people that just hadn't seen each other for a while. It never once felt like I was meeting a stranger," he said.

"I'm interested in seeing where this goes as well. But...I do want us to become friends first. I guess I'm old fashioned like that. It's been a great month though."

"I agree and that's understandable. You and I have a lot to learn about each other, but I'm an open book and willing to tell you everything you want to know. I don't have any secrets."

Ansley leaned in closer. Her eyes dancing. She was happy to hear that he was fine with her request.

"I just have one question though," he said while rubbing his beard.

"Yeah, what's up?"

Davis smirked. "Valentine's Day is coming up soon, so can we spend that day together or would that be moving too fast?"

She responded by tugging on his beard, beckoning for him to seal the evening off with a kiss.

Once they came up for air they started using their mouths to communicate intimate details about their life. He told her about his family. That he was the eldest of two boys and that he had a younger sister that was currently in her sophomore year at Howard University. He and his brother both attended college up north as well. His biological father passed right before he went off to college and Davis had to leave school early to help his family.

She told him that her parents were happily, retired educators, who had been married for thirty-five years and were still living in their family home in North Fulton County. She shared with him that she had only one sister, and that her family was extremely close. She told him that she'd almost been engaged, but it ended when she chose her career over love. She hadn't planned to share so much with Davis, but he showed that he was a good listener and non-judgmental. She was enjoying their conversation, so much so that she didn't even realize they were holding hands across the table. The band was wrapping up and people were beginning to leave. Time escaped them and it was well past midnight.

"Well, Davis, I had a really good time, but it's well

passed my bedtime."

"Oh wow, I didn't realize how late it was either. I guess I should agree. Let me walk you to your car," he said.

"Okay you can walk me to my car," she said with a mischievous grin.

As they left the café, Davis gently enclosed his large hands around hers. The walk was actually nice and romantic. The stars lead their way as the symphony of conversations, cars passing by, along with the live music from local bars, created a great soundtrack for their moonlight stroll. After they were about a two blocks from the café, Davis looked at her and said, "Okay where exactly did you park, woman?"

She giggled and pointed to the upcoming building, "In this parking garage. I live right there. Thanks for walking me home."

He wagged his finger at her. "Oh...you're a piece of work miss lady."

She felt breathless as he bent down and kissed her on the forehead. He lingered in her space, taking his hands and caressing her shoulders as he pulled her into a warm embrace.

She closed her eyes, laid her head on his chest, and inhaled his scent. They stayed that way for a moment. His arms around her waist and her head nestled against his chest. She allowed herself to get lost in that moment...and she liked it.

As they put some space between them, she allowed her fingers to linger on his back, caressing his spine and letting him know she wanted him near. He stole her breath when he looked into her eyes while pushing her long tresses behind her ears.

"Go ahead inside so I can make sure you got in safely," he said.

She kissed him on the cheek before she walked up the stairs to go inside. She looked back and watched Davis heading back towards the café. She briefly thought that she should have invited him inside if only for a second, but she was glad that she ended the night the way that she had.

"Hey Ansley," he called out to her, "I'm looking forward to spending the day with you. We'll have to do something unforgettable."

She got a warm, fuzzy feeling at the thought of spending more time with him. "That sounds very doable."

Once behind the door she giggled with glee and then exhaled as her toes let her know that they agreed. A toe curl never stirs me wrong.

She waved over at the door attendant as she passed the entryway. Her feet glided towards the elevator. She pressed the button for the elevator, still smiling at the evening she just had.

Ansley's phone vibrated, tearing her away from her thoughts and back to the present. She grabbed her phone off the nightstand.

Ansley broke into a smile when she saw the message from Davis. She touched her lips, thinking about the kiss that they shared.

Davis: Had a great time last night. I can't wait to see you again. Let's talk soon.

As much as she wanted to bask in this moment, it was time for her to get up and get moving.

Ansley left her place an hour later.

Her feet floated toward the elevator. As she waited on the doors to part, she felt weightless. She had not crushed on a guy this hard since Ryan. There was something about the way Davis made her feel at ease and brought out those romantic feelings that just made her certain that she was ready for another relationship.

Chapter 7

As he sat on the bench waiting for the bus to arrive, Davis could not stop thinking about Ansley and their time together. He had just sent a text to let her know that he was thinking about her. As he thought about last night, he felt a twinge of sadness thinking about how different their lives were and wondered if she could ever love someone like him.

She was a college graduate, and he never finished due to the financial troubles his family experienced after his father's death. Her family was all college educated and his family just tried to make it each month. At times it was a struggle just to make it through the week.

He loved hearing how her family always got together for church on Sunday, often had weekend meet ups, and celebrated most major holidays together. Davis loved that family was so important to her. He wished his family had that same dynamic—wished that they cared about his future and what he did with his life.

His mom made a pretty decent living working for the United States Postal Service in Chicago, but after his father passed away when he was eighteen, his mother informed him of the situation they were dealing with and announced that he needed to help out financially. He never anticipated at that age that he was to become the man of the house while she spent the majority of her time working or trying to find a new man to head their household.

Davis' heart filled with bitterness as he thought about his father. The ugly truth was that the man had checked out on his family long before he died. Get rich quick schemes and women without morals were his father's drug of choice. Davis used to want a relationship with his father, but the man could not be bothered to take time to build a bond with him or his brother.

It wasn't always like that. His father used to take him and his brother out to hoop on local basketball courts or to toss around the football. But once he was laid off, his love for his family was no longer a priority. Davis detested his father for that, and he soon started to resent his mother as well. He didn't understand why she did nothing to hold the family together.

It was because of her that he never gave a woman more of himself than was required. He was there for his mother, and even as a child she took from him and his brother. Was not there to show his little sister how to be a woman, she used her curves to take care of her personal needs and treated her children like a distraction.

Davis wanted to be different though, he did not want to be a man that hated women and treated them as disposable goods. He blamed his mother for showing him that only one person really benefitted in a relationship. There had to be someone that loss in order for the other to gain, he recalled her telling him and his siblings that one evening. She would go from one man to the next, and stay gone for days. Leaving him to fend for his family. He promised that he would never let a woman take advantage of him. He would always take what he needed before they got the chance to hurt him.

Coming out of his dark memories, he grinned when

his phone lit up and he saw that Ansley had responded to his text.

Ansley: I had a wonderful time with you, too. I can't wait to see you again.

Seeing her message lifted his spirits. Ansley gave him hope that there were women out there that did not come with an agenda. Her heart was pure gold and it showed. Ansley would be the one to change him for the better; he just needed to make a few life changes to ensure that once he got her, she wouldn't abandon him. He needed her to keep him at a peaceful state. He couldn't take on any more drama in his life.

Just as he was about to put his phone away, it rang. The number on the screen was showing restricted. He went ahead and answered it, with the people he rolled with, it was not unheard of to have a burner phone or two.

"Yeah, you got Davis… who this?"

"Davis, huh? Is that what you're calling yourself these days? I don't know what's wrong with the name I gave you, chile. Oh, that's right. Someone is running from the law like a buffoon."

His lips turned downward. "Hello Ma."

"I don't know why you insist on throwing your life away like this," she responded, continuing her rant. "You use to be about something. I'm shocked you're still using this number. I hope you didn't forget that you're scheduled to appear in court next week. Are you coming into town? You can't keep prolonging this."

"I'll be there, Ma. Why you trippin' like this?"

"I know I didn't raise you to be this way. It just breaks my heart. It really does. Men are supposed to take care of their responsibilities. This just don't make no kind of sense, son."

"I'm fine. Thanks for asking," he said his tone laced with sarcasm. His mother never seemed to have anything nice to say. He was not perfect. He messed up just like the next person, but she could never understand that.

"Boy, you must think I'm slow or something. I know sarcasm when I hear it, and you best keep that smart mouth of yours under control. With all that I know, you should think twice about treating me any kind of way."

"Ma, I appreciate you calling, but I'll take care of it. Don't worry," he said, not hiding his agitation.

"That girl keeps calling here, wanting me to deliver messages to you and I'm sick of it. You need to handle your mess and leave your father and me out of it, ya hear?"

"I don't have a father, and when have y'all ever helped me out with anything?"

When he told Ansley that his father was dead, Davis meant it. The man was dead to him.

"Sometimes I feel like Beau is the only family that I have," he said, feeling defensive. "Your first husband completely abandoned me. Your current, disowned me, and with both of them openly denouncing me whenever they had a chance, you took your love away from me, too. But my cousin—he's always got my back. Just stop calling me."

"I love you, Lord knows I do, but you are so ungrateful. Harold might not be your biological father, but he did more than your sperm donor ever did. Harold provided a way for us to pay for your tuition, books and student housing and what did you do to show your appreciation? You didn't even finish."

He winced. Davis was tired of her not taking ownership for the way his life turned out.

"How soon you forget that I had to leave school to help you? You let my siblings continue their education while I worked to help you pay for them to remain enrolled. So you can stop hanging that over my head."

"Boy please. You got caught up running the streets with Beau, you coulda gone back to school. Don't you ever fix your mouth to say we didn't do anything for you. We just stopped trying to help cause' I learnt a long time ago that you can't help the helpless. Handle your business and tell that girl don't call here no more," she said before disconnecting the call.

Just when things were going well—his mother called him to make him feel worthless. Bringing up drama that he did not want to be bothered with now. Most mothers were supportive of their children, but not his mother—that husband of hers, Harold, had taken prime real estate in her mind. That is where all of her attention went. She did not have time for her oldest son, but in comparison, his siblings were always a priority.

It was okay, though. He did not need her for much anyway. He was his own man. He had to go back to Chicago to resolve a few issues, but planned to come back to resume his new life in Georgia and his plan to make Ansley his woman.

Davis was starting to feel like he was getting his life on track, and he wanted to make sure the problem went away forever. Using the Delta Airlines application on his iPhone, Davis searched for flights to Chicago. He was not sure how he was going to finance this trip, but he had to figure out a way. His cousin, Beau came to mind.

Beau Cannon was infamous in the family and there was no situation too large for him to handle—for a small fee, of course. Davis already owed Beau at least a thousand dollars, but Davis hoped that he could work out another deal with his cousin. He had to get to Chicago, and he knew asking Beau for help meant terms and conditions, but what choice did he have?

The phone rang twice before a woman answered, "Yeah, who dis?"

Davis thought he had the wrong number. Beau changed his number at least once every two or three months, but he always answered the phone.

Davis paused. "Umm... is Beau there? This is his cousin, Davis."

He heard a conversation going on in the background before Beau came to the phone.

"Fool, if you're not calling to make a payment, then you don't need to be calling," Beau said, without prolonging the awkward moment Davis anticipated.

"Listen man, I know I owe you and I'm working on a come up right now, but check it out, I need to catch a flight to Chicago tonight. Old girl tossing my name around and I need to get her to withdraw this lawsuit." Davis was desperate and did not have another option.

He knew that Beau would request that he make a drop in Chicago to repay the debt. Right now, Davis had no choice but to do whatever Beau requested. He just hoped that it was not a large ticket item or one of those dummy missions. "I can bring you in on this job I'm working on and give you a majority of the profit, if I have to, but I need you to make this happen for me."

Beau roared with laughter. "Man, you stay in trouble... you know that? You owe me more than a percentage, brother. I've always kept your name clean and took the hard hits for you. So I tell you what; I got some business to take care of in Chicago as well. You handle a few things for me and I'll give you a hand."

Davis swallowed hard. He knew any task that Beau would assign could be risky. He was running out of time and opportunities to end this situation, and doing work for his cousin was his best and only choice. "Alright, man. What do you need me to do?"

Chapter 8

It was Ansley's turn to host girl's night out at her place. She and her girls tried to get together for an evening of fun, food and relaxation at least every other month. Her house was the neutral zone because Simeon and Lanae always found a reason to disagree on just about everything. The day the two of them agreed on something would be the day that Ansley accepted a White House nomination.

With Valentine's Day approaching, she wanted to do something with the girls. With Davis out of town, she invited them for dinner on Sunday evening. In the past, they normally got together on a Friday or Saturday, but she wanted to leave her Valentine's weekend open. Last year, she and Simeon did something together, but now that she was dating Davis, Ansley figured this would be a great way to still spend time with Simeon since she mentioned having a tough time with her man. It would not replace their Valentine's Day tradition for the past few years, dinner and a movie, but she hoped that it would soften the sting of the truth once Ansley told Simeon she had plans.

She asked Simeon to come early so that they could discuss the incident. A week had passed since their awkward exchange at Tin Lizzy's. Ansley was glad that Simeon agreed to come over and she hoped that they could resolve the tension and get back to way they were before.

There was a knock at the door.

Ansley rushed to answer it. She assumed it was Simeon since the doorman did not ring her before sending up a guest, which was normal protocol. She had given him permission to allow Simeon and Lanae to come up whenever they visited.

She looked through the peephole. Simeon was standing with her arms crossed and eyes downcast.

Ansley opened the door and greeted her. "Hello lovely. C'mon in. The wine is chilled, mimosas are strong, and I put your favorite goblet on the counter."

"I brought red wine," Simeon said as she entered the condo. She handed Ansley the bottle and walked toward the living room.

Her voice seemed void of emotion. Still, Ansley was glad to see her. "Thank you for coming."

Ansley considered going in for a hug, but she feared that Sugar Shane Simeon would reemerge. Words will do just fine.

Simeon turned to face Ansley. Her hands crossed over her chest. "I'm sorry about pushing you. I shouldn't have done that."

Ansley walked pass Simeon and over to the kitchen. "No you shouldn't have. I would be lying if I didn't say I'm sorry I didn't push back." She smirked. "Care to tell me what the heck that was about?"

"That was just a bad day for me," Simeon responded. "I'm really sorry."

Ansley took her hand. "Let's have a seat in the kitchen, and then you can give me a real answer instead of that crap you just tried."

Once Simeon was seated at the kitchen table. Ansley opened the merlot that Simeon had brought over. As she poured them both a glass, Simeon unloaded.

"Monty…that's the guy's name. The one that stood me up? He had my head all scrambled. He hasn't returned any of my calls or text, and finally, I know what's been keeping him from me."

Ansley handed Simeon her glass and sat across from her. "I don't know what this has to do with you treating me the way you did, but go ahead—what's his issue? Married?"

Simeon sipped and squished the wine around, allowing her palate to savor the flavor before speaking. "Him being married would be easier to digest." Meeting Ansley's gaze, she stated, "It's him dating you that I'm having an issue with."

Ansley choked on her wine as her tears filled with eyes. "Wait, what now?"

Simeon pressed her hands to her cheeks. "The man you're dating is the same man I met at a conference in Chicago. He introduced himself as Monty. We went out for drinks…he and I did a lot of drinking…"

Ansley felt her heart beating fast. She held up her palms. "But the guy I'm seeing is Davis—not Monty—they aren't the same people." She hoped that Simeon would realize that she was mistaken.

"I'm not crazy, Ansley. Monty and Davis are the same man. I should know. He and I went back to my suite and had an intense night of lovemaking," Simeon said. "When I woke up the next day, Monty was gone and I didn't see him again until he showed up at Tin Lizzy's the same day that you got laid off. I had hoped that he wanted to reconnect with me, but I guess after seeing you at the New Year's Eve Party, he chose you over me."

Ansley took a deep breath. She couldn't believe what

she was hearing. Her shoulders tensed and she began to rub her temples. "Why did you wait until now to say something? If you knew it was the same guy. You could've said this at the restaurant instead of trying to knock me down."

Simeon leaned back against the chair, setting her hands flat on the table. "I just realized who he was when I left the restaurant and saw him getting on the bus."

Ansley was still having a hard time comprehending. None of this felt real and with Simeon's unpredictable behavior, she just was not sure what to believe.

She began running her fingers through her hair. Ansley stood and walked over to the island in her kitchen. She nibbled on her bottom lip.

"Simeon—when was the last time you were with him?" Ansley questioned. Although she posed the question, she didn't know if she was ready to know the answer.

Ansley saw how Simeon's leg bounced underneath the table. She took a calming breath as she prepared to hear the answer.

"He came over a couple of weeks after the party, and stayed the night and even had breakfast with me the next day. I thought he was going to give us a chance, but instead he wanted you."

Ansley slapped her hand to her forehead. "Oh my goodness, Simeon who cares who he wanted," she yelled. She slammed her hands on the table. "He's playing us both. I know him as Davis, who knows what other names he's using or how many women are out there. Unbelievable."

Simeon gave a half shrug. "I didn't want to ruin things for you two, but I have to be honest."

Ansley pinched the bridge of her nose. This was all just too daunting. She shook her head.

"Simeon…I don't even know what to say. Wow…I mean…wow." She didn't want to believe what she had just heard. "This is a lot to take in all at once."

An image of Simeon in bed with Davis materialized in her mind. Ansley dismissed the thought. She slumped down in the chair next to Simeon.

Simeon waved her hand. "Now you know the truth."

"I wish I had never gone out with him. I can't believe this—what a jerk."

"I'm glad to hear you say that because now that you're out of the picture I believe me and him could have a future."

Ansley squinted her eyes and frowned.

Simeon stared straight in her face. "I can see that you're concerned, but don't worry about me. I know you may be thinking I'm weak or pathetic, but you don't know my connection to him. I know how to handle a man like him. The type that may tweak the truth not to hurt you. I'm not sure why he lied about his name, but I know my feelings have not changed behind his behavior. He's not your type anyway."

Ansley guffawed. "I'm sorry, but you can't be that desperate for love that you still want him after this?" Ansley inquired. Not hiding her growing irritation with Simeon's nonchalant attitude, she said, "You deserve better, and I've seen you with better. This still doesn't explain why you put your hands on me though."

They sat in silence for a moment, the tension mounting between them.

"Let-it-go," Simeon hissed.

The doorbell sounded.

"That's Lanae," Ansley announced. She walked over

to let Lanae in while talking to Simeon over her shoulder. "We can finish this later."

"Whatever," Simeon uttered.

She rose to her feet and strode into the kitchen to pour herself a glass of wine before walking over near the windows.

Ansley unlocked the door and welcomed Lanae inside.

"Hey, sweetie," she said while embracing her. "Come on in."

"Hello, hello," Lanae said. "It seems like it's been a minute since I visited Chateau Ansley. I see you have some new art pieces. Very nice." Lanae glanced at Simeon. "How are you, lady?"

"I'm fine," she responded, but never bothered to turn around to face her.

Lanae looked at Ansley and then shrugged. "What's her problem? Not that I'm surprised—forever shady."

"Excuse me? What exactly are you trying to say?" Simeon said turning away from the window. "Ansley, you might want to get your friend before I do." She glared at Lanae.

"Okay, why don't you have a seat in the living room, Lanae and I'll get you something to drink," Ansley said, trying to diffuse the situation. "Simeon, you look like you could use a refill too. I didn't think I would have to separate you two this early."

Simeon rolled her eyes at Ansley and turned back toward the window.

Lanae and Simeon had a love hate relationship. It usually started just with one making a joke which the other didn't receive well. Ansley tried to avoid confrontation with either of them because they could drag a disagreement into the ground, kill it, resuscitate it, and beat it some more.

"Not that anyone asked, but I have salad for starters and honey pecan chicken with grilled asparagus for the main dish."

"That sounds delicious. Where'd you find the recipe for the chicken?" Lanae asked, while positioning her body to face the kitchen from where she sat in the living room.

Lanae and Simeon both tried to convince her to buy some cookbooks, but she had an addiction to finding recipes on Pinterest. This was her hobby. Along with taking photos of the food she cooked and posting it on Instagram. She was a proud foodie.

"And please tell me that we won't be the first to try it 'cause I did not bring my Zantac," Simeon said. She walked away from the window long enough to feign a stomach ache. "Lanae, you remember when she tried to make sushi rolls? My tummy is still mad at me for that one."

"You mean the shouldn't-have-tried-it rolls? How could I forget? Girl, I barely made it home without having to stop a few times," Lanae said with a chuckle. "It's crazy to me—as much as you love to cook, you don't have any cookbooks around here."

"Right… all she has is that raggedy manila folder." Simeon walked over to the counter and picked up the folder and grabbed a stack of recipes. "You almost have a full cookbook right here."

Lanae got up and joined them in the kitchen. "Now see—that's pitiful. I have to agree with Simeon. Why don't you just get the real thing? I'm sure there's one out there with half the recipes you have printed."

"I have to get my daily fix, and I can't do that with a book sitting at home on the shelf," she told them.

"Okay, enough boring talk. What's up with Davis?" Lanae asked.

Ansley glanced over at Simeon, who was waiting for a response. "Let me fix these salad plates for y'all, and then I'll check on the chicken again. It should be about done." She really did not want to discuss Davis, or at least not with Simeon being there.

Ansley tossed the salad and fixed three plates. She walked over to the table and placed one on the servers for each of them.

"Ain't nobody thinking about that salad right now. This story must be juicy. I can read between the lines. Let me go get comfortable," Lanae said walking back towards the living room grabbing her glass and the wine bottle. Simeon was not far behind.

"I'm curious to hear this too Lanae. Go ahead Ansley."

Ansley looked over at Simeon as she sat up tall, eyeing her like a hawk studies its prey. She could see a slight glint in Simeon's eyes too. It was clear that she was relishing this moment, hoping to get full disclosure. While Ansley had nothing to hide, she was not planning to say much because that was a conversation she wanted to have with Simeon alone.

Lanae threw a pillow in Ansley's direction. "If you don't come on with the goods I'm going to get very anxious and might have an accident with this red wine on this beige carpet," she threatened, pretending to tip her glass.

"I know you won't do that 'cause then you'll have to explain to Jacob why you had to pay to have my carpet cleaned. Or I guess you could roll up those sleeves and get to scrubbing. Either way, you'll be cleaning up that wine stain."

Simeon remained silent.

Lanae did not seem to notice, but Ansley knew that Simeon's silence was deliberate, she was not wanting this moment to pass without Ansley divulging more information.

"Yeah, yeah... get to the deets on this evening with Davis."

Ansley's eyebrow rose. "Um...deets?"

"She's talking details and you know it. Why you stallin'?"

She glanced in Simeon's direction. She didn't want to have this conversation, but Lanae was adamant and there seemed to be no way to avoid it. Besides, Simeon had plans to still pursue him anyway, so she may as well give her what she wanted.

"Okay fine. We met up at the café down the street. We talked, ate and listened to live music," Ansley said. "We had a great time and then he walked me home."

"Did he spend the night?" Simeon asked.

Lanae stared wide-eyed at Simeon for her bold question, and then looked back over to Ansley awaiting her answer.

Ansley pursed her lips. "No Simeon, he didn't," she responded. "He went home afterwards."

Ansley tried not to wear her emotions on her face, but right now she was over Simeon's passive aggressive behind. She took the chicken out of the oven, and removed the asparagus from her mini George Foreman grill. Ansley was not going to allow Simeon to disrupt this evening—not over a guy that she was no longer planning to date.

She and Simeon never had a problem when it came to men. They had different preferences in that department, but now there was Davis, and he was proving to be the catalyst for change in that area.

"Though you attempted to water down those details, it seems like you are really smitten with him," Lanae stated. "Outside of today, the mention of his name would have you smiling all hard and blushing. Did you not enjoy the date?"

"I did have a good time," Ansley was reluctant to admit. "And I do like him, I don't think I realized just how much until he left for Chicago. I really miss him."

Even though she was upset that he had deceived her, she was struggling with how her heart felt about him and Simeon. Though Simeon was acting out of character, she still cared about her, but her heart wanted to know what Davis and Ansley looked like in the long run.

"Davis is in Chicago?" Simeon asked, interrupting her thoughts. "For how long?"

"I took him to the airport this morning. He said he'd be gone through Thursday, but that he would be back in time—for Valentine's Day," Ansley responded.

"I haven't met Davis, but don't rush into anything. Take time and really get to know this man—"

Simeon cut Lanae off before she could finish. "Before you start this episode of Iyanla Fix My Life, can we please eat?" She rose, walked into the kitchen and grabbed a plate. Lanae shrugged and followed Simeon over to the table.

"Lanae, you might as well keep your advice to yourself. This girl here is a grown woman. She'll do whatever she wants, regardless of what you say or how you feel. Ain't that right, Ansley?"

Ansley sent a sharp glare in Simeon's direction, but who was she kidding, she wanted to at least hear him out. Every story had two sides, and his story may have a different ending.

Ansley plastered on a fake smile. "Yes, let's go ahead and fix our plates so Simeon can find a better use for her trap."

Simeon smirked as if she had just won a battle, but Ansley was not even trying to escalate this conversation. "Get over it, already," she uttered loud enough for Simeon to hear. Ansley could see Lanae tossing glances between the two, but she was not asking any questions. She knew Ansley would tell her everything later, just like she always did when she and Simeon had a disagreement.

Ansley could not believe she was being so catty. Simeon confessed that she slept with Davis and the man disappeared on her while she was sleeping—it's not like they had a real relationship. It was a one-night stand.

She fixed her plate after Lanae, and joined them at the table. Ansley felt like she was in an old western as Simeon stared her down. This year was getting off to an interesting start, and by the hint of anger building behind Simeon's eyes, it was only the beginning.

Chapter 9

It was eight o'clock at night, and Ansley had just finished washing the dishes from her dinner party. She was exhausted, but there was work to be done. She was two hours into her assignment, and her legs were beginning to ache from sitting on the floor crossed legged with her feet tucked under her thighs.

Ansley pulled her hair up into a messy bun and began rubbing the back of her neck. She adjusted her laptop which was sitting in her lap and placed it on the chocolate, leather ottoman in the center of her living room. She felt a tad bit overwhelmed.

She had yet to begin working on her article submission for Grind House, and she didn't want to keep Jason waiting. Her goal was to have her article submitted before the Tuesday deadline. It was important that Jason and the other writers saw her a great contribution to the team.

Rubbing her eyes, Ansley decided it was time to take a break. She stood to stretch and legs, and walked into the kitchen to grab a glass of water. Taking a couple of sips, Ansley stared at her phone on the island charging. She considered calling Davis back and telling him that he could lose her number. He had called her a couple of times during the dinner party, but in light of recent events, she had yet to commit to reaching out to him.

As if on cue, her phone rang.

It was Davis.

She answered on the second ring.

"What a pleasant surprise," he said. "Ms. Wright, what do I owe the pleasure of actually hearing your voice and not your voicemail on this evening?"

Ansley exhaled. "It's been a little hectic with the new job kicking into gear, and then there's school. I'm still trying to find balance," she said. "You caught me at a good time. I'm taking a break from my paper."

"How was your day?

She unplugged the phone and hopped up on the counter top to sit. "Busy. I have a demanding schedule this week. I have a couple of deadlines that I need to meet for school and work, and I just need to manage my time wisely to get everything done."

"You sound stressed," Davis said. "When was the last time you had a massage? Maybe you need someone to help you alleviate some of that tension."

Ansley scrunched her nose. The idea of him touching her was not a tempting offer considering he had been with Simeon. Then again, she wasn't even sure if that was even true. Simeon didn't have a reason to lie to her, but she had been shifting moods on her lately, so Ansley wasn't sure which way to think. All she knew was that she planned to keep it cordial until she got some answers.

"It's been a minute. I'll have to get that planned in the near future. But listen, I really need to get back focused."

She heard him draw in a breath.

"I'll let you get to work, but don't forget I'm kidnapping you for a Valentine's Day. We'll start out with a morning walk through the Atlanta Botanical Gardens, and then brunch at The West Egg in Midtown. Midday, we can hit up the Art Stroll in Atlantic Station, and following that,

I was thinking we would catch a movie," Davis told her. "And if we get hungry again, we can have dinner or dessert somewhere. Are you up for that?"

Ansley pretended to strangle herself. He was saying the right things, but all she could think about was getting some clarity. Timing was not on her side.

"Davis, it all sounds wonderful. We'll see how the week unfolds. Okay?

Again, she could hear the life deflating out of him, but until they had a chance to speak in person she had to try to reel in her emotions.

"I see," he replied. "Well you're a grinder. I know you'll have your work done before I get back. We are doing this," he claimed. "Besides, I really miss you, and this...we can't wait another minute. I'll call you when I return on Thursday."

He disconnected the call before she could protest.

Her heart melted. Ansley wanted to dismiss her desire to connect with him further, but she could not just turn off the feelings she was developing. She drew in a long breath. So much for getting back to work, her mind was fully concentrated on Davis. Hearing the deep timbre of his voice sent her pulse racing. Dang it, Simeon.

As long as Simeon kept popping into her head, she knew she would have a temporary block on her desires. Ansley shook away the thoughts that made her lips quiver in anticipation of a kiss that would not come.

"Davis, what are you doing to me?" she whispered.

Chapter 10

After leaving Ansley's house, Simeon rushed home to pack her bags. She decided to hop on the first thing out of Atlanta heading to Chicago. It was time she and Davis had a real conversation. She managed to get his itinerary from Ansley. Simeon was actually grateful that Lanae had been around because Ansley might not have shared as much information, which assisted her in setting her plan into motion. Before darting out of Ansley's house, Simeon managed to purchase a ticket on her Delta Airlines app, and stop by the boutique across the street from Ansley's place to grab a sexy new dress and some lingerie.

The next morning she was hustling through Atlanta Hartsfield International to catch her flight. She smiled to herself as he showed her boarding pass to the attendant. The thought of being tangled between the sheets with her future boo was enough to make this impromptu purchase worth it.

With her bags secured in the overhead, Simeon sat and nuzzled her neck against the chair. *Wheels up and we are out.*

Two hours later she was pulling into Chicago O'Hare and wiping the sleep out of her eyes. She planned to get checked into the hotel and get some rest before reaching out to Davis. She wanted to make sure she had her energy for tonight. She wasn't sure why he was there and what his plans were for the day, she thought it would be best to inform him of her arrival later in the evening. Simeon hoped that asking to meet him later would limit his options of saying he was too busy.

"What are you doing in Chicago?" he asked when she called to inform him that she was in town.

"I'm here on business," Simeon lied. "I was surprised when Ansley told me that you were in town as well.

"Huh? Ansley told you?" he stammered.

"Yes I know all about Davis, and she knows all about Monty." Simeon informed him. Not deterred from her mission she continued, "I was thinking, since I'm in town, we should have dinner together. We have a lot to discuss."

He huffed. "Nah, I'm not hungry. Enjoy your trip."

"Oh stop it Monty. Or is it Davis?" She laughed at her own joke. The deafening silence on the other end let her know that she had regained his attention. "I guess it doesn't really matter now, right? What matters is that you're dating my best friend—don't you think she would want us to get along? Listen, we need to figure out a way to be friends—for Ansley's sake."

More silence and then, "I suppose you're right," he agreed.

"Excellent. There's a great restaurant at the hotel where I'm stayin'. I'll text you the address."

They arranged to meet at eight o' clock that night.

Simeon hung up with a huge grin on her face. She clapped her hands with delight as she stood to prepare for his arrival.

Davis didn't know it, but they were going to have dinner in her suite. She glanced at the sexy, barely-there, burgundy dress laid out on the bed. Ansley may have stolen his attention with her conversation, but Simeon knew she could entice all of his senses in a way that Ansley would never do. Ansley was too much of a good girl.

She met Davis first, and by all rights, it makes sense that Ansley be erased out of the equation. Simeon could tell that Ansley was still not one hundred on letting things end with Davis even after she told her that he was the man in her life. This would be the push Ansley needed to let go and move on to the next man.

Ansley would soon realize that she never had Davis—she was just temporary. Simeon figured that he must have known they were friends and wanted to get a reaction out of her. That's why he stood her up at the party, he wanted to see if she would fight for his affection and she failed to do so. She didn't even realize it was the same guy.

Simeon smirked as she eyed the tiny video recorder hidden in the bouquet of flowers on the dresser. While she knew it would hurt Ansley to see the footage, she had a feeling she was going to need it to help Ansley let go of him. After tonight, Davis would belong to her.

He arrived an hour later.

When she opened the door, Davis's eyes roamed up her long limbs, firm thighs, and continued up to the plunging neckline of her dress and lingered on her breast. "You couldn't afford the whole dress?" he joked.

She stepped back to allow him to come inside the suite. He hesitated before taking a few steps inside the door frame.

Simeon laughed. "This is the whole dress. Don't you like it?" She modeled for him, stopping short to give him the full view of her firm behind.

Davis rubbed his hand across his beard. "You're going

to break up a few marriages and quite a few necks tonight dressed like that."

"You're looking pretty, darn sexy yourself." She lusted over his fit physique, even in a fitted tan dress shirt and olive green corduroy blazer, his body was on display. His tweed slacks fit his sculpted frame. They would be the perfect fit couple.

He gestured towards the door. "Shall we go?"

"Well, I hope you won't mind but...," Simeon closed the door behind him. "I ordered room service."

He turned around to face her, his arms folded across his chest. "What are you up to?"

She threw her hands up, professing her innocence. "I'm not up to anything at all. I thought we should have some privacy when we talk."

Davis met her gaze. "About what?"

"Us," Simeon responded.

He gave her a look of puzzlement. "There is no us. There never was."

"So you're saying that you were only interested in sex? Because that's not what you said that night."

"Simeon, we were both drunk," Davis uttered. "I don't remember much about that night and I doubt that you do either. Let's just go eat."

She closed the gap between them. Pressing her breast against him, she murmured, "We had a connection."

"What we had was sex," he said. Taking a few steps back, Davis said, "Simeon, I need you to get past this little infatuation of yours. I have real feelings for Ansley."

Red-hot anger coursed in her veins. "I don't believe that for a second. You're only using her to upset me. I know that's exactly what you're doing." She began to pace back and forth in front of him. "You didn't even tell her your real name."

Davis shook his head and grabbed Simeon by the shoulders. "You're wrong. I'm into her, and I wasn't lying to her, or at least not anymore." He released his grip on her and hung his head. "I went through the process to have my name changed legally. So it is Davis. I wasn't trying to hurt anyone. Not you or her—I'm sorry if I hurt you."

Her glare softened as she heard the defeated tone in his voice. "It's okay baby." Simeon cupped his face and looked into his eyes. "Apology accepted, but tell me why? Why did you need to change your name? Are you in trouble?"

He backed away from her touch.

"Tell me. I can help you. Is someone after you?"

"There's nothing you can do for me."

He brushed pass her and walked over to the queen size bed, and sat down. Simeon walked over and climbed onto the bed, pulling her legs underneath her.

"I came here hoping to work out a payment plan with my kid's mom. I was a little late on payments and she started harassing me."

Simeon began rubbing his back. "I didn't know you had a child. At least you're trying to do the right thing. How behind are you in paying her?"

Davis clasped his hands together. "I haven't made a payment in about two years—or well not full payments. I've been giving her money when I could so she gave me a pass. Once those payments got lacks, she got her hood cousins to come rob my place and rough me up."

Her eyes saddened. "I'm so sorry. Is there anything I can do to help?"

Davis muttered a curse. "Not unless you have six thousand dollars sitting around.

The corners of Simeon's eyes crinkled. "I don't have it on me, but I can transfer it to your account."

He shook his head. "I can't let you do that."

"See that's where you're confused. You're not letting me do anything, I'm offering it to you. No strings…well, maybe just one string."

"I'll help you if you make love to me one last time." Davis stood and Simeon scrambled to her feet as well.

"Wait don't leave. Think about it. You could eliminate that debt. I just need you to keep seeing me."

"What? You sound crazy." He started toward the door and Simeon pulled his arm.

Davis spun in her direction. There was a combination of rage and lust in his eyes. She looked over her shoulder toward the camcorder. There was no way she could allow him to walk out the door. She had to make him agree to this.

She leaned in and kissed him. When he didn't resist she pressed into him. His hands slid to her waist and gripped her tighter. Her heart rate quickened as their kisses became more intense. He began unzipping her dress and she stepped out of it as it fell in a heap around her ankles.

Simeon panted as his hands roamed her body. He guided her towards the bed and started to undress. She leaned up to help him with his shirt. He leaned down and regained her lips, beads of sweat formed on his forehead. He lowered himself on to the bed, wrapping her legs around his waist she whispered in his ear, "Call me Ansley."

"What?" he pushed away from her.

She pulled him back down. "Calm down. I can be her for tonight. Come on, don't stop now."

Davis was bewildered. He removed Simeon's hands from around his neck and began getting dressed. He was shaking his head in disgust. "I'm out."

"Don't you dare walk out on me. How will you pay your baby mama, huh? You need me too," she yelled. She hopped off the bed and followed behind him.

"I'll tell Ansley everything. Don't be an idiot."

Davis paused and looked at Simeon once more before walking out.

As the door closed, Simeon picked up a wine bottle and threw it. She stood there trembling with fury as she watched the red liquid run down the white door.

His walking out reminded her of her father. It was all he ever did—walk in and out of her life. A man of great financial means, her dad acted as if he didn't have to answer to anyone. He was a horrible husband and a not-so-great father to her. Maybe if she'd been a boy…

Simeon shook the pain-filled thoughts from her mind. Thinking about all that had happened during her childhood only made her angry. She didn't like when she got angry—her fury raged out of control. Simeon's chest rose and fell, as she walked over to her purse, grabbing one of the prescription bottles out. She shook out a pill and held it in her hand, before discarding it. She didn't want to not feel her disappointment. Maybe Ansley was right, he was out to hurt them both.

Images of Davis appeared in her head, prompting her to strip the comforter from the bed, toss the pillows across the room, and to attempt to push the mattress off the bed. She eyed the video recorder that would not help in getting what she wanted and threw it against the wall. She looked at the cracked screen and shards laying on the floor. Simeon lowered herself to the floor and sat among the wreckage. It mirrored how she felt.

There was a knock at the door.

Simeon took several deep breaths...she needed to calm down. She grimaced looking around at the room that was now a complete mess from the wine stained walls, to the shards of glass and plastic surrounding the door. Simeon figured that someone must have complained about the noise.

She looked through the peephole to see Montgomery. Simeon cracked the door. She didn't want him to see how she had trashed the room.

"Did you mean what you said? About being there for me, and helping me through all of this. Did you mean it?"

Simeon did not respond.

Instead she opened the door and pulled him into her arms. She sobbed on his shoulder. He came back for her.

For them.

His lips found hers and sealed their love contract. Simeon planned to take care of him, so long as he took care of her heart. She knew she could not survive another heartache. Ansley would have to find a way to understand. Now that she had him back in her arms, she got confirmation that her desire had not mislead her. They were meant to be together. She would make sure nothing came between them again.

The next day, Simeon woke up and gazed over at Montgomery lying next to her. *He didn't leave me*. It was all she could do to keep from screaming. She raked her fingers through her hair, her eyes dancing as she thought of the love they made. Simeon laid there staring at him with adoration. She was taken with him and in pure bliss that he was the one to make her feel this way.

As he stirred, she slid her body closer to him. She stroked the side of his face with the back of her hand and allowed her hand to continue down to his bare chest.

"Good morning handsome."

He opened one eye and smirked at her. "Morning beautiful."

Simeon winked at him before sliding out of the bed and padding nude across the room to her overnight bag.

"It's about time you woke up." She joshed. "I thought I would be flying back to Georgia alone."

Montgomery turned on his side to face her. "I still need to figure that out. My plans are to be here until Thursday. I still have to work out these payments. Besides I only had enough for a one-way ticket."

"I went ahead and booked us a flight departing at ten a.m. I'm about to jump in the shower. It's a little after seven now, so we need to get a move on," she said over her shoulder.

"Simeon I can't leave that soon, but I appreciate the offer. I'll figure out a way to pay you back."

Turning around with her toiletries in hand, she licked her lips as Montgomery stretched out in the bed studying her fit frame. The sunlight managed to highlight her assets through the slit in the blinds. She loved the way he was looking at her. *Got him.*

"I want us to be friends, and more than anything I want us to connect pass the physical. You don't have to pay me back, but I do want you to sever ties with Ansley. That's all that I'm asking of you."

He covered his eyes with his hands. As he lay there mute, Simeon became anxious shifting from one foot to another.

"It might be hard to believe, but I do care about her feelings and our friendship. It's just that I met you first—and it seems only fair that..."

"I'll tell her," he mumbled.

Her eyes lit up. "Tell her what?"

Uncovering his eyes, he said, "I'll let her know that I can't see her anymore."

Simeon's shoulders relaxed and she exhaled. "Thank you. And you don't even have to mention me, I think that will make it less painful that way."

He had no clue how much it meant to her that he would make her his number one. His priority. Simeon hoped Ansley would be able to forgive the methods she used to win him back, but matters of the heart required extreme measures. Simeon gave him a come-hither look.

"If you don't stop looking at me like that, you won't be making that flight."

"I'm not messing with you," she said in between laughing. "I'll tell you what. I'll change our flight to Wednesday night or Thursday morning."

"They'll charge you for that Simeon, and don't you have to get back to work."

"Don't worry. I got you." She continued to the bathroom to take a shower. "Care to join me in the shower?"

He propped himself up with his elbows resting on the mattress. "And you know it, now go ahead and get the water started. I'll be right there."

She blew a kiss over her shoulder before entering the bathroom and turning the shower knobs. A smiled danced across her lips. As she tested the water, she felt more content than she had in years. Sorrowed closed up her throat as doubt seeped in, she could only hope nothing would steal this moment. Whatever almost happened with Ansley was not important, she wanted to live in the now with him.

It dawned on her, that she had no evidence of his new found commitment to building their relationship.

A frown formed on her face.

Simeon hated that she didn't have that security net, but then she remembered that she was not letting that past interrupt her plans for the future. What's love without unrelenting trust? He said he would break things off with Ansley for good and she had to trust him. She didn't want the possibility of not being with him to be an option—she couldn't handle that.

Chapter 11

Laying in bed, Montgomery couldn't believe his luck. Had Simeon not dropped into town, he would've been forced to find another place to lay his head for the night. He spent the first night at a motel, and was planning to see if his brother could make room for him. While he found her to be very annoying, in this instance she turned out to be a major blessing.

Montgomery laughed to himself. He'd almost said too much the other night. He was simply planning to use Ansley for her money, but couldn't afford to let Simeon in on that particular truth.

Montgomery got out of the bed and started towards the bathroom, but stopped short and went over to Simeon's bag. He cocked his head to the side as he noticed that she only had one outfit in her bag, which he thought was surprising considering she said she was there on business. As he thought more about it, they never did discuss what she was there to do.

He didn't make much of it. Instead he took advantage of the time and went through Simeon's purse as well. She didn't have any cash in her wallet, and her purse was filled with opened mail, receipts, invoices, and a few pill bottles.

He picked up one of the bottles and tried to read the prescription. He had never heard of it before, but planned to look it up to see what she used it for, dependent upon its strength and use, it might have some street value and he could offer it to Beau. Anything he could do to get his debt paid down, he would do it. He grabbed his phone from the outlet on the bedside nightstand and took a picture of her prescription label.

"Monty, what's taking you so long?" Simeon called out.

He jerked his head towards the bathroom.

"On my way," he said before sending the picture to his cousin. He knew if anyone knew the value of that bottle it would be Beau.

He put the bottle back in her purse the way he found it, and opened her wallet and took one of the credit cards out. Davis was sure to take one of the cards tucked behind another card. *She won't miss it.*

Davis slid the shower door open and snuck behind Simeon. He planted a few kisses on her collar bone. He smirked as she squirmed. Lathering up, he felt overjoyed that his plan was coming together. *I'll ask for forgiveness later.*

Chapter 12

On Wednesday morning, Ansley received her first major assignment for the July issue. They had just started working on the March issue, so she was surprised that Jason wanted to talk to her so far in advance about work for July. Since starting her job with Grind House, she had been writing fluff pieces that no one else wanted to cover. Ansley did not mind because it was an opportunity to display her talent and build publishing credit. Her efforts had paid off and now she had this new piece to write.

It was great being back in a deadline driven environment. Jason was expecting her, so she waved to the receptionist in passing as she made her way to his office.

Ansley tapped on the open door.

"C'mon in," Jason whispered as he gestured for her to enter. "I'll be wrapping up this call shortly."

She sat down in one of the plush, visitor chairs, and her eyes traveled around his office. She hadn't realized how many awards had been won by Grind House. It felt great to be a part of a company with accolades.

Jason ended his call. "How are things going with you?"

Ansley smiled. "Great actually! I really like it here."

"Glad to hear it," he responded. "I must say the pieces you submitted are interesting. I can see one out of the three you submitted being featured in our upcoming issue. The other two need more development, but the one you wrote on women's health would be an excellent contribution. Can you have it ready for the March issue?"

"Absolutely," she responded. "I'm really passionate about women's health topics and this article is going to blow you away. I will need to check out a camera to take a few editorial shots. I hope that you will allow me to cover more healthy-living topics in future issues if this one appeals to the readers." Ansley paused, and said, "Jason, you also mentioned an assignment for the July issue?"

He gave a slight nod. "Ah yes… the July issue. I recall you writing some amazing pieces on the Essence Festival last year for New Breed. Are you interested in taking on New Orleans again?"

Ansley thought she might faint. Not only had he shown interest in one of her submissions, but also he trusted her to cover one of the major events of the year. Her mind was racing with questions she would ask and who she wanted to interview. She could not wait to get to work.

"Ansley… is that a yes or a no?" he joked. "I'm sure some of the other writers would love to take your place—that is if you're too busy."

"Oh, no… I'm sorry—I mean, yes I'm free to cover the event. Thank you for the offer and I'll do my best to make the publication proud," she said sitting up taller in the chair.

"I'm sure you will. We need you to cover several events around the city, as well as get some backstage interviews for our live video stream. Use your contacts to go ahead and get everything booked. No harm in getting a jump on the other media."

"Thank you again for the opportunity and I'll get right on it," she said, no longer able to contain her excitement.

"I'm glad to see that you're so eager because you have a deadline to meet," he said.

"Yes, I do." Ansley rose to her feet.

"I look forward to reading your work."

Her smile was radiating through her entire being—she had a glow. Life for Ansley was looking up. She only wished that she could share her happiness with Davis or even Simeon for that matter. Ansley wanted to wait until Davis returned to talk to him about Simeon. He was still in Chicago, so Ansley used this time apart to try and figure out how to have that conversation.

It dawned on her that she was not even sure if his name was actually Davis or if it was Monty. If they were going to manage to become something, Ansley had to address several areas of concern with him. For all she knew, Simeon could be lying and nothing even happened. She was not sure what to believe, but soon she would have all the answers she needed whether she was ready or not.

Chapter 13

After wrapping up her interviews, Ansley felt she had more than enough information to finish her article. She drove over to the Starbucks on North Druid Hills to organize her work.

She hoped a change of environment might be good to get the creative juices flowing. Ansley walked up to the counter and ordered a skinny vanilla latte and a brownie. Ansley loved her sweets, she skimped on one and indulged in the other. Chocolate was her vice.

While waiting on the barista to call her order out, Ansley set her laptop at a table near the window. She loved the ambience of coffee shops. The music was always a blend of mellow and mid-tempo grooves that matched her writing mood. The sounds of briefcases opening and closing; friends laughing over good times, and the awkward exchange of first dates meeting in a neutral zone filled the air. Her favorite was the hum of the coffee being brewed and foam being dispensed.

"Ansley," the barista called.

Sipping on her drink, she began to type. She had gotten a lot accomplished over the past few days—a good thing too because Davis would be home later this evening. Talking with him was a task alone, she didn't want any distractions.

She was nine hundred words in, Jason requested fifteen hundred, and the article was coming together. Ansley reached into her bag when she felt her phone vibrating. It was Lanae.

"Hey, what's going on, sis?"

"Nothing much just working on this feature about working mothers in the Y Generation."

"Sounds interesting," she responded. "I'm over here grinding out an article too. I'm working to get it wrapped up today."

"Awesome," Lanae said. "Listen, there's a singles mixer going on at The High Museum tonight. I can get you two passes if you want to take Simeon. I could sense some tension the other night, but you know me, I stay in my designated zone. If nothing else you'll both be able to enjoy some art and music."

"That sounds cool. I'll see if she's available and get back in touch with you later." Ansley paused and added. "And yes, there was some back and forth, she and I still need to talk so this will be a good way to revisit some unfinished business."

She chatted with Lanae for a few minutes more before getting back to her article.

Ansley remained at the coffee shop for another hour and was able to finish her final draft, which she emailed to the copy editor.

She checked her watch. Davis's flight was scheduled to leave around six p.m., central time. With him getting in late, she planned to get with him in the morning. It was unlikely they would have their heart to heart tonight, because he might be a little jet lagged and she wanted him at his best for this conversation.

As of late, Ansley could not think of Davis without Simeon crossing her mind.

She pulled out her phone to call her. It was time they put an end to this Davis drama. This whole thing was getting stale.

The call went straight to voice mail. Ansley tried the office next. Simeon's assistant answered the call.

"Hi Grace. Is Simeon available?" Ansley said.

"I'm sorry, but she's not expected back into the office until tomorrow. Is there a message?"

"No," she responded. "I'll try her cell again."

She sent Simeon a text, asking her to call when she got a chance. It dawned on her that her friend may be curving her attempts at communication. Ansley gave a slight shrug. They had been friends for too long to let something like this come between them. Besides, it was pointless to assume Simeon was avoiding her when she wasn't sure.

She packed away her laptop and left for home.

Chapter 14

Ansley woke up early Saturday morning.

She and Davis were spending the day together. It would be their first time connecting since his return to Georgia, and since Simeon revealed some truths about him. While she knew it wouldn't make sense to some, she had every intention of going on this date with him and before it was over, she would confront him. He needed to see how it felt to be duped. To think she knew his intentions, only to find out that he wasn't being forthright, really bothered Ansley.

He had a full day planned for them. She had been looking forward to this since Davis mentioned it, and after wising up to the mess he was pulling, she felt that she deserved to enjoy every second of it. First on the agenda was the Atlanta Botanical Gardens.

Ansley chose a pair of fitted jeans, a light, long sleeve blouse, and a light blazer since it was a bit windy outside. She took a final glance in the mirror and applied a sheer M.A.C. lip gloss. She sprayed on some Rebel Fleur perfume and was on her way.

Stepping onto the elevator to head to the parking garage, she rummaged through her tote bag for her car keys. *I can't find anything in this huge bag.*

She sighed when her phone rang. By the time she located it, the call had gone to voicemail. Ansley checked her messages in case it was Davis.

"Ansley, this is Davis. I had to run a quick errand over in Midtown so I'm just going to meet you there. I can't wait to see you."

Ansley was disappointed. The original plan was that she would pick him up at his place. She was curious to see where and how Davis lived. Now that she knew he was fronting as two eligible bachelors, she wanted to know more about his lifestyle. Ansley believed that one could learn a lot about a person by their choices in home décor, music, even what was in the refrigerator. Yes, she wanted to be nosy, but there was always next time—if there was a next time.

Ansley got in her car and headed over to the botanical gardens. She thought about trying Simeon again, but decided against it considering she had a date with Davis and her dating him was an unresolved issue between them.

Ansley wasn't sure if Simeon would agree to her plan or assume her sole purpose for going was to continue dating him. This was not the case. Ansley intended to pretend like everything was copasetic, and then call him out to see if he would be honest.

Arriving at the Atlanta Botanical Gardens, seemed to drive away her anxiety over seeing him. The chemistry between her and Davis was strong. They walked and talked along the budding red roses, the dancing tulips and finally they entered the exotic orchid garden. This was Ansley's favorite site at the Gardens thus far.

"I absolutely love orchids. I can just stay in this area for hours. It's so tranquil," she said, looking up into Davis's eyes.

"I'm glad we are sharing this together."

"I thought you had come here before?"

"Nope," Davis said. "I heard about it from a friend and thought it would be romantic. Just think about it, this is just the first part of our date—there's more to come. They have an orchid drawing class at ten o'clock; we can make it if we hurry."

"Oh, I'm down. Let's go." She beamed.

He scanned the program and screwed up his face. "Uh...on second thought, maybe we should walk around a little more. I need a little more commitment from you before I spend a hundred and eighty dollars."

"Oh...yeah. And my love is not for sale," she said before laughing. "It's cool. I'm fine with walking around. There's plenty to see."

They continued from one floral exhibit to the next sculpted art piece, from the desert rose to the Algerian iris. They explored every bud and bloom the gardens had to offer.

She was impressed with his knowledge about horticulture and botany. He told her that his mother had a green thumb, and gardening with her heightened his exposure and interest in plants and flowers. "Does your mother have a garden?" Ansley asked.

"No, but she used to plant flowers in my grandmother's yard. We lived in the city, but I'm sure if mom had one of her own that she would've had me waist deep in soil," he said with a laugh.

"I totally get it," Ansley responded. "My mother has a garden, but she ain't trying to let anyone touch her precious babies. My sister and I almost lost our lives for accidentally stepping in her garden bed. While I didn't do the work, I always appreciated the beauty. You know what I mean?"

"I know exactly what you mean," he said looking down

at her as they walked. He gestured for her to have a seat on one of the benches near the Parterre Fountain installation.

"This place is so picturesque. The artwork, the flowers, and the water features… it's breathtaking," she murmured while looking around.

They sat in silence, enjoying their serenity.

He reached for her hand and enclosed his around it. "I'm glad we came."

"I am, too," she responded. "Oh shoot. I've been taking photos of everything but us. Come on let's get a selfie."

He jerked his face in the other direction and covered his face. "Whoa, nah I'm good. How about I take a photo of you though?"

Ansley scrunched her nose. "What? No, this is a memory that I'm sharing with you and I want to capture us in this moment."

"Listen I said I don't want to take any freaking pictures," he snapped.

Ansley frowned. She knew some people were camera shy but he was a tad intense.

He looked at her and noted her lips forming a straight line. "I'm sorry about that. I'm just grouchy from lack of nourishment. Are you ready to go eat?"

He rubbed his hands together.

"Uh sure, I guess so."

They walked back toward Ansley's car. She was very curious about his reaction to the selfie request, but up until now everything was going really well. Then there was still the need to talk to him about Simeon, which was certain to curb the mood.

They pulled into the parking lot of the West Egg, one of her favorite places for brunch.

"Okay, Davis, the botanical gardens were one thing, and now we're having lunch at one of my favorite spots." Ansley gave him a sidelong glance. "Have you been spying on me?"

He laughed and held up his hands in defense. "Honestly...someone at work suggested the gardens and this place for brunch. I've never been to either one, but I'll have to thank my coworker for these excellent choices."

"Oh okay. I was just thinking it's crazy that we have these interest in common. I guess I need to meet your coworker. Sounds like we would get along great."

He squinted at her with mock anger. Her brows moved up and down. Ansley loved how she could be playful with him. He got her humor. They just seemed to work.

The waiter came over and took their order. Ansley got the shrimp and grits, and a side of fruit. Davis chose the short rib hash, fried green tomatoes, skillet potatoes, sausage and a biscuit. She didn't know he ate like that. It was a tad heavy for her.

While they waited for their food to arrive, he asked, "Ansley, do you think you could get use to the idea of us?"

She looked up at him. "I think you're extremely charming and we have fun together." As much as Ansley was trying to fight it, she was smitten with him. The more time they spent together, the more she wanted to be with him. She settled back in her chair. "I'd like to see where this goes, but we have time to figure all that out."

He looked at her, his eyes filled with longing.

Once their meal was served, they continued to chat and get to know one another. While she loved hearing about his sister and brother, and their adventures in his grandma's garden, the story she was most eager to hear was about that one time in Chicago when he hooked up with Simeon.

Ansley watched as Davis waved the waiter over to settle their bill. As they walked toward the exit, Davis excused himself to go to the men's restroom.

She decided to wait for him outside. Ansley knew there would never be a perfect time to ask him about Simeon, so she thought, why not attack it head on?

Davis crept up from behind, and kissed Ansley on the cheek.

"You ready, pretty lady?"

"Sure," she started toward the car, turning backward to look at him while she spoke. "So, Simeon told me you two got together in Chicago, and that your name is really Monty. Care to elaborate?"

She stopped in front of him, placing her hands on her hips. Davis avoided looking at her, he pivoted around her and proceeded to walk toward the car.

"Yeah, I-uh. You know—I guess, um," he stammered, looking over his shoulder. "It must have slipped my mind."

Ansley caught up to Davis, stepped in front of him and poked him in the chest. "You… forgot… y'all slept together or you forgot to tell me your real name?"

There, everything was out in the open. She stood there hoping he wouldn't disappoint her with a lie.

He shrugged in nonchalance. "Please don't start creating unnecessary drama, Ansley. Today has been great, so don't start acting like a jealous teenage girl."

"Come again?" Her tone was chilly. She threw her hands up dismissing him. "You know what I don't even know why I came. I wanted to make you feel what Simeon and I felt, finding out you were playing us to get what you needed. Or at least I know what you wanted from her, not sure what your plans were for me. "

She turned away from him and walked to the driver side of the car. She got inside, slamming her door shut. He hustled to open the passenger side door and slide inside.

"Uh—the bus stop is down that way. You might want to catch out and go find you a seat."

Davis grabbed her hand, rubbing her fingers in between his, and turned her toward him. "Listen Ansley, I really like you, and I'm sorry about what I said. I didn't mean to come off that way."

She snatched her hand away. "You had a chance to come clean, at least earn forgiveness. You and I didn't get that far, but you knew that Simeon was my girl and gave her false hope and now you got me all in the mix. It's not cool what you did."

"Do we really have to do this right now? Let's just go to the art stroll, okay?"

"Davis, I can't believe you chose to be a coward." She threw up her hands in defeat.

"While I would love to go to the art stroll, I doubt I'll enjoy the company—without continuing to fake it."

"Are you serious?"

Ansley nodded. "Very."

"Can you at least take me home and we can talk more?" he pleaded.

She rolled her eyes and turned the ignition, starting the car. *Lord, I need an extra blessing for this one.*

Chapter 15

The ride to his townhouse was a quiet one. He wasn't saying another word; he didn't want to tick her off any further. Davis was grateful that she was driving him home and he didn't have to take the bus.

Davis used the time to try to figure out his next move. He needed to make sure that he and Ansley were good. He was frustrated for the way he behaved. He had overreacted in response to her question.

She navigated her car his driveway and parked. The silence between them was thicker than morning fog.

"I'm sorry," Davis stated. "The last thing I wanted to do was ruin this day for you."

Ansley took a calming breath. "I got what I needed and wanted out of today because I went to my favorite places, but this is on an indefinite pause. Maybe we could be friends somewhere in the future, when I can laugh about this but that day is not today."

"Pause, as in you want me to back off?" Davis questioned.

"Instead of trying to decipher what I mean by pause, you need to be calling Simeon and apologizing to her. What you did to her was wrong? You toyed with her heart and it really messed her up."

"I don't want to mess this up. That's what I care about right now," he responded. "We will talk about everything, but for right now... can we table this?"

"I'm not one for drama either," she told him. "I guess we can discuss later, but we can't ignore this. The three of us will have to come together on this. Simeon really likes you, and I get it. The thought of you two sleeping together, it's against girl code that I'm even here with you right now. Regardless of my plan to jack with your emotions."

"You're right and I'm sorry Ansley." He squeezed her hand. Davis looked out the front window. "Did you want to come in so we can talk some more?"

Ansley shook her head. He released a harsh breath. "I figured as much." He tapped his fingers on the dashboard before opening the car door. "I know this is a stretch, considering, but can I have a parting kiss?"

She rolled her eyes, but couldn't help but smile, he knew that meant she wanted to let him but just couldn't allow it to happen.

Davis leaned across the seat and kissed her on the cheek before stepping out of the car and walking into the house.

He hadn't managed to smooth things out with Ansley, but he could tell it wouldn't be hard to get back in her good graces. She appeared to be dissolving right there in front of him. He had a bigger dilemma to tackle—Simeon. He had to give her what she wanted without letting on that he was still going after Ansley. There was something about her that threw him off of his game, and for once in his life, he wasn't afraid to allow love into his life again.

He gave a bitter laugh. For once he found a woman that makes him want to act right, and it happens to be the friend of a fling. He spat a string of expletives, slamming his fist into the door.

"Whoa. You act a fool at your own place," Beau

growled. Then laughed heartily. "That is if you can ever afford a place of your own."

"Whatever man."

"I'm gonna let you slide only cause you did what I asked, and you managed to not attract attention. That's what I like to see playa. Now about them pills, we might be able to work that out but if you digging the chick you might not want to steal from her."

"Nah, we just kicking it. What you find out?"

"Gotcha. Well, dude, she might be bipolar so you can't be juking her around. You remember Aunt Catherine was bipolar and she wasn't on medication. Nah, don't take nothing off this broad."

"Since when you got some morals," Davis joked.

"Aye man, I do have some standards. Now run me that money," Beau said with his hand extended.

Chapter 16

"Hello, mommy's phone," Kennedy announced.

Her goddaughter always picked up her mother's cell phone when she saw Ansley's name on the screen.

"Hey, Kennedy. How are you, doll?"

"Good. Mommy and Daddy are playing Candy Land with me. Daddy was cheating," she said.

Ansley's heart melted every time she spoke to this little girl.

"Your daddy needs to go sit in time out," she teased. "Well lovey—can I talk to your mommy please? I won't hold her long."

"Yes, she's right here. I love you, Ashy," she said.

Ansley laughed. Kennedy had come a long way, but she still could not quite pronounce Ansley's name.

"Love you right back, sweetie," she responded.

"What's going on, Ashy?" Lanae joked.

Ansley laughed along with her.

"I know y'all having family time so I'll try to be brief," she said. "I want to hear your thoughts on something."

"What's going on?"

"Davis and I went out earlier today—we had a great time. Or at least we were before I confronted him about a woman from his past," Ansley stated. "We got a little heated, and we ended the night lukewarm. I still have questions for him about this woman, but don't want to push the issue."

"Let me excuse myself for a second," she said. Ansley heard her asking Jacob if he would go ahead and get Kennedy something to eat before returning to the call.

"I'm back." Lanae continued, "What made you ask about this woman and what did he say that got you upset?"

Ansley ignored the infliction on the word woman. She wasn't giving up anything. Lanae knew there was tension between her, and Simeon but there had been no conversation detailing their mutual connection to Davis.

"Well I let him know that I heard they had a one-night stand, and he played dumb, acting like he forgot it happened. He said I was acting like a jealous teenage girl."

"Hmm. Were you jealous?"

Ansley responded. "It's not that I'm jealous, it's just that—I wanted him to say it wasn't true. I hoped Si—she was lying."

Ansley could hear a faint giggle in the background and she knew it didn't belong to Kennedy. Her slip of tongue had sold her out.

"Well, he didn't confirm or deny it, so now you just have to wait. A conversation is in order and you all need to talk this out and not let the subject linger—all three of you," Lanae advised.

Ansley chuckled.

"You're right. You're right." Ansley raised her hands toward heaven. "I tried talking to Simeon the night of the dinner but that didn't go well at all. I said Davis was no good, and I know that I haven't known Davis very long, but I enjoy being with him. There's like a magnetic draw when we are together. As much as I try to pull away, I'm forced back—it's such a strong feeling."

"You don't have to rush into anything with this man. Figure out what's going on with them and talk to Simeon. How long have you two been friends now?"

Ansley nodded as if Lanae could see her. "It's been about five months now, and we have become close."

"Well, you have to be careful, you can't be loose with using the term friend. Everyone is not deserving of that title. Do you entrust her with your secrets? That's something to consider, you should be asking yourself is he worth losing a friend?"

"I know. You're on target with that one. I guess I have some thinking to do," Ansley responded. "Go back to your game. I'll give you a call tomorrow."

She hung up the phone. Left with her thoughts, Ansley knew that she needed to talk to Simeon minus the emotions. If that was even possible. Simeon seemed very adamant about pursuing Davis and she was in fact the one to meet him first. This was against everything she believed to want someone that a friend had been intimate with and had she known what happened before they started dating, she never would've given him a second thought.

But that wasn't Ansley's reality, her reality consisted of the basic girl meets boy and girl falls for boy scenario. She could've never predicted the one that made her feel a tingle in her spine would've had the same effect on her friend.

Davis called Ansley early Sunday morning. "What are you doing today?" he inquired.

"Working on my article," Ansley responded, "Then I'm going to run some errands and try to catch up on some chores around the house."

"Sounds like you have a busy day."

"That I do," she agreed. "What's up with you?"

"I was hoping to spend some time with you today."

"Oh, no can do. I really need to get some work done around here, Davis."

"Are you sure you're not just trying to avoid me?"

"Yep. I told you we were good and I meant that."

"Alright, cool. So sometime next week then?" he queried.

She smiled at his eagerness. "We'll see. Maybe I'll cook dinner. I found this great new recipe for chicken marsala that I've been wanting to try."

"I can't wait."

They talked a few minutes more before hanging up.

Ansley returned her attention to her work. She made corrections suggested by the copy editor and planned to submit the revisions tomorrow. She really enjoyed working at Grind House because she was learning a lot.

When the article was completed, Ansley logged into her virtual classroom to see the schedule for her upcoming course. After ordering her e-books and downloading the syllabus, she got up to start working on her chores.

Three hours breezed by. Ansley plopped down on the sofa to rest. She managed to wash and dry three loads of laundry, vacuum, sweep, and dust around the house. If her mother was here she would be telling her it's not officially clean until she mopped the floors and cleaned the windows. Ansley looked around the room and felt she'd done enough for the day, or at least the soles of her feet proclaimed as much.

She got up, walked into the kitchen, to grab a bottle of water and make a sandwich. Ansley was cutting up an apple when her phone rang.

It was Simeon.

"Hey, girl," Ansley greeted.

"You lost a hand or something?"

Her smile disappeared. "Huh?"

"I haven't heard from you."

"Actually I called your cell and sent you a text on last week. I called your office and receptionist said you were out of town. You didn't get my messages?"

"Oh, yeah, sorry about that. I've just been keeping to myself. I needed some time to think some things over."

"Like what?"

"Just the last conversation we had was a little tense, and we haven't spoken since then about the whole Davis thing. That conversation was never resolved. So it's been weighing on me. I apologize for my part in this mess. Davis or Monty to me anyway, he was never my man. I shouldn't have come at you like that. You're my friend. About the only one I have if I'm being honest."

"Is that how you really feel?"

"Absolutely," she confirmed.

"I never wanted to hurt you."

"I know. I wasn't trying to—well I'm lying, at the time I was wanting to hurt your feelings. I was being petty."

Ansley chuckled. "It's cool. I just want us to get back on good terms. I've missed you."

"I missed you too." Simeon cleared her throat. "Speaking of Davis, when was the last time you spoke to him anyway?"

Ansley started chewing on her nail. She should have lead with this information. This could put a hold on the love fest they were having.

"He called me when he got back in town, and then we met on Saturday."

"This past Saturday? As in Valentine's Day?" Simeon quizzed.

"Yeah. When he got back in town, I had every intention of asking him about his history with you, but the rest of the week was busy for me and we didn't get to talk. Saturday came, and when I asked about you, he just avoided the subject all together."

"I see. What all did you tell him?"

"I told him that I knew you two hooked up in Chicago, but like I said, he didn't confirm one way or another."

Ansley was met with silence on the other end.

"I know you're probably thinking why did I even need to verify anything with him, and my response is I guess it's just the writer in me. I wanted to hear him out, and get his side."

Simeon's laughter was solemn. "It's no biggie. I get it. I would've done the same thing." A beat and then. "Well listen, if you have time on Monday, let's meet at Tin Lizzy's for drinks after work."

"Yes, let's make that happen for sure," Ansley said.

As the call ended, Ansley couldn't help but feel as if her friendship was ending also. Though Simeon was acting brave, there was something in her tone that let Ansley know their relationship would never be the same.

With the laundry folded and put away an hour later, she made some popcorn, poured a glass of wine, and settled in for a Lifetime movie.

Ansley released a soft groan at the interruption of the phone ringing. "Hello."

"Ms. Wright, you have a visitor. A Davis Montclair."

"Davis is here?" She could not contain her surprise.

"Yes ma'am," the doorman responded. "Should I send him away?"

"No, I'll come down." Ansley rushed into the bathroom.

She brushed her teeth and rinsed out her mouth, tucked away the loose strands of hair fighting for freedom from her ponytail, and straightened her t-shirt before heading down to the lobby.

Ansley greeted the doorman in passing as she hurried to meet Davis. He began walking towards her, meeting her halfway. He looked like he had just been out running errands. He wore a worn, heather gray, Chicago Bears hoodie and dark blue jogging pants.

"Hey," she said. "Umm, I thought we said we'd try to make plans for next week."

"I couldn't wait to see you."

She could not help but smile; he had that effect on her.

"You look nice," he said.

Ansley glanced down at her gray sweatpants and wrinkled, white tee shirt. Her hair was in a messy ponytail; she wore no make-up.

"Whatever..."

"You could wear a trash bag and still look beautiful," Davis told her.

"Thanks—I guess," she said not believing a single word he said.

She gestured for him to come with her. "You can only stay for an hour, Davis. I have an early start tomorrow."

"An hour?"

Ansley held up her index finger.

They stepped inside of the awaiting elevator.

"I was just about to eat a snack when you called," she announced. "Are you hungry? I can warm up something."

"No, being here with you is satisfying enough."

On her floor, Ansley unlocked the door and stood to the side to let Davis enter. "You can have a seat anywhere. Would you like a something to drink? A glass of wine or cup of coffee?" she offered. "Umm—I have Pinot Noir, Beringer Merlot, Chardonnay, and Moscato…"

"Do you have a wine cellar?" he said, teasing her. "I'll have whatever you're having," he said. His eyes filled with desire, Ansley turned away to go get his glass of wine.

Ansley felt him watching her. Her heart was pumping out of her chest like a fist thrusting in the air on the Arsenio Hall show. This man was a natural master of seduction—it took no effort at all. Everything about him from his voice; the way he walked, his eyes, and the way he said her name engaged all of her erogenous zones. She had to keep close watch over him or she might give him access to areas of her body that she was not ready for him to explore.

Ansley poured two glasses of wine before joining Davis in the living room. She handed him the glass and took a seat adjacent to his.

"I hope you don't mind my just dropping by like this."

"Just don't make it a habit," Ansley said.

"You have that guard dog downstairs…the man couldn't even get my name right."

Ansley laughed. "Don't be mean."

He awarded her a devilish grin before taking a huge swallow of wine.

She looked at him. "You're sure you don't want anything to eat?"

"I'm fine."

"So, what's up with the impromptu visit?" Ansley inquired.

He took a deep breath. "I didn't like the way things ended yesterday and I needed to see you. I don't want any misunderstandings between us."

Looks like everyone wanted to wrap up loose ends today. First Simeon, now Davis. Ansley reached for her wine and took a sip.

"I needed to see you to make sure that things were really okay between us," Davis stated. "I really care about you."

"I'm not that fickle," she said. "We're good, although I do think there is something we need to discuss."

"What's that?"

"Simeon."

Davis almost choked on his wine. It was apparent that he hoped Ansley had let that go.

"C'mon, I know what happened in Chicago," she announced. "Remember, I know that you two slept together. Just come off it already and tell the truth."

He cleared his throat. "She told you that! She came on to me. I never tried to go after her."

Ansley shook her head. Confusion shown all over her face. "So, you're saying that you two didn't sleep together when you met at that conference?"

"Oh… that." Davis cleared his throat. "Umm, yes we had that one night together and that's all it was. I promise you that," he said.

Ansley tilted her head to the side, lifting her eyebrows up in surprise. His response led her to wonder if they had more than a one-night stand.

"Simeon is one of my best friends, so we talked about what happened. But it sounds like you're referencing another night, have you all been together more than once?"

"What does it matter? Simeon was a mistake in my past, and I'm trying to look ahead at my future. I'm here with you now. I'm trying to show you that I desire you. I want us. Are you really going to pass up on this? Tell me now and I'll leave you alone."

Deep down it bothered her that Simeon had experienced his passion—something she had yet to do. She took another sip of her wine.

"If you two had dated seriously, then she would've told me about you and this would not be happening." *Who am I fooling even this is a stretch.* "You would not be here with me right now. It goes against the friend code. I hate that I met you second, and she met you first. This—this is just wrong."

Ansley shook her head.

"You're the only woman for me," Davis declared.

"Would you have ever told me about the one-night stand?"

"No, I probably wouldn't have," he answered. "It's because I don't kiss and tell." Davis paused a moment before saying, "Despite what happened between me and Simeon, I didn't feel a connection with her. It's nothing like what I feel when I'm with you."

"And what do you feel when you're with me?" she wondered aloud.

His eyes gleamed. "You have a big heart. You're intelligent, and you're beautiful. I've never met anybody like you, Ansley. My ex and I dated for two years. It was great at first, but she wasn't supportive, was very possessive, and we eventually parted ways. That's when I found out that she was crazy."

"Thankfully, I've been spared all that. I've only been in love once, and I let that relationship go for my own selfish reasons. He was a really good guy."

The one that got away. Man if I could hit the retry button I would.

Chapter 17

Davis thought he glimpsed a hint of sadness in Ansley's eyes as she talked about her ex. It bothered him because it meant she still cared for this man.

He had invested a lot of time and energy into this relationship, and he was not going to allow someone else to take her from him. They should be together, and she soon would come to realize that he was the only man for her.

"Do you still see him?" he wanted to know.

"No," she answered. "I ran into him back in January and that was my first time seeing him in years. He has his life and I have mine."

"Why did you two break up? Did he hurt you? I know it's not my business, but I want you to know that I would never do anything to hurt you," he said as he took her hand.

Ansley pulled her hand free. "You barely know me Davis, and the things you're saying to me…I don't want to rush into anything. Also, I think we should all get together and talk—you, me, and Simeon. I'm tired of all the confusion and back and forth."

"Sure. Whatever it takes to make this work. We can take our time," he said leaning in attempting to kiss her on the lips.

She turned her head away and started to protest, but he pulled her back into his arms and his eyes bore into her.

"Ansley, I'm not going anywhere. You should know this

by now. I'm here to claim you as my woman. I saw something in you the first day we met and I see even more in you now. If you let me…I will show you that you can have everything your heart desires. I can make you happy."

This time she didn't move away from his advances.

Ansley surrendered as his lips took full custody of her mouth. She allowed his hands to surround her waist. Their tongues danced and her heart rate increased.

Their connection was fluid. He brought her in closer to him and she could feel his intensity growing.

Davis gently stroked her hair with his free hand while the other explored her hips and thighs. He allowed her mouth to take rest as he slowly guided his lips and tongue to her neck.

A soft moan escaped her lips, and she knew then that he had won and so she didn't fight, she gave in.

Chapter 18

Davis woke up feeling invigorated. He peeked over at Ansley, who lay sleeping peacefully, and smiled to himself. He adjusted the cover over her body.

She belonged to him.

He worried that Simeon would somehow mess up what he was building with Ansley. Davis couldn't believe that he almost slipped up and told her about Simeon's attempt to lure him into her bed. Ansley didn't know about that, so Simeon must have been keeping that to herself, or perhaps she was embarrassed because she had given him six grand. Some of which he used to finance his date with Ansley.

If Simeon thought anything like him, she was keeping that information, just in case she needed to use it against him later. He shook his head in frustration. He had to get Simeon out of his head and just focus on making Ansley happy.

It was unfortunate, but he had to sleep with Simeon this time. It was more for business than pleasing his own flesh. If he hadn't let her get another sample, he would've been stuck in Chicago without a way to get back home. It was common sense to take advantage of that situation.

Davis just had to plan ahead, make sure that he was never in a place or situation where both women would be present. He told Simeon that he would break things off with Ansley, and he would make sure it appeared that way.

He did feel a twinge of guilt though after finding out she was taking medication for her anxiety, or whatever she had going on but he couldn't help it that he fell for her friend.

As he watched her sleeping, Davis decided that he would show her, yet another, side of him and prepare breakfast for her.

Breakfast in bed, every woman wanted to experience that. This would be a great start to her day and another way to push Simeon further back in her thoughts. He hoped that if he wooed her, and showed her what it would be like if they were a couple, she wouldn't continue to worry about his past with Simeon.

Chapter 19

Ansley woke up to the smell of bacon and eggs cooking in the kitchen. She sat up in bed and cringed when she realized she was naked. She clutched the sheets against her bare bosom.

Her head started to throb at the reminder that she had slept with Davis. This was never a part of her plan. As Ansley summoned the courage to get out of bed, she winced when she saw a condom wrapper on the floor.

She tiptoed to her closet to grab her robe.

Ansley walked into her bathroom and took a quick shower. She tried to lather away her embarrassment. Last night was coming back to her, the blurry details were coming together.

Fifteen minutes later, she strolled into the kitchen with her robe tied securely over a pair of pajamas. Davis had on the pull-over hoodie, and jeans he wore when he came over last night. His feet were still bare, he hadn't put on any socks or shoes yet.

"Good morning, beautiful," he greeted. "I took the liberty of preparing breakfast this morning. We have scrambled egg whites, turkey bacon, toast and fresh fruit."

Ansley stood in silence. This was a lovely gesture, but she was at a loss for words.

"Ansley, are you okay? Is this going too fast for you? I know last night was unexpected," he said approaching her with caution.

"Last night was not supposed to happen."

"True, but we both wanted it," he said closing the space between them. "Right? Tell me I'm not alone here." He pulled out a chair at the table and gestured for her to have a seat.

She obliged him.

He gave her a little room, grabbed the plate he had prepared and sat it before her. Davis then prepared a plate for himself before joining her.

Ansley bowed her head to say grace.

When she was finished, the first thing she said was, "Davis, last night—never should've happened, regardless of how much we wanted to make love. We were just talking about you and Simeon being intimate."

"I apologize if you felt pressured or that I took advantage of you in any way," he responded.

"No, I'm not blaming you," Ansley stated. "We were in this together." She searched for the right words. "I really like you, but I did not want to rush into anything."

"Liquid courage is a helluva drug," he said attempting to cut the tension with humor. Ansley's hard stare let him know that his joke was not welcomed. "My bad, that was supposed to be funny, but I guess it's too soon for that joke. I honestly wasn't expecting what happened between us last night, but I don't want it to stop. Please give us a fighting chance. I promise we can move at your pace."

Before she could respond, her phone rang, and Ansley couldn't be happier for the interruption.

"I need to take this call. It might be my job."

She walked back into her bedroom, leaving Davis sitting at the table.

Ansley answered on the third ring.

"Hello," she answered.

"Hi Ansley, this is Jason. I hope I didn't catch you at a bad time."

"Your timing is perfect," she said looking over her shoulder towards the kitchen.

"Great. Are you free to cover an event at the Compound tonight?"

"Sure. Will they have an area to pick up press passes or shall I come by the office?"

"We have a press pass here at the office for you. One of the photographers and a videographer will be coming with you to get some footage for the live web-stream. Thanks again for taking this on."

"No problem Jason. See you in a few," Ansley said, ending the call.

She returned to the kitchen. "Sorry about that."

"Ansley…"

She held up her hand wanting to pause him. Ansley didn't want to discuss the events of last night one more minute.

Davis couldn't be deterred though, and proceeded to say, "Do you want to be with me?"

Meeting his gaze, Ansley responded, "Yes and no. The yes comes with expectations, and the no is based on uncertainty. Yes, I like you but there's a kink in this chain that is breaking the hold you were having on my heart. I don't know that I can do this."

"I understand, and I plan to adhere to your expectations, which I know is to be faithful and honest. I know your concern is whether or not I'm still interested in your friend and if I'm worth the trouble that this will cause for you and Simeon. The answer is yes. I'm worth it, baby."

Ansley buried her fingers in her long tresses. "Davis, please just stop talking. Please, I just—I just need a minute."

She sat down and he lowered himself into the chair across from her.

She couldn't believe she lost control of the situation. Now that the physical was added to their love equation, it felt that much more complex. *Stupid wine.*

While his joke was tacky, he was right, liquid stimulation mixed with one part cuddling and one-part kissing was the ultimate aphrodisiac. Davis had been so tender with her. He was a wonderful lover. There was a part of her that resented him for being with Simeon first. Try as she might, it was hard for Ansley to push the thought away.

Ansley looked down at the breakfast he had prepared. It was no longer hot.

Any other time, this would have been the perfect way to start her morning, but right now she was too deep in her feelings to enjoy it. She grabbed a piece of bacon and took a bite. More as a means of stalling their nourishment.

"I have to be at work in two hours," she said avoiding eye contact with him.

"Yeah, I need to get home," he said. "Shower and change clothes ..."

She wiped her mouth on her napkin. "Last night was—unexpected. Again, I'm a big girl and don't regret what happened and I'm glad that we met. I still want to get to know you—but slowly."

Ansley took note of Davis' defeated expression as he looked heavenward, and blew out an exasperated breath.

"You know how you just don't want to mess things up?" When he nodded, she continued, "I made many mistakes in my last one. I don't want to do the same with you. I would love to be friends, and we can just start there."

"It's a leap of faith. Take this leap with me and I promise you won't regret it, Ansley," he pleaded.

Ansley gave him an askance look. "Don't make me regret this, Davis."

The corners of Davis's mouth went up into a Cheshire cat like smile. "I won't."

He leaned forward, kissing her on the top of her head.

She inhaled his scent.

Ansley and Davis both rose to their feet, and she walked him to the door.

"I'll try to call you later," she said, her tone full of apprehension.

He pulled her into his arms once more, he searched her eyes for any sign of trust.

"You know I got you, right? This will work. We will work."

Ansley couldn't find the words to express how she felt. She felt like she was in purgatory, caught between love and loyalty.

Davis lowered his lips onto hers, and she melted. The emotions he expressed came through his kiss and she felt all of the desire he had for her.

Ansley could feel herself getting caught up in the moment, and struggled to maintain her equanimity. She stepped out of his embrace.

"I'm not going to let you make me late."

He laughed, backing away and waving goodbye as he walked toward the elevator.

Ansley closed the door behind him and replayed everything that happened this morning. Though Ansley wasn't sure what the future held for her and Davis, she couldn't deny that he had implanted himself in her life and her heart.

Chapter 20

After stopping by Grind House to get her credentials, Ansley made her way to the event at the Compound. She wore a pair of red pumps, cropped, distressed denim jeans that hugged her full hips and accentuated her firm behind, and a black and white, off the shoulder top. She dressed up the outfit with multi-colored bangle and some eighties inspired door-knocker earrings. She styled her hair in a pompadour, and her makeup was natural using earth tones that made her skin tone shimmer.

Ansley took in the crowd. The Who's Who of Atlanta were mingling in every corner of the room, including Simeon. Ansley was not surprised to see her nor was she shocked to see her on the arm of a player for the Atlanta Falcons.

Their eyes locked and Ansley waved over at Simeon. She flashed her press pass to let Simeon know that she was working.

Ansley located her entourage, and found the man of the hour, Joseph Baptiste.

They were able to get several sound bites and enough dialogue for live footage and a spotlight in the upcoming issue. She made her rounds and interviewed several others in the building for potential features in the future.

Two hours later, Ansley was finally off the clock and just wanted to unwind. Simeon seemed into her date, so she decided to give her friend some space.

"Ansley..."

She turned around to face Davis. "What are you doing here?"

They embraced.

He looked handsome as ever, wearing a short-sleeve black button down shirt, exposing his firm arms and chest tucked into a pair of stone-washed denim jeans. His cologne held her captive.

Before Davis could respond, another voice caught Ansley's attention. She turned to face her ex.

"I guess I need to go play the Georgia lottery because there's no way that I'm this lucky," Ryan said with a laugh. "This is a pleasant surprise."

"Hey, Ryan," she said accepting a hug from him.

"Are you solo tonight or is Simeon your plus one?"

"No, she's not alone," Davis stated. "Come on, Ansley, we need to talk." He guided Ansley away from Ryan and toward the exit.

She looked over her shoulder and mouthed, "I'm sorry," to a bewildered Ryan.

Once outside, Davis turned to look at her, but his face was unreadable. She approached him unsure of what to expect once their eyes met.

"Is that him?" he growled.

"If you mean my ex, yes that's him."

"I guess that's why you won't give me a fair chance. This isn't about Simeon at all."

"Whoa. I told you I haven't spoken to him like that. You're bugging out right now and it's unwarranted."

"My feelings are validated. I'm falling for you. No I haven't said it in so many words, but you have to feel that and this run around you keep giving me. Come on man."

Ansley stood with her hands at her side and her mouth agape. He couldn't possibly be jealous of Ryan. Could he?

"Do you want him back?" He looked downward, and backed away.

She walked into his space and took his face into her hands. Looking him in the eyes, she said, "Let's go somewhere and talk, okay?"

He hesitated, but took her hand and they walked out of the club together.

Chapter 21

Simeon's eyes burned with rage as she saw Ansley and Davis in an embrace. He promised her exclusivity, but from the way he had his arms wrapped around Ansley's waist was too familiar. They looked too comfortable.

She fumed. To think she invited him out to this event, and once again, he ends up with Ansley and not with her. This was so embarrassing. She was there entertaining a potential client from the Atlanta Falcons, and now she was leaving him to fend for himself with groupies and photogs while she stormed the venue looking for Davis' trifling behind.

She pushed her way through the club. If Davis was going to be a coward and not tell Ansley the truth, then she was more than willing to lay it all out for her to see. Simeon refused to be mistreated, after all she did for him, and she would not be ignored.

Just as she was within arm's reach, she saw Ryan, Ansley's ex-boyfriend approach. She paused after seeing the exchange. Simeon knew how Ansley felt about Ryan and if he was there, Davis would be a non-factor.

Simeon looked over her shoulder to check and see if her client was still waiting for her.

He was there, but the scowl on his face let her know that he was not pleased that she abandoned him. She held up her index finger to let him know she would be right back.

Turning back, her view was obstructed by a passerby, but as the sea of patrons thinned out, she realized Davis and Ansley were gone. She looked and saw Ryan, and went to catch up with him, hoping that Ansley was on his arm.

"Ryan!" she called out. "Ryan, hey. Uh—I thought I saw Ansley with you. Do you know where she went?"

"Hey Simeon, right? Sorry it's been a minute," he said. "How are you?"

"Good, um, Ansley?" she said placing her hands on her hips.

"Oh my bad. She left with some dude. Is that her boyfriend?"

"Not if I can help it," Simeon said as she hurried toward the exit. Once outside she was met with the same fate that Davis had placed her in once again—alone.

Chapter 22

Davis unlocked the door to his place and held it open for Ansley. He walked toward the kitchen as she stood near the entryway, taking in the view. He had impeccable taste. Ansley had not expected him to have raw photography and original art pieces on the wall. She was impressed.

"Would you like something to drink?" he asked holding up a bottle of water from the refrigerator.

She walked toward him and accepted the water.

"Please have a seat, Ansley." He passed her the water as he sat down at the bar in the kitchen. "So the art showcase was pretty amazing, wasn't it?"

She tilted her head to the side. "Now you know that is not what we should discuss." Ansley pointed in his direction. "What was that back at the club? You appeared to be upset because Ryan approached me. True or False?"

Davis shrugged.

Ansley frowned. "I would've introduced you, but you didn't give me a chance."

"I don't need to meet him."

Ansley bit her bottom lip, trying to not to laugh. "You're jealous."

"So what if I am." He laughed at himself once he saw the way Ansley's eyes danced. "Nice attempt on trying to hold back your laugh. You might as well let it go."

Ansley was tickled. She covered her mouth with her

right hand. "I'm sorry. I didn't mean to laugh."

"It's cool, but to answer your question, I did get a little jealous. You're an amazing woman and any man would be lucky to be with you—I just want that man to be me."

Ansley walked around the bar, and reached up to touch the side of Davis' face. "I see you, and I hear you. I'm not reuniting with Ryan and I meant what I said earlier. I want us to get to know each other. I don't want to rush."

"Like I said, I'm not going anywhere. It's just nice to know that you plan to stick around to get to know me, too."

She wrapped her arms around his neck and allowed him to kiss her. As their lips locked, she didn't worry about anything but that moment and vowed that she would just allow herself to be. Be in the now and relish the moments that came, speed bumps and all.

Chapter 23

Four months later...

Ansley's relationship with Davis was going well to the point they had become inseparable. Taking it slow and building their friendship had proven to be effective for them. Ansley could have never anticipated having this strong bond with him after everything they had gone through to get to this place in their relationship.

Ansley wanted to introduce him to Lanae and Jacob, so she decided to throw a dinner party at her house. Up until now, Lanae had only met him in passing but had not gotten the chance to talk with him in an intimate setting.

Her guests were due to arrive within the hour. She also invited Simeon, who much to her relief, was dating someone new.

As expected, their relationship was tested, strained, dead, and revived. Simeon seldom called or invited her out for drinks. And their interaction at Tin Lizzy's resembled that of a revolving door. It continuously went around in circles, widening the gulf between them.

Deep down, Ansley knew that she was hanging onto this friendship out of guilt. She had chosen her heart over friendship. They went through a period where they didn't talk, but they continued to work on their friendship, although it would never be the same.

"Davis, would you mind setting the table?" she asked while checking on the baked ziti.

"Of course, baby. Are you using the fine china or Chinette?"

"Ha, Ha. You're funny," she said, throwing an oven mitt at him. "Just put the plates on the table, silly."

"Ansley, I'm glad you finally decided to officially introduce me to your friends—as your man," he said. "It assures me that things are moving in the right direction."

She walked over and kissed him on the cheek. "Everyone should be here shortly, so I'm going to finish getting ready," she announced as she headed toward her bedroom.

She had requested that everyone dress up. Ansley wanted a reason to wear the navy polka dot dress from Anne Taylor that Davis purchased for her.

She turned from side to side to get a look at her physique from every angle.

Not bad. The boy's got taste.

The dress accentuated her shape and hugged her in all the right areas. All of her fat rolls were behaving. *No Spanx needed tonight. Thank God.*

Davis walked in the room just as she was attempting to zip up her dress.

"You look beautiful," he said.

"Thank you," she responded.

He walked up behind her to help her get dressed.

Davis deliberately took his time pulling the zipper up. Pressing his body into hers, his touch was gentle as his fingers gripped her waist as he leaned in closer, tracing circles on her neck with his tongue.

Ansley closed her eyes and allowed herself to enjoy their closeness.

He turned her around to face him and kissed her with great fervor.

Her arms fell limp at her side.

Before Davis could take things any further, there was a knock on the door.

Ansley pulled away from him. "Our gucsts have arrived. Why don't you pour a couple of glasses of wine?"

"I have a few places that I would like to pour a bottle of wine, and it's definitely not in those glasses," he whispered before turning away.

"Boy, go get the door." She laughed. "You're a mess."

He had gotten all gussied up for her friends and looked quite handsome. He chose a pair of tan trousers, a beige button down, with a preacher tie as Ansley liked to call paisley print ties, and a suit jacket.

She stole a quick glance at her reflection before heading to the front.

Ansley's steps slowed, when she saw that Simeon was the first to arrive.

They greeted one another cordially, then she was introduced to Charles, Simeon's date.

"Davis, you might know him since he's the new Financial Analyst at Lowell Myer, LLC." Simeon said with a devious smile. "Isn't that where you said you worked?"

Ansley raised a brow. She wasn't sure what that Simeon was up to—she knew exactly where Davis worked.

"Oh, do you work for Lowell?" Charles asked. "I haven't met everyone yet. Maybe you can show me around next week. I'm still getting my feet wet."

Davis shifted his weight from one side to the other. "Um...yeah sure," he replied. "I'm not always in the office though. I'm a private contractor."

There was another knock.

Ansley opened the door.

"Davis, this is Lanae and Jacob, as you may have guessed," she said with a grin.

"It's nice to finally meet you," Lanae said.

"So as much as I love Ansley, I must ask you…why didn't you run while you had the chance?" Jacob teased.

"I'll save that conversation for dinner." Davis laughed. "But in all honesty, something about her just took my breath away."

"And on that note… dinner is ready," Ansley said interrupting the embarrassing conversation.

"Good because I'm starving," Jacob said. "This looks good, but I'll wait until I take a few bites to tell you what I really think."

Everyone laughed.

Minutes later, wine was flowing, and dinner was going better than Ansley could've hoped.

Ansley settled back, observing Davis as he interacted with her friends. Even Simeon was being pleasant to him. There were a few instances where she caught Simeon eyeing them, a scowl on her face, but Ansley wasn't surprised. She simply chose to ignore those moments.

She got up from the table and grabbed her phone to take a few live action shots of everyone. As soon as she got one of Davis and Jacob talking, she saw his mood shift. She grinned and walked over to show him that the photo turned out great.

"Ansley, what are you doing?" He asked in a low voice. "You know I don't like photos."

Ansley pouted. "I know, I know, but we don't have any together where you're looking at the camera and look, you're smiling and it's natural. It's a great photo."

Her gaze pleaded for him to just relax and go with the flow. When she saw the corner of his mouth go up, she felt relieved that he wasn't going to pitch a fit over it.

"Let's go ahead and get this selfie while I'm in a smiling mood."

Jacob walked over and offered to take the photo for them. "Nah, no selfies. Let me get that for you."

Ansley was content with how it turned out. The photo made their relationship even more official.

Lanae broke into her thoughts with a story about an article she read.

"Ansley, you should interview that woman in Oregon for your next Health and Wellness feature. Did you hear about her lawsuit?" Lanae asked, looking around the table to see if anyone else had heard the story.

"No what happened? I haven't looked at the news today," Ansley said, in between bites.

"A jury awarded this woman $900,000 in damages after she sued the man who gave her herpes. She met him online and they went out a few times. Shortly after sleeping with him, she started to have outbreaks. You can find the story on OregonLive.com and several other news outlets."

Davis cleared his throat and being coughing.

"Are you okay, sweetie?" Ansley inquired.

"I'm fine."

She turned back to Lanae. "I hadn't heard anything about it. Thanks for the tip. I'll have to see if I can do a follow-up story." Ansley shook her head. "That's a shame. Some people have no respect for—"

"Dinner is delicious," Davis interjected.

She blew a kiss at him. "Thanks, love."

"The baked ziti is on point," Simeon stated. "You're going to have to give me the recipe."

She laughed. "Since when are you interested in cooking?"

"Hey, I cook every now and then." Simeon glanced at her date. "Don't I, baby?"

Lanae and Ansley exchanged looks of surprise. Simeon was the queen of dining out and ordering in.

Everyone continued making small talk over dinner.

"So, is everyone ready for dessert?" Ansley questioned. "I have brownies and ice cream, or New York Cheesecake and you can add your own toppings."

Taking her cue, everyone cleared their dinner plates to make room for dessert.

She laughed. "I'll take that as a yes."

Ansley glanced over at Davis and winked. As far as she could tell, he had made a good first impression on Lanae and Jacob.

At times, her relationship with Davis felt surreal, but he continued to keep his promise and she had no regrets about letting him get close to her. He was worth all the trouble that came with giving him her heart.

Chapter 24

"Your friends are cool, Ansley," Davis said later when they were alone. "Even Simeon was chill tonight." He was relieved that she hadn't tried to cause any drama.

She chuckled. "She and Charles looked like they were quite cozy. I like him for her. They were giggling and fawning all over each other all night. It was cute."

"He seems like a nice guy. "I'll definitely check him out at the office before I leave there."

"What do you mean leave?" Ansley asked. She turned off the water and began drying the last of the dishes.

"I've gotten a great offer from another company," he said. "I thought I had mentioned it to you. Anyway, I think it's a much better opportunity for me."

"Oh okay. Is it high-rises or what kind of buildings?"

Davis shook his head. "No, not really. It's smaller retail space or something," he stifled a yawn, then said, "Man I'm beat. I think I'm going to head home."

"You could always just sleep here...and I do mean sleep," she said with a grin.

He threw up his hands in mock defense.

Together, they walked toward the bedroom.

Davis bit back his irritation. It seemed like every time he felt like he was moving ahead, something tried to pull him back down. It started with Simeon oversharing, telling Ansley about their tryst. He still felt as if he were waiting for the other shoe to drop—that Simeon might decide to tell Ansley about their most recent hookup in Chicago. He thought for a short time that Ansley's ex would be another obstacle, but once he took control of the situation at the Compound, she hadn't mentioned Ryan. He was going to have to say goodbye to his Lowell Myers cover before Charles innocently started asking questions which could expose his secret.

Truth is, Davis had not been working there or anywhere for that matter. He made his money through other means that Ansley would never understand. If Charles became a threat to his happiness, he would have to figure out a way to deal with that.

"Sweetie, are you planning on taking a bath or shower right now?" Davis inquired. "I'd love to get in, but will wait if you were about to go first."

"Actually, I'm going to watch a bit of the late night news before I get in, so you can go ahead," she said.

He walked over to the vanity where she was sitting, and kissed her forehead before padding barefoot into the bathroom.

Davis turned on the water and waited until he heard her turn the television on before reaching in his pants pocket for his cellphone. Hoping the water and television combined would muffle his voice, he returned a missed call from Beau.

"What's up?" Davis knew if his cousin was calling, it was not going to be good.

"I need you to go back to Chicago," Beau commanded.

Davis ran his hand across the top of his head. "I don't know about that. There was almost a situation last time. Dude pulled a gun and then—"

"Aye man, remember the rules. Less is more on the phone, you got me?" Beau barked.

"My bad, but Beau—you never mentioned that someone could get killed. I'm not down with that type of work. So I'm not going to be able to do this again. Anything else and I got you."

"Man up, D. When you work fo' me, things can get messy. Besides, it's not like your soft behind stepped up to handle bid'ness anyway." He let out a sinister laugh.

"I'll handle money transfers, but I'm not a killer." Davis paused when Beau didn't respond. "I appreciate everything, but I'm done. I'll find another way to pay you back."

"You done? You still owe me, which means I own you. When I call you for something, you best be ready," Beau snarled before hanging up.

Davis stood there, taking a moment to reflect on his current situation. He never expected his life to be this way. He was from Chicago Heights, a suburban town right outside of the city.

Growing up, Davis tried to do things the right way, but everyone assumed the worse, wanting to box him in with his family lineage of ex-cons. Even with his ex-girlfriend Bree; Davis tried to be a good man, but she didn't appreciate him. She always accused him of being a dog like Beau, who was a blatant womanizer.

There was a point in his life where he loved Bree beyond words, but she chose to make him feel irrelevant, so he became the man she wanted—a scumbag.

Once they called it quits, Davis decided to start fresh and find a way to be happy again, and so he moved to Georgia.

Having Ansley in his life restored his hope for the kind

of life he desired. She made him want to be better, be more than what the world, his mother, and Bree tried to say he was. Then Simeon presented a piece of his past to Ansley on a silver platter hoping to steal his newfound joy.

There was a chance that Bree was working her way to Georgia to find him. He couldn't let that happen. Davis knew that Bree felt that he owed her something. He wished her well and hoped she would just move on and let him live his life.

All the years of lies and scheming were beginning to take a toll on him. He didn't want to wait until it was too late to make some changes. He had to start somewhere.

Davis stepped into the shower and prayed that the water would wash away all of his dirt and when he stepped out that he would truly be clean.

Chapter 25

Ansley looked toward the bathroom door. *What is taking him so long?*

He was usually in and out.

As if on cue, she heard the water stop and Davis reemerged.

"What were you doing in there? Trying to make the Guinness Book of World Records for the longest shower?"

His lips twisted. "I missed you too."

She took him by the hand and guided him away from the bathroom door. "Yeah, yeah. Now move it. I need to get in there."

Davis pulled her into his arms. "I don't know what I'd do if I ever lost you."

Ansley tilted her head, showing her confusion. "What made you say that? Is everything okay?"

"Everything is fine. I just felt the need to tell you that," Davis said before kissing her on the cheek. She studied him from behind as he padded over to the Cherrywood dresser where he had a designated drawer to grab a pair of boxers.

She shrugged and turned to walk into the bathroom. As she walked over to turn on the water, she heard a beep.

On the counter, was Davis's cellphone. Ansley was surprised to see that his screen was not secure. He must have just used it before coming out.

Ansley was two-seconds from snooping, but she didn't allow herself to invade his privacy. Since the Simeon incident, he had been very forthcoming and she had no reason to think he was keeping secrets again.

No. She wouldn't be that woman; theirs was a trusting relationship. Ansley was proud of her decision.

He can be trusted.

She had to believe this.

Chapter 26

Ansley rushed out the door the next morning without breakfast.

Jason's assistant called to notify the staff of an impromptu staff meeting. Davis had just finished preparing breakfast, she hated to have to miss out, but she didn't want to be late.

She walked into the building and took the elevator to the 4th floor.

As soon as the doors opened, Ansley jetted down the short hall and into the large meeting room.

A few other staff members straggled in behind her. She wasn't the only one dragging.

"Good morning, everyone," Jason greeted as he strolled into the room. "First, I want to thank everyone for the amazing work done on the last three issues. We have some great reviews on several of the articles. Readers were very vocal about one article in particular—they want to see more like it. Ansley, would you like to be our new Health and Wellness Feature Writer?"

Ansley stared at Jason with her mouth gaping open. She was only able to compose herself enough to nod her acceptance.

The other staffers started to laugh and congratulate her on the good news.

Inside, Ansley wanted to get up and do the wobble. It was hard, but she restrained herself and maintained her composure.

Throughout the meeting, her mind was dancing with ideas for future features for her section in the publication. Her section. She loved the sound of that.

After the meeting, Ansley went to her cubicle to digest all that had just happened. Her phone rang. It was Simeon and Ansley could not wait to share with her the good news.

"Hey girl," she said. "You won't believe what just happened. Jason gave me a feature section that is mine and only mine. I'm so excited."

"That's great news, Ans. We haven't talked much since you're all booed up."

"Oh," she replied. "You've been pretty busy yourself."

"Yeah, I guess. Being with Charles has been fun, but I miss hanging out with you. You know some girls' time," Simeon responded.

"Same here," Ansley stated. Their friendship was still on the mend, so an outing might be just what they needed.

"Are you free on Friday? There's a new boutique that I represent opening in Buckhead and we are hosting a grand opening soiree."

"That sounds awesome," she responded. "I'd love to come. Let me just check to see what Davis has planned and I'll give you a solid answer."

"Wow… are you serious? Your schedule is solely based on what he wants now?" Simeon asked, her tone laced with disappointment. "Listen, before you think I'm jealous… I'm totally not, by the way, but since you and Davis made it official, it's like you lost some of yourself. It's like y'all are Velcro. Just so you know, it's okay to still have a life outside of him."

Ansley rolled her eyes heavenward. "That's not fair,

Simeon. I still do things solo all the time. We both have been pretty busy, but why don't we meet for lunch today… that is, if you're free."

"I guess that's fine. I have an appointment around two o'clock, so I can meet you before noon for an early lunch."

"That works for me," Ansley responded. "We can meet at Yard House in Atlantic Station."

The call left Ansley wondering if she had been neglecting her friends. She tried to remember the last time she spent time with or had a long chat with Simeon or Lanae. She and Davis did spend a lot of time together, but that is what usually happened with couples. Lanae hadn't complained, but the difference is that Lanae was married with children. Ansley decided to make a concerted effort to work on her relationship with Simeon. Starting today.

Ansley arrived at Yard House a little before 11:30am.

Simeon was already there and was about to be seated at a table. "I guess this is perfect timing," she said.

"Hey lady," Ansley said, and they embraced.

As they released, she noticed that Simeon seemed a little melancholy. She had dark circles under her eyes, and her fit frame now appeared gaunt. Her hair lacked luster, and was a tad disheveled in comparison to the well coifed, luminous appearance of Simeon's dark brown hair. "You don't look like yourself. What's bothering you?"

They were seated on the patio. As soon as the server took their drink order and walked away, Simeon opened up. "I'm just tired, honestly. I lost a major account last week and my boss is livid. This boutique grand opening is days away and the marketing campaign has not gone as planned. I can't afford another slip up."

"What happened?" Ansley asked puzzled.

Simeon rolled her eyes. Her face set in a deep frown. "They took an account I was assigned to work and gave it to this other guy Rick, who has been trying to steal it from me. Anyway, once I found out, I exploded on the guy." She paused. "I apologized, but since then, they have been punishing me with mediocre accounts."

Ansley recalled when Simeon flipped out on her at Tin Lizzy's. This erratic behavior was not characteristic of the Simeon she called friend.

"I hate to hear that....is there anything I can do? Maybe I can pitch the story to Jason for our live stream and do a video interview with the boutique owners at the launch party. Do you have a lot of media coverage?"

"No, I don't...," Simeon said. "I didn't even think to ask Jason myself. I've just been so stressed out."

"I'll definitely talk to him about it today," Ansley replied. "That story could help both of our jobs."

"Congratulations again on the promotion. You totally deserve it," Simeon said her voice lacking emotion. If anyone were to have walked by and heard her, they would have assumed she was being sarcastic, but Ansley knew Simeon was hurting and didn't take it personal.

"Thanks. I do deserve it, don't I?" she said with a chuckle. "But in all seriousness, I'm sorry if I've been neglecting our friendship."

"Girl, I was just tripping," she said. Simeon's eyes lit up. "I should be used to being without. I'm never first on anyone's list. I don't know why I thought you should worry about speaking with me. I'm no Lanae, I'm not on her level."

Simeon's shoulder lifted in a half shrug. She sighed audibly.

"Charles is such a sweetheart. He's been really great. I'm inviting him to the party too. You should bring Davis if you want, but we can leave them both at home and mix and mingle like we use to. Goodness, I'm so hungry. I really want dessert, though. What are you ordering?" Simeon searched the menu. "Girl, have you tried these Firecracker Wings? I'm about to have a cheat day and get that. You decided yet?"

Ansley scrunched her face. She shook her head, but did not acknowledge Simeon's shift from brooding to upbeat. If she had to choose, she'd much rather see her friend happy.

The server returned with their drinks.

Simeon took a sip of her drink. "Cheers to your promotion and to—our friendship."

"I'll drink to that," Ansley said, while raising her glass.

Davis made himself at home in Ansley's condominium. He had hoped by now that they would be living together. He was getting tired of motel stays and bumming on the sofa at Beau's midtown townhouse. Since Ansley had not given him a key, he decided to do it himself. A couple of days ago, when she was cooking and ran out of ingredients, Ansley sent Davis to the store to get what she needed.

While he was out, he stopped to have a key made at a nearby Walmart. This was the first time he had used the key; he needed money and knew he just where to get it.

Davis had taken Ansley's checkbook out of her purse the night before, and placed it somewhere he could access it. Since they first met, she seldom reached for her check book. She paid her bills online and purchased everything with cash or credit. He figured he would have some time to do what he needed before she noticed. Plus, she was always misplacing things in that oversized tote she carried, he felt certain he would be able to replace it before she noticed it was gone.

Pulling the checkbook from behind one of the portraits on the mantel, Davis wrote out a check addressed to cash, so that he could take it to the check-cashing spot up the street. He needed funds fast, so he did what he had to do. While he wanted to turn his life around, he still had to take care of debts. Besides, they were a couple now, what was hers was now his. He would be able to explain away her doubts like he did with them all.

Chapter 27

Ansley was an unexpected delight in his life. When he attended that conference in Chicago, his goal was to conquer the infamous Simeon Harris. Her family was one of the wealthiest in the city of Atlanta. It was easy to find her. Beau had provided him with enough information and details on the parties she attended and people that she associated with for business and pleasure. He studied her and got what he needed. Simeon could have provided the money he needed to get his life in order, but he met Ansley and got distracted.

Davis was not one to settle with one woman unless she could ensure his life as a kept man. He didn't bother to get a job; he was strategic in dating. Davis stayed abreast of the socialites, entrepreneurs, and the other "IT" girls in the city. While he didn't have the pedigree of the other men in this world, he was well-spoken, and had the looks and charm that allowed him to hobnob with the best of them. He planned to date Simeon to meet her friends and make connections that would benefit him in some way or another.

Ansley's family wasn't rich like Simeon's, which is why he felt some guilt about what he was doing. He wouldn't have done it, if the credit card he'd taken from Simeon hadn't been denied. When he first took the card, he held off on using it right away. He started with small purchases and then a few larger ones once he felt comfortable.

All was well, up until his recent trip to the supermarket. He was trying to buy some groceries through the self-checkout lane when the card was denied. As the clerk approached to assist him, he mentioned needing to grab a few more things but never returned.

Simeon must have realized it was gone and called to report the card missing.

He was kind of happy to be rid of that connection to her. Davis wanted to change, and using that card was linking him to his old ways. After today, he would be all set with his final payment to Beau.

Davis held the check up admiring his penmanship. It didn't take long for him to learn how to do her signature. Once he was confident that it matched, he was ready to start collecting from her account. For a moment, he wondered what he would say if she ever found out. He could not worry about that right now, he needed to get this money so he could pay Beau.

Davis had researched the check cashing store up the street from Ansley's place. He knew that the surveillance camera was out of order, but was scheduled for repairs later that afternoon. He chatted up the woman who worked there earlier that morning to ensure that he would have enough time to get in and out of the store. With Ansley leaving early for work, he knew he would have time to get the check and make it to the check cashing place.

Things are looking up for your boy.

There had been a few instances where Davis was almost outed but he managed to sustain. He never had to worry about Charles after all—Simeon dropped him a few days after the dinner. Davis had not heard anything from Bree either. She was content for the time being since he gave her some money. He allowed himself to relax and focus on getting things with Beau resolved.

Just as he was about to leave Ansley's home, he heard his phone ringing. He searched his pockets, realizing he must have laid it down somewhere. He looked around and grabbed it off the kitchen counter right before it went to voicemail.

"Beau, I'm about to get you some money right now," Davis stammered.

"Good, but I might need you to put in some work tonight. Keep your phone on."

"I told you I'm done, man. I'll have your money. I'm heading to the check cashing store as we speak."

Beau laughed. "That's not how this works, until I have money in my hands, I own you and I have a job for you. Be ready."

Up until now, Davis thought he had some normalcy. He hadn't heard from Beau since the last time he tried to tell him he was not doing any more dirt. Davis pushed the check in his pocket and rushed out of the condo. Being in the same state as Beau, was proving to be a disadvantage to his desire to have a new life. He had to find a way out of this mess, even if it meant leaving Georgia and Ansley behind.

Hours later, Davis met Beau at Magic City, one of Atlanta's most popular strip clubs. Walking into the club, Davis was met with the bass from Lil' Wayne's hit single *Lollipop*. The darkness of the club was illuminated by the coruscating red and blue lights, which created purple rays across the ceiling. Girls were arching their backs and wiggle their behinds in skyscraper length heels. He looked overhead and was in awe as he saw one dancer hanging from a rod in the ceiling while another dancer was below her swinging around pole with one hand.

For a second he felt he was at a Cirque show. These girls could give the acrobats in that show some real competition. The crowd was thick tonight. There were men and women pouring, sipping, and making it rain from every corner of the room.

It took him a minute to find Beau, who was sitting at his VIP table in the back right of the club. Beau insisted on meeting here, he believed that they could meet there without anyone getting suspicious. His cousin had taken the liberty of ordering for them.

"Listen man," Davis yelled over the music. "This isn't everything, but its five hundred toward my balance. I'm good for the rest by this weekend, but I'm telling you—I can't work for you, fam."

Although he was listening, Beau's eyes traveled the room. He was always aware of his surroundings and liked to stay one-step ahead at all times. Beau had an intimidating look. He was tall, round, and had deep sunken eyes and a full black beard. The lights in the club illuminated his toffee complexion.

Davis watched as Beau combed through the stack of bills that he handed to him.

"I've always looked out for you. I went to jail because of you. I wanted you to have the chance to finish college without a rap sheet." Beau said in an elevated voice, not making eye contact. "I gave you life, by taking away my own."

Davis opened his mouth to respond, but Beau held up a hand.

"When you deny me, not wanting to join my bid'ness—that hurts, man. Is my life worth nuffin? The things I've done for you. " He laughed. "Don't you think you owe me more than cash deposits?"

Davis remained quiet because he didn't know how to respond in a way that would not make things worse. He had to choose his words.

"Beau—I've thanked you repeatedly over the years. I know that you've sacrificed a lot for me—for our family. I know my words are never enough. While I can't work for you… I will pay off my debt."

When Beau hadn't responded, Davis took that as his cue to leave. Just as he rose from his seat, Beau placed a heavy hand firmly on his shoulder.

"You see that guy over there? That's Johnny. Up until recent, he's been loyal, but I heard he's been talking to the police. I need you to handle that for me."

Davis's eyes widened. He felt as if he couldn't breathe. Davis looked over at Johnny, who was picking up empty glasses from a table across the way. He didn't know what this guy had done, but the way Beau handled things meant that this guy was going to be missing soon. This was never going to end. He was starting to realize that he would never be free of his cousin's rule, even if he paid him off for this debt, Beau was always going to feel entitled to more.

"Handle how?" Davis replied, his voice cracking. "I just told you I'm not about that life."

"Just handle it. I want him quiet and I want him to know that his days are limited if he keeps running his mouth," Beau said, while passing Davis a gun.

"Whoa—put that away," Davis said looking around the room. "I'm cool man. I-I got my own," Davis lied.

Beau rubbed his hands together before putting his arm around Davis shoulders. "Well do work then lil' cuz. Oh, and if you don't get this right, then I'll have someone get you right. Ya' feel me?" Beau said with a menacing stare before breaking into laughter. "Nah I'm just joking. I would never go after family. We all we got in this world, right?"

Davis dapped up his cousin before walking away. He could feel Beau's eyes on him with each step. It felt like he had on fifty-pound ankle weights. As he was nearing the exit, he peered over at Johnny.

He watched as a girl in street clothes walked up to Johnny, carrying an overnight bag in her hand. As the two left the building, Davis strolled toward the exit to see what kind of car they were getting into.

Davis wasn't sure how he would complete Beau's demands, but unlike his cousin—he wasn't a killer. There had to be a way to shut this guy up, without putting both of their lives at risk.

Chapter 28

Ansley hadn't spoken to Davis since that morning, which was unusual since he normally called or texted at least twice a day. In the evenings, he had started staying at her place. She noticed he was leaving more and more items there. It was time to have a discussion with Davis because she felt that he was slowly moving into her home. Ansley cared for him, but she was not ready to cohabitate—she liked her space.

She took off her heels and walked barefoot to her bedroom. Ansley left work early because she needed to finish an assignment for school. Just as she was about to sit down and start working, the phone rang. Ansley felt a twinge of guilt because she hoped that it was not Davis. She didn't want any distractions. Looking at the caller ID, she saw the call was coming from the lobby and picked up.

"Hello, Ms. Wright. There are two detectives here to see you," the door attendant responded.

Her mouth fell open. "Um, did they say what they wanted? I didn't call them here."

"No ma'am, shall I ask them or do you want me to send them away?"

She began chewing on her nail. Ansley searched her mind to think of why they might be wanting to speak with her. Then fear set in, and she started to wonder if someone she knew was hurt or in danger.

"Oh no it's alright—please send them up. I'll meet

them at the elevators," she said perplexed. Ansley had no idea why detectives would want to speak to her. She sent up a silent prayer as she walked to meet them.

The elevator doors opened.

"Ms. Wright?"

When Ansley nodded, he said, "I'm Detective Leon Bower and this is Detective James Benson. We have a few questions and I hope you can help us out."

"I'll do what I can," she responded. "Can you tell me what this is all about?"

"Do you mind if we talk in your home?"

"I'd like to see your badges please."

The one named Bower had a grin on his face that resembled the Joker. "Here you go."

The other detective followed suit.

Ansley had no idea if the badges were real, but they looked official. "Did you show the attendant your badges?"

"Yes," Bower responded, "he refused to call you before he verified that we were indeed with the police department."

She knew he was telling the truth. The doorman was a retired policeman and he was very cautious about who came and went under his watch.

"I just live down the hall here," she said.

They followed her back to her condominium.

Ansley opened the door and let them inside. She gestured for them to have a seat before jumping into the conversation. "I'd like to know why you came to see me."

Bower, tall and lanky with ginger red hair, spoke first. He pulled a photo out of an envelope. "Can you tell me about this photo?"

Ansley could not disguise her surprise. It was a photo of

her and Davis. She swallowed hard before asking, "Where did you get this? Oh Lord, has something happened to Davis?"

"That would definitely make our job easier," Benson said, the other detective, who was short and portly with a strong resemblance to Spanky from the Little Rascals.

"I beg your pardon?" Ansley looked from one man to the other. "What does that mean? Why are you even here?" Ansley inquired.

"Excuse my partner, we received a tip that you may know of his whereabouts. How well do you know him?" Detective Bower asked.

"He's my boyfriend," Ansley inhaled, and then blew out a calming breath. "Is he okay?"

"My apologies for alarming you. We need to speak with him, about an acquaintance. Could you please give him my card when you see him again?"

"Sure, but why are you looking for him here?"

Benson scoffed. "As if he's not basically living here with you," he said gesturing toward a pair of Davis's shoes sitting near the door.

Ansley folded her arms across her chest. "This is ridiculous. You're here with empty comments, no questions, and no answers—and you're being rude. Please stop wasting my time, detectives."

"Thank you for speaking with us, Ms. Wright. We may come back once we have some clarity on the information that we need from you. Right now we just need to talk to—I'm sorry, what did you say his name was?" Bower asked.

Her brows knitted. "You came here asking me about Davis, how do you not even know his name? Are you profiling? Do you even have the right man?"

"Davis, right…it just slipped my mind," Bower replied. "Thank you again."

"By the way, where does this uh Davis work? Maybe we can just meet him there."

Ansley passed the detectives and opened her front door.

"I'll give him your card and let him provide that information," Ansley stated. Not that she was trying to hide anything, but these detectives were sketchy.

"Ah yes—here's my card. We will talk with you again soon," Detective Benson said as both detectives passed their cards to her.

After they left, Ansley shuddered with her back against the door. She walked over to her desk and picked up her phone to call Davis. He needed to know that something strange was going on—she hoped he had not gotten into any trouble.

Unsettled from a lack of sleep and her racing thoughts, Ansley decided to work from home the next day. She reached over to her nightstand to grab her phone. After the police left, Ansley tried to call Davis but got his voicemail and he had yet to call her back. If she did not hear from him by noon, she would call him again. Speaking to him would help to put her mind at ease.

She sat cross-legged in the middle of her bed and turned on her laptop. Ansley froze with fear when she heard her front door opening. The doorman had not called to announce any visitors, and the only two people who had keys to her place were Simeon and Lanae. They would never just drop by without letting her know about it.

She reached over and saw that her cellphone was not on the nightstand, but on the dresser by the door. She slid off the bed and tip-toed across the room to grab her phone, preparing to call the police. Ansley realized she was holding her breath the entire time, she feared that her floor would creak, and make the intruder aware that she was home.

Ansley quickly peeked around the corner.

She was relieved to see it was just Davis in her living room, but her relief was short-lived at his using a key to gain entrance into her home.

Ansley had never given him a key. She made a mental note to check the drawer of her nightstand where she stashed her spare key. Before she could go confront him, he got a phone call.

"Yo, what's good with you, fam? I guess you heard the news?" he asked.

Her eyes narrowed, as she watched with disgust as he acted so cavalier as if he lived there and was not intruding. Ansley remained behind the wall, standing in place, listening to his side of the conversation.

"Good, so everything is taken care of then?" Another beat and then, "That's what's up. I told you I would handle it my way. By the way, I'm about to get you the rest of the money today. Alright, bet."

Davis hung up, walked over to the mantel, and reached behind one of her photos.

Ansley had no idea what he was up to and decided that she would remain hidden. She couldn't believe what she saw next.

At first, Ansley couldn't make out what was in his

hands, she saw a thin rectangular object but it wasn't until she saw him remove the check he had written out that she knew what he had taken.

Ansley's hands shook as she lifted the phone to take a picture of Davis committing the crime in her home—the place where she welcomed him.

He had the nerve to whistle as he left, locking the door behind him.

Ansley wanted to go after him, but her anger paralyzed her.

She felt like such a fool. Ansley hadn't realized that her checkbook was missing, mostly because she rarely used it. Walking over to the mantel, she pulled the checkbook out and began reviewing the check registry to see how many checks Davis had taken. She could tell by her check registry that he had taken one other check prior to today. Ansley had carbon copies of each check, and was happy to see that he had neglected to remove the copy from the check he had just written in his haste to leave.

Ansley called the bank to report the stolen check and the amount that was written out to cash. After speaking with a representative, Ansley froze the account so that Davis could not access it, she wished she would be able to see his face once he realized that check was no good. Ansley had another account opened in her name, she had the bank move everything over to that account until she had taken care of this mess.

Next, Ansley arranged to have a locksmith come out to change her locks. Her third call was to the doorman, she informed him that Davis was no longer welcomed to her home and asked him to put a BE ON THE LOOKOUT notice to all of the residence so that he couldn't manage to get into the building from the parking garage. The call that Ansley regretted the most was to the detectives that had come by looking for Davis. That pill was going to choke her as it went down, the truth was hard to swallow and those gentlemen knew Davis was seedy but she was too wide open to see it at the time.

Ansley was furious, but mostly with herself. She had fallen for Davis' charm, his intelligence, handsome features, smooth words, and sweet kisses. She chose him over her friendship with Simeon. Ansley was humiliated. Nothing he could say could repair the damage done today.

"Yes hello, Detective Bower? Hi, this is Ansley Wright. I need to talk to you about Davis Montclair."

Chapter 29

Davis released a sigh of relief. He was getting closer to having his debt to Beau paid off, and then he could just focus on Ansley. Focus on being a better man altogether. That's all he wanted was to be a better person. He hated using her. Davis could not deny that he was catching genuine feelings for her, and if he lived a straight life, maybe they could have something real.

Maybe.

He took the bus across town trying to find a nearby check-cashing store. He never went to the same one twice; he didn't want to leave any trails. He walked inside and was elated to see that there was no line. Typically, when he came on paydays, the line was almost out the front door.

He walked to the counter, provided his identification and the check he had stolen from Ansley. The clerk, slid the glass away so that she could take the check and ID and began processing the transaction.

While waiting, he walked over to the bulletin board and pulled a few of the job announcements. If he really wanted to be an honest man, he knew he had to earn an honest living. Today was his beginning, and once he got this cash in hand, he planned to live free of the drama.

He glanced back toward the counter, wondering why it was taking so long for her to process his request.

The cashier was gone.

Davis walked over and peered through the glass. He did not see the check or his identification.

This was not a good sign.

He made a hasty exit.

Davis walked down to the next block where he climbed on the first bus that stopped. He looked back in time to see a police car pull in front of the check cashing shop. He did not relax until the bus pulled away and merged into traffic.

He was glad that he had used a fake ID, he removed the Bulls hat that he had on and tucked in under his shirt and jeans upon leaving the store. Davis cursed as he realized he hadn't even scoped that place to see how many cameras were in the store before doing any business. Now, he had to try to get another check. Davis checked his watch.

It was still early. He considered going back to the condominium, but with everything that had just transpired it might be better to wait until tomorrow. He needed some time to figure out if today's events were associated with his fake ID or had Ansley realized her checks were missing?

Chapter 30

Ansley spoke to the doorman who informed her that he thought Davis had moved in because he had a key. In reviewing the surveillance footage from the parking garage, she saw there were a few times that Davis walked in right behind other tenants and made his way up to her place. She still couldn't figure out how he managed to get a set of keys made without her knowledge, but then as she thought it over if he were able to get in her bag to get her checkbook then why not her keys?

After speaking with the detectives, she promised to come down to the station after she verified the total amount of money Davis had taken. Ansley tossed on a teal maxi dress and headed to the bank.

In reviewing her checking account, with the banker, Ansley learned that the other check Davis had written was also for five hundred dollars. Had she not been home to discover Davis' devious plan, he would've gotten away with one thousand. After spending hours at the bank, they assured Ansley that they would do their best to get all of the money returned.

She had just gotten back from speaking with the bank, when she saw detectives, Benson and Bower, standing right in front of the parking garage entrance. She pulled into a space and got out of the car. Ansley peered over her sunglasses at them, she felt a headache coming on. Exhaling, she stepped out of her truck and walked over to them. Her steps felt long and weary, her legs unstable and baby fawn-like, she didn't feel able to do this.

Ansley always thought she had a discerning spirit, Davis had proven her wrong today. Davis was who she thought he was after Simeon told her that he was lying about his name. But she chose to follow her heart, it was clear to her now that she was clinging to something that was never there. It was just infatuation, and she was the silly fool who let him juggle with her emotions.

"Ms. Wright, thanks for calling us. Did everything check out with Davis? Get it? Cause he took some checks from you." Benson bent over laughing at his own corny joke.

Ansley clicked her teeth. *I'm not here for this foolishness today.*

"Excuse my partner. Can you tell us what happened?" Benson asked.

"I was home today, which is different from my normal routine. I seldom work from home. Anyway, I was in my bedroom when I heard someone enter and so I—."

"Whoa, hold up there," Detective Benson requested. "You mean to tell me you heard someone enter your home and didn't call the police ASAP?"

Ansley cut him a dirty look. "As I was saying, I reached over to call the police, but realized my phone was on my dresser, which is by the door leading to the living room. Once I got up to grab the phone, I looked around the corner and saw Davis. At first glance, I felt relieved but then I remembered that I have never given him a key to my home. He must have made one. Anyway, he was there because he had taken my checkbook and placed it behind a frame on my mantel. He had written out and cashed one check for five hundred, and was preparing another for the same amount today. Only today I was home and he was unable to cash that check."

Detective Benson took a glance over at Detective Bower. "What happened after you confronted him?"

"I didn't," Ansley said looking away. She knew Spanky was judging her. "After he left, I called my bank and then went down there to complete some paperwork. They're going to assist in recouping the stolen money."

"Do you know where he might be now?" Detective Bower asked.

"I have no clue, but I'm sure he'll be snooping around here. I haven't heard from him yet."

Detective Benson nodded. "If he reaches out to you, act normal as if nothing has changed. If you can get him to meet you somewhere, we can be there and we can have someone surveillance your home if you like."

Ansley shook her head before taking out a pen and paper. Her head was spinning and she just wanted this to be over with. "I can't do that. Here you go. This is his phone number. I'm sorry. I'm willing to point him out of a line up, or identify him in court, but that's all I'm mentally prepared to do right now. I don't want to speak to him. I don't want him in my home and I don't want to be alone with him anywhere, ever again," she spat.

Her hands began to shake. She hated that she allowed this to happen. Had she broken things off from the jump, none of this would have happened. He would be ruining some other woman's day.

"I understand that you're overwhelmed, we'll be in touch Ms. Wright," Detective Benson said.

She walked through the building entrance from the

parking garage, and got onto an awaiting elevator. Hurt and anger escalated inside of her. Ansley could not believe how naïve she had been. One thing for sure, her eyes were wide open now.

Chapter 31

Davis woke up early the next day to get a head start. He had a busy day ahead of him.

He showered and slipped on a pair of black jeans and a fitted, button down, red, black, and white flannel shirt.

It was risky, but he needed to go by Ansley's house to get another check. It had been two days since his failed attempt at the check cashing store.

He hadn't heard from Ansley, and neglected to return her call after everything went down. He thought it was best to lay low. He would call her soon, but right now he had other matters requiring his attention.

Davis had spent the past few days working to get Johnny out of state. He called Beau to let him know that he would be late with his money, only to receive an earful about Johnny still being careless, and discussing Beau's business with those outside of their circle. Davis found out that the stripper he saw talking to Johnny often traveled for out of state appearances. Davis arranged for Johnny to join her when she went to Charlotte, but his plan was for Johnny to go there and never returned. So far, his plan was working.

Davis figured his plan would work best if he had a man to man conversation, and he let him know that Beau had a hit out on him.

Johnny agreed that it was for the best that he relocate

considering his life was in jeopardy, and he took the money and left with no argument.

With a stack of cash, he'd taken from Beau's secret stash that he shouldn't have known about, he paid for Johnny's travel and accommodations in North Carolina. He had to break off a few dollars for the dancer as well, and her silence was not cheap, but he made it happen for his cousin.

Problem solved.

Davis walked out of his extended stay motel room just as his neighbor was leaving.

"Aye man, you had some visitors yesterday," the man announced.

"Serious?" Davis was instantly on guard. "What did they look like?"

"Two suits. Looked like some Law and Order type jokers."

"They couldn't have been looking for me," he responded with a forced chuckle. "I'm a law-abiding citizen."

His neighbor laughed. "Sure. Aren't we all?"

Heart beating rapidly, Davis returned to his room where he hurried to pack a bag. He wasn't planning to return to this place. If it was one thing that he learned from Beau, with the life they lived routines were trouble. It was Johnny's routine that got him caught up. He would've been an easy target for Beau to find. He did the same thing every day. Visited the same people. He was a walking target. Davis wasn't planning to be an easy catch.

His cell phone rang.

He didn't recognize the number, so Davis didn't answer.

What if they are watching me? He was in panic mode, looking around the parking lot and across the street at the motel adjacent to the one where he was staying. Seeing a taxi pulling up to let someone out in front of the lobby, Davis picked up his bag and took the steps down, two at a time. He flagged the driver down, and got inside, giving the driver Ansley's address.

On the way over to Ansley's house, Davis tried calling and texting her. She never answered or responded. Davis hoped her silence didn't mean that she knew that he had stolen money from her. He let go of that theory. She must have been busy or perhaps she was mad that he didn't call her back. It had been a few days.

Shaking off the thought, he began to formulate alternatives to his financial needs. Davis thought that it might be a good idea to steal some of her credit cards out of her wallet as well. Then when she realized that cards were missing—she would just assume they were stolen along with her checkbook.

The more he thought this over, the more it made sense to him. In fact, he planned to call Beau and see if he could arrange a burglary at her place. He didn't want Ansley hurt, but it really needed to be authentic. As he thought it over more, it would look even better if the job was done while she was with him. That would give him an alibi and it would help in proving his innocence, pending she suspected that he stole from her.

He tipped the driver and asked him to wait while he ran inside.

Davis walked to the door and pressed the button to be let into the building.

He looked over at the doorman and waved, but the elderly man peered at him over his glasses, picked up the phone and turned his back to Davis.

A thread of apprehension snaked down his back. This

was a bad sign.

She knows.

Ansley must have known, that was the only way he could explain why the doorman was acting as if he didn't just see Davis waiting there for him to open the door.

Davis muttered a curse. *What am I going to do now?*

Chapter 32

Ansley paced back and forth in her living room. The doorman called to let her know that Davis was downstairs. She didn't want to see him, but she did want answers.

She wanted to know why he did this, and Ansley planned to get her answers but not without having a little fun catching him in the act first. She instructed the doorman to make up an excuse for not letting him in right away. Ansley wanted Davis to think that she was not home, to see if he would attempt to get upstairs and use the key again.

Ansley was hurt, but she forced that particular emotion to the back of her mind and focused instead on her anger. Fury fueled her now. She eyed the large candlestick holder on her sofa table. If Davis tried anything, she had no problem using it on him—she was that angry.

Her telephone rang.

It was Simeon. Ansley silenced the ringer, she didn't want her phone to be going off with Davis coming up within minutes. Her friend knew her well enough to know when she was upset. Answering the phone would have led to a long drawn out conversation and Ansley unloading all that had occurred this morning. She wasn't ready for anyone to know what a fool she had been.

Chapter 33

Davis was about to leave when the doorman buzzed him inside the building.

He walked in with his hands raised. "What's up man? I didn't think you were going to let me in for a second there."

"I had to deal with a crazy woman on the phone. Sorry 'bout that."

He eyed the elderly man. "Been there... done that." Davis paused, then asked, "Do you know if Ansley's at home?"

"I believe she already left for work."

"Good. I have something special planned for her this evening," he lied.

Davis stood there beaming like a man who really had romancing his woman on the brain, but the doorman didn't look embarrassed or interested in the details.

"Well alright. Good talking to you too," said Davis, his tone full of sarcasm. He stepped onto the elevator as the doors parted.

Davis planned to be in and out of Ansley's place. There was no need to linger. He knew what he wanted to accomplish, and that did not involve getting caught because he wanted to take more of her personal effects.

On her floor, he strolled at a casual pace, as if he were one of the residents. He had spent so much time there, he had gotten to know a couple of her neighbors.

Davis stuck his key into the lock.

It didn't work.

He swallowed hard and glanced around, although he was the only one in the hallway, he felt as if the walls were narrowing by the second. *Stop being paranoid.*

Davis inhaled as he prepared to try the lock again. When the door swung open, he barely had time to react.

"Did you come to steal more money, Davis?" Ansley asked, holding the checkbook in her hand, and giving him a death glare.

"Hey babe. What are you taking about?" he said, wearing a puzzled expression.

Shaking her head, she laughed. "Wow. Are you for real right now? You have a lot of nerve."

Davis decided to try another tactic. "Whoa…slow down."

He reached for her and she jerked away. Davis held his hands up in defense. "Listen Ansley, if you'll just sit down so we can talk…it'll all make sense. I was planning to tell you about the money."

She poked him in the chest. "So you admit it. Un-freaking believable." She looked heavenward. "There is nothing you can say that I'll believe or that I even want to hear right now," she responded. "I will say this—you are going to give me back my money. You've got one week."

She pushed him back toward the hallway. He caught the door with his hand before she could close it on him.

"Ansley, listen to me, baby. I lost my job and-and, I was just ashamed to tell you," he said as he moved closer to her. "I should've told you I needed help. I'm sorry." Davis lowered his eyes to the floor.

Silence. He wasn't expecting her not to respond at all.

Lifting his eyes to hers, he hoped that she would have some pity on him. That's not what he got from Ansley though.

"Boy, please!" Ansley said as she reached across the threshold, mushing him in the face. "Get out my house. I want all of the money you stole from me within seven days or you will be sorry. Oh, and there are two detectives wanting to talk to you."

Davis glanced up at her. "About what?"

"You need to ask them," Ansley responded. "I can't believe what a liar you are, Davis. Simeon doesn't realize how lucky she was to just deal with you for one night."

He tried to look wounded by her words.

She glared at him. "You have no idea just how much I regret the day you walked into my life."

"You're angry now," Davis stated. "I know I can't take back what I did, but you need to know that I care for you and wouldn't do anything to hurt us. I messed up big time, but if you'll give me another chance—."

"That won't be happening," she said, interrupting him. "I don't want anything else to do with you."

Davis walked toward her.

Ansley backed away from his reach and redirected him to the door. "I want you out of my life."

"You don't mean that."

She looked into his eyes. "Oh, I mean it. There is no way I can ever trust you, Davis. You're a liar and a thief…I have a feeling that your deceit goes even deeper."

Davis knew when to walk away and this was one of those times. Ansley had won this round, but he had no intentions of giving up. When she calmed down, he would be waiting to resume his rightful place in her heart.

As soon as he stepped back into the hallway, she

slammed the door. Davis could hear her securing the locks.

This was not what he needed.

Davis got on the elevator and headed back to the lobby. He wasn't sure if Ansley was bluffing about the detectives waiting for him outside, but his plan was to go straight to the taxi and head far away from there.

As the elevator door opened, he got hit with a dose of clarity about what transpired with the doorman. Ansley must have banned him from the building, this is why the doorman was hesitant to let him in, and it was even more evident now that he saw the smug look on the doorman's face as he exited.

Once outside, the only thing waiting for him were the detectives. His taxi left him stranded. Davis uttered a curse. The two men approached him.

It made sense now. The only reason Ansley had him come up was to keep him from leaving before the detectives arrived. "Davis Montclair, I'm Detective Bower. You're a hard man to find."

Must be the guys that were snooping around the motel.

"You've been looking for me, may I ask why?" he asked trying to keep his tone level.

"We would like to ask you some questions about your connection to Beau Cannon," Detective Bower said.

His brows snapped together. "I'm sorry, who?"

Detective Benson chuckled. "Are you saying you don't know your own blood?"

"I'm afraid I don't know anyone by that name. Did he say he knew me?"

The detectives exchanged looks.

"I actually have to get back to work gentlemen, so if there's nothing else, I'm going to get going," Davis said walking around them.

"Over at Lowell Myer, LLC, right?" Detective Benson asked with a smirk. "I'm sure they could miss you for a couple more hours. From what we know, they've been missing you forever, since you're not on their employee roster."

Davis wanted to wipe that haughty look off the detective's face. He wasn't sure what this guy thought he knew, but he refused to flinch.

"Detective honestly, I do have some errands to run. I'm not sure how I can help you?"

"So you have to get back to work or run errands? Which one is it, pal?" Detective Benson asked.

"What my partner means to say is that it all depends on you, Mr. Montclair," he said gesturing toward their car. "We'd like you to come down to the station with us."

This day was not going as planned.

"Sure, no problem." Davis walked with them to the car. As they walked, he sent a quick message to one of Beau's girls so they would let him know what was going on. Davis knew from previous experience to never call or text Beau directly in situations like this.

Before Davis got into the back of their black, unmarked sedan, he looked up to see Ansley staring down at them from her window.

He gave her one of his signature smiles. Davis was not done with her yet. Not even close.

Beau watched from a nearby car as Davis got into the back of an unmarked police car. He knew that joker would manage to get in trouble. His hands clenched into fists.

He better not mention my name.

Beau didn't want the beautiful woman Davis was chasing to become collateral damage for his mistakes.

Chapter 34

Davis was silent the entire ride to the station and maintained his unflappable demeanor. The short detective was entrenched in his bad cop role, but Davis was no stranger to police stations and did not intimidate easy. He still found it hard to believe that Ansley had manipulated him this way. Davis was usually two steps ahead when it came to women. He would have to give Ansley some time alone. She would come around, one way or another.

"Davis… it is still Davis, right?" Detective Benson asked, interrupting his thoughts. "Do you need to call your job and inform them that you'll be late?"

Does he know my real name?

"I sent them an email from my phone," he responded. Davis smirked. He knew the detective was really trying to push his buttons. It was working. Davis was using everything within him to resist the temptation to sucker punch him.

At the police station, they sat him in one of the interrogation rooms.

He was not nervous because there was nothing they could pin on him. His hands were clean. There was nothing connecting Davis to Beau, he wasn't sure how they made a connection.

Davis and Beau had minimal interaction. They used burner phones when they needed to speak, and they only met in person if it was a situation that required an in-person conversation. The detectives broke into his thoughts when Detectives Bower and Benson returned to the room.

"Davis... Montclair is it?" Bower said when he entered the room, carrying a folder.

What do they know? Don't show weakness, you got this.

He leaned back in the chair and sat expressionless. "Yes, that's correct. Now how can I assist you?" Davis said.

Detective Benson sat down at the table facing him. "Mr. Montclair, can you tell us how you know Beau Cannon?"

"I told you that I didn't know him." Davis stared at the two men. Trying to gauge what they knew and what they were trying to get him to admit.

"So this isn't you leaving Mr. Cannon's home? Or talking to Mr. Cannon at Magic City a few days ago?" Detective Bower said, sliding a few photos across the table.

"Oh, that guy. I never got his name. He sat by me at the bar," Davis lied.

"I see. And how do you explain going to and from his home?"

"I've never been to his home. I'm not sure whose home that is in the photo," Davis said pretending to study the picture. "Was this done in Photoshop? The image seems distorted in a few spots, but overall—nice job."

"You're from Chicago, correct?" Benson inquired.

"What is this about?" Davis asked, trying to buy time.

"You know... Beau is also from Chicago," Bower stated as he joined them at the table. "This is what I think—I think you do know him very well. Blood relatives or old friends from the hometown. Maybe he followed you here... or perhaps he requested you move down here to work for him."

"You don't have any idea what you're talking about. Perhaps, I should allow you all to speak to my lawyer." Davis rose to his feet. "I don't know what you're seeking, but you're not going to pin anything on me just because I'm from Chicago. That is all that you know about me, so if you'll excuse me, I'm done talking."

"Whoa. Where's the fire, Mr. Montclair?" Detective Bower asked. "You're not under arrest. We are just trying to understand your connection to Mr. Cannon."

"By the way, what made you change your name, Montgomery?" Detective Benson chimed in.

"I think it would be best that you contact my lawyer."

As if on cue, LaRue Baker, the lawyer Beau had on retainer, walked into the interrogation room. LaRue had been Beau's lawyer for several years and had gotten him dismissed from multiple charges from drugs to attempted murder.

"You're exactly right, Davis," she said. "Good afternoon, gentleman."

"As the Detective just said, you're not under arrest and so you don't have to tell them anything. Let's go."

Davis left the room without looking back.

He was glad that he got a message out to Beau during the ride to the station. Beau always came through. Davis debated whether he should leave town, but decided against it for now. A quick departure would only make him look guilty.

Chapter 35

Ansley spent the rest of the week consumed with her job and school. She was the first to arrive and the last to leave each day.

It was after six o'clock, and she was just leaving Grind House. As she stepped into her Range Rover, on her way to Lanae's house for dinner, her phone range.

She reached for her Bluetooth to answer the call. "Hello."

There was silence on the call, and then it disconnected.

She grabbed her phone from her purse to see who the call was from, but the number was listed as unknown. Ansley shrugged it off as nothing and started to call Lanae to see if she needed anything from the store when her phone rang again.

This time, Ansley checked to see who was calling before she answered, and again the number was showing as unknown.

She answered on the third ring, a woman spoke. "Hello Ansley, my name is Bree Spellman. I'm your man's ex-girlfriend. I think we should talk."

Ansley's hands gripped the steering wheel.

After everything that happened with Davis, Ansley probably shouldn't have been surprised by this phone call, but she was taken off guard and was not at all prepared. Now what.

"Hello, are you there?" Bree spoke into the phone.

"Oh—I'm sorry, I'm here." She sighed. "First off, you should know that I'm not seeing Davis anymore, so what can I do for you?"

"Davis... I'm talking about Monty," Bree stated.

Ansley frowned in confusion. "I don't know a Monty. The man I dated was Davis Montclair."

"Is this Ansley Wright? He told me that you two were a couple when he came to Chicago back in February," Bree stated.

Ansley grunted as reality set in. It had been almost a month since she last spoke to Davis, and he was still haunting her.

She recalled the day that Simeon told her his name was Monty. She didn't dig into the details or make him proclaim anything. Instead they argued and his lies made it through another day. Then there's the lie about the type of business he went to Chicago to handle. The more she learned about him, the more she realized she hadn't learned anything at all.

"I'm sorry. I just remembered a friend of mine saying he went by the name Monty. I must have blocked that out."

"I should have known that he lied about his identity. That explains why I had trouble serving him to appear."

"Serving him—as in court papers?" Ansley inquired.

"He's a con-artist. Of course he lied about who he was." She could tell that Bree must have been processing everything she was learning as well.

"I'm sorry...what are you talking about?" Ansley sat confused.

"He stole money from me. He was mentally, physically and verbally abusive. I ended up losing my job because I was in and out of hospitals. Monty caused me to have a miscarriage with all that I endured. Bet you didn't know that, or did you?"

Ansley was not surprised about the theft portion of this story, but Davis had never raised a hand to her nor had he ever spoken to her in a harsh tone. This was a surprise to her.

"I'm sorry you experienced such trauma. No one should have to go through that." Ansley paused before continuing. She didn't want to come off as being insensitive but she wasn't sure what Bree was looking for her to do. "As I said earlier, we are no longer a couple. Listen Bree…thanks for reaching out to me, but I really have to go."

"Ansley wait… there's more to the story," she said. "You need to know that he has—"

The phone went silent, but her screen still showed the call as active. "Hello Bree?" she called out.

When Ansley did not get a response, she ended the call. She figured that Bree would call her back, however, she did not.

Ansley pulled into Lanae's driveway empty-handed. After Bree's phone call, she could not think about anything else.

Before she could knock, Jacob opened the door. "Whoa... hey, Ansley. Lanae is in the kitchen." He stepped aside to let her enter.

Ansley sat down on a barstool at the island in the kitchen.

"It took you long enough." Lanae walked over to greet Ansley with a hug.

"Yeah. I know. Sorry about that. I had an unexpected phone call," she explained.

"Uh-oh," Lanae said as she grabbed two empty wine

glasses and a bottle of Beringer Merlot. As she poured she asked, "What's going on?"

"Well, Davis and I are done." She paused to take a long sip of her wine.

Lanae took the bottle and topped off Ansley's glass. Ansley took that as her cue to continue.

"He stole money from me, and then I get a call from his ex-girlfriend today and find out his name is really Monty. If I'm being honest, Simeon said that a long time ago, but I breezed right pass collecting the facts on that one."

Lanae pursed her lips. "Wow. I'm sorry, sweetie. Geesh. He stole from you? How much if you don't mind my asking?"

Ansley raked her fingers through her bangs. "Well it would've been one thousand, had I not caught him in the act but he got five hundred which the bank recovered." She ran her fingers across the top of her wine glass. "How did I get here?" she asked. "You hear stories like this, but I've never been involved in anything this crazy. I feel violated."

"You still care about him, don't you?" Lanae asked.

"Honestly, I don't know what I feel or think outside of anger. One minute we were working on developing something and then next thing I know he's helping himself to my money."

Lanae got up to remove a pot roast and broccoli rice casserole from the oven. "Well beloved… I would feel the same way."

"I just wanted to go with the flow for once, you know," Ansley said.

Lanae put the two dishes in the warmer. She turned toward Ansley. "Well, you know Jacob and I were always team Ryan. He was the man you were supposed to marry.

Fine too. I still believe that's who you will be with one day."

Ansley would never forgive herself for breaking Ryan's heart. Lately, she had thought a lot about him and the decisions she made. She was young and selfish and didn't want to rewrite how her dreams played out in order to be with him and watch him follow his own.

Lanae left her kitchen and stood in front of Ansley. "For as long as I've known you, you've always been in a rush. You've never prayed, fasted, or felt compelled to wait on God for anything."

Ansley pondered over Lanae's words. "I can't even argue with you. I guess I just wanted to fulfill my and my mother's dreams. She always wanted to be a writer, but she put her career second to marriage. I didn't want to be married and look back at dreams unfulfilled."

"I get that Ansley, but again I ask you, why just assume that you couldn't have it all?"

Ansley's eyes welled with tears. Lanae was right. Living with tunnel vision had blinded her from opportunities in her career and love life. With Davis stealing from her and this revelation about her life choices, Ansley knew that she needed to assess some things about her life if she wanted to keep putting herself in the role of victim. She was tired of living with regrets.

Two hours later, she left Lanae's house and drove home.

Her phone rang a few minutes after she walked into her bedroom. "Hello."

"What's going on with you?"

"Simeon, hey…" Ansley said, taking a seat on the edge of her bed. "I was thinking about calling you."

"You sound upset."

"I found out some things about Davis. He's not the

man I thought he was," she said. "I'm sure none of this surprises you."

"Actually, it does," Simeon responded. "I thought he was different—at least with you. What happened?"

"He stole money out of my checking account."

"What..."

"Yeah, that was pretty much my initial reaction. Then to top that off, I received a phone call from his ex-girlfriend."

"Are you serious?" Simeon asked.

"She called me earlier..." Ansley's voice died.

"And?"

"He stole from her, too. He was also abusive."

Simeon gasped.

"I should've listened to you. You were right, his name really is... or was Monty. I guess he changed his name when he moved to Georgia."

"This is scary. Do you think he's on the run or something?" Simeon quizzed.

Ansley gave a dismissive wave of her hand as if Simeon could see her. "All I know is that he's a liar and a thief."

"Wow, what a loser," Simeon seethed. "Are you okay?"

"I'm fine," Ansley assured her friend. "This is what I get for rushing into the relationship—and for choosing to pursue that relationship over our friendship. I'm sorry and I know that's not enough, but I hope you'll accept this as a start."

Simeon chuckled. "I'm so over that whole situation and there's no need to rehash any of that. We are good."

She paused a moment, then said, "Thank you. I'm just glad the truth was revealed before I lost my heart to him completely."

"He better hope I don't run into him anytime soon."

"Simeon, don't get involved," Ansley said with a short sigh. "He's out of my life and I just want to move forward."

"You sure you're okay?"

"I am," Ansley said. "What's going on with you?"

"I've been having some health issues. Going to see my doctor tomorrow morning."

"Do you want me to go with you?" Ansley asked out of concern.

"No, it's not anything serious," Simeon responded. "I just need a wellness checkup."

Ansley didn't pry. If her friend wanted her to know specifics, she would have given details.

They talked a few minutes more before hanging up.

She sat cross-legged in the middle of her bed, pondering over her future. She had the Essence Festival coming up, and this was an unwelcomed distraction.

Ansley picked up a pillow and threw it across the room. She hated being made out to look like a fool—Davis had not paid her back yet, but then she did not really expect that he would. However, she was not going to let him get away with stealing from her. He needed to learn that bad behavior came with repercussions.

Chapter 36

Ansley was embarking on the second month of not speaking with Davis. He had attempted to call her a few times while she was at the festival, but she always sent the calls straight to voicemail. She didn't need the distraction. While she wanted to erase him from her memory, Ansley knew she had to get closure first. She wanted him to take responsibility for his actions and tell her the truth about everything. Ansley knew it was a stretch to think that he would do right by her, but she had to try to get some clarity for her own peace.

Ansley decided that she was going to shower, dress and go to his townhouse. She needed to confront him. Sitting around trying to figure out what caused him to deceive her, was no longer sufficient, she wanted the truth behind his lies.

Thirty minutes later, she was at the door. She couldn't believe she had only been to his place twice, and of those two visits, she had only gone inside once. Just as she was about to knock, two women walked out. Ansley took them both in, one had Poetic Justice dookie braids and the other woman appeared to have started getting her hair braided, but from the looks of it she must have ran out of hair. Or whoever was doing her hair must have taken a break.

"Umm...is you lost or sumptin?" one of the women with the braids asked. Ansley couldn't take her eyes off the woman's front snaggle tooth, but then she saw the gold cap on the bottom row and became even more distracted.

"She said is you lost?" the other with the hair struggle quizzed.

"Oh my bad. I'm here to see Davis. Is he home?"

"No one named Davis lives here. This my man's house. You trying to see one of his boys? Because I know you ain't sniffing 'round my man," she said with an attitude.

"I'm sorry, but this is the person I'm here to see," she said holding up her phone to show the woman a picture of Davis. Ansley remembered the day she took this photo of him, she had to sneak and get it. He never liked to take pictures, and she was beginning to think it had a lot to do with his seedy lifestyle.

The woman took the phone and showed it to her friend, who glanced at the picture and then back at the other woman. "Naw, we don't know him. Maybe he was just here for a party or sumptin'. Sorry you got the wrong place," she said before walking off.

The other woman went back inside without acknowledging her any further.

It was possible that he had moved away. Especially since he owed her money.

Coward.

Just as she was about to drive away, the woman with the unfinished braids, was now waving her over. She must have darted around the house and waited for the other woman to leave. The woman motioned with her hands for Ansley to drive around the corner.

Ansley wasn't sure what the woman wanted, but nodded and did as the woman requested. A few minutes passed before the girl came walking toward her car. Ansley rolled her window down and leaned across the passenger side to see what the woman had to say.

"Excuse me, but you mind if I get in the car? I don't want anyone to see me," she said, her eyes shifting around.

Ansley unlocked the door on the passenger side.

"I'll make dis quick. I know the dude in the picture, but when NeNe said she ain't recognize him, I knew that was my cue to keep my mouth shut. You look so innocent and church lady-like, I don't think you deserve to be caught up in his mess."

Ansley wanted to know what a church-lady dressed like, but this was not the time to focus on petty details. She took a deep breath. She couldn't imagine what she was about to hear, but she braced herself.

The woman continued, "His real name Montgomery Davis. He work fo' my boss sometimes and hustle people out of money—he's a carn-artist," she said. "He always in and out of trouble from what I've heard, but yet he always gets his cousin to get him out of jams. Dis here is one of his cousin's places, but you ain't heard any of dis from me. I ain't even post to be talking to you," she whispered. Chewing on her nails, she peered over the backseat to ensure no one crept up behind the car. "I gotta go, but look him up. I'm sure you'll find some dirt on him. We never spoke, understand?"

Ansley swallowed hard and nodded her understanding. The woman got out of the car and disappeared the same way she came.

Ansley let out a sigh of relief. That didn't go as bad as she had anticipated, but yet there was another layer of mystery to Davis Montclair—or Montgomery Davis. She had done a Google search when they first met, but that yielded no results. Ansley figured it was because that's not his name, and perhaps he only just started using this alias. She couldn't make it back to her condo fast enough. It was time for her to do a little investigating of her own.

Ansley was not sure what she would find, but she decided that a bottle of wine might help settle her nervous stomach.

She grabbed a glass, popped the cork, and logged into her laptop.

She went to Google.com and performed a search. There were several Montgomery Davises in Chicago, and several sites willing to share everything for a small fee. After Ansley found nothing of concrete value, she decided to take a break and turn on the radio. Her favorite on-air personality was on and she seldom missed her show.

"Okay ladies, stay tuned. I hope that you all were listening to the segment when we brought in the creator of Don't Date Him Girl.com. Well today, we actually have women in the studio who have used the site and found out more than their share of scandal on these men they were dating. You do not want to miss this."

Ansley had forgotten about that radio segment and never even thought about looking at the website.

As the radio continued to blare in the background, Ansley walked back over to her laptop, keyed in the website, and waited for the site to load. She could not believe how many scorned women were out there. It was nice to have some company along with her misery, but at the same time, it was very sad.

She read a few of the entries and decided that some of the women were just bitter.

She typed in Montgomery Davis and found several entries.

Ansley narrowed her search by listing Chicago and Atlanta as the last known cities where he may have resided. This brought her results down from 50 to 20 entries.

She went through each entry and was just about to give up when she found what she needed. There was a photo of him sitting beside a gorgeous woman with raven black hair. Ansley stared at the picture. It was the only one in the profile. The rest included details about their relationship. Ansley's eyes widened as she read the first line

Ladies, beware of this predator. He preys on women when they are at their most vulnerable state and then tries to wine and dine you into believing he's the romantic type. But honestly, he's a lothario who can't be trusted.

I guess you're wondering how he was able to wine and dine a woman when he has no job, and to answer your question, I'll get to the point and say he's a con artist. He's a bum. Watch your purses ladies, he's all about the five finger discount. He stole over $3000 from me before I realized what was happening.

He's an intelligent guy and managed to hack into my computer and steal my information. He's also verbally and physically abusive. I was in and out of hospitals because he decided to show his love by pushing me down the stairs when I confronted him about stealing my money. Then there was the time when he punched me in my face because he was having a bad day. This man cannot be trusted and you should avoid him at all costs. In addition, for the finale—the final nail in the coffin, this man has a STD and he knows he has an STD. He would never tell a woman that because he thinks that a condom would be enough to protect women instead of honesty. A majority of the time, he uses his charm to coax a woman into letting him have his way free of a raincoat. Or maybe he will do what he did to me, and take it off during the act. I'm currently trying to sue him for damages because I lost my job from having to be out so much to recover from his abuse and I suffered from severe depression once I found out about the STD. Ladies, you've been warned. He cannot be trusted.

Ansley read and re-read the last part of the woman's comments. This had to be Bree. She had mentioned the abuse in her phone call, but the part about Davis having a STD—she must have made that up, Ansley didn't want this to be true. She refused to believe it.

This had to be a lie. Davis... Montgomery, or whatever his name was, he was a horrible person, but this was effecting someone's health—would he really be so cavalier to put others at risk? Ansley knew the answer to this, but she was in denial. Her head began to throb. She needed to get tested immediately. She scheduled an appointment online to meet with her doctor.

Chapter 37

Ansley avoided talking to her friends and worked from home over the next two days. She was not in the right mindset to deal with people. She couldn't bring herself to tell Lanae or Simeon about the latest information she'd discovered about Davis...Montgomery or whoever he was.

She was a complete wreck as she dressed for her doctor's appointment. She had the first appointment of the day, and she was ready to get it over with. Ansley looked at herself in the mirror and shook her head as she saw the uncoordinated buttons on her white blouse and mismatched navy and black shoes she wore. She exhaled and grabbed her purse from the dresser to head out.

An hour and a half later, she sat in a chair while the phlebotomist drew her blood. She'd already completed a pap smear and provided the doctor with a urine sample. It would be a couple of days before she would know her fate.

Ansley wanted to scream.

Although the doctor assured her that she wasn't currently exhibiting any signs of a STD, which was relief, but Ansley still wanted to get those test results so she would know for sure that she was negative. Leaving the doctor's office, Ansley decided that she would not worry. She had prayed about it and believed she would be fine.

Wherever Davis is hiding, he had better stay there...

Chapter 38

Davis thought it was best to keep a low profile. He'd heard from his cousin that the police were showing up at places that he frequented, but other than that, they hadn't approached him.

It looked like they were hitting their heads on the ceiling with this investigation, there wasn't room to go any further which alleviated Davis. He wasn't sure exactly why they were looking for Beau. It could be anything—drugs, money-laundering, murder—he dabbled in several things.

Davis was distancing himself from Beau. The last thing he needed was for his cousin to be arrested and he be charged as well since he'd lied about their relationship. Beau had been taking charges for Davis since they were young. When Davis turned eighteen-years old, Beau told him that he would not be doing any more time for him. Of course, Beau still got his hands dirty for the family, but Davis knew if Beau ever got arrested again, he would be heading to prison for an extended term.

Davis decided to walk to the nearby Landmark Diner to grab a bite to eat. He loved this place, and its old school appeal with its checkerboard floors, fluorescent lighting, and the round swivel tools. His favorite part was the jukebox in the corner, and the pay phone near the door. They designed this place like a time warp, and if he had a choice, he would have preferred to be in any other time zone but the present.

He chose a booth in the back corner away from the windows. Davis glanced around the restaurant, it was lunch hour so it was very busy and with it being summer time, several student were out of school and taking up space.

Davis picked up the menu, though he knew he planned to get a cheeseburger with no onion, no tomato, and fries. Condiments on the side. It was the same every time he came here. He scanned the room to get the attention of a waitress, instead he saw the last person he wanted to see.

He frowned, wondering what Johnny was doing back. He had arranged to get him out of the state, but he didn't follow through to make sure there were no slip-ups with his plan. Seeing Johnny here meant, that something had gone wrong.

Davis placed his order with the waitress, and almost died when he saw Detectives Bower and Benson heading in his direction. He was tired of being harassed.

Thinking they were there for him, he prepared to get up to leave when he saw them have a seat in the same booth as Johnny. Davis worried that Johnny's return meant he was cooperating with the police. *Guess this guy does need to be watched.*

As a large party walked into the restaurant in search of a table to accommodate their group of ten, Davis used the opportunity to slide into the booth behind the two detectives. His back was to them, and he hoped that he could find out why they were meeting with Johnny.

The server came over.

"Is everything okay? Was something wrong with the other table?" she asked.

The last thing he wanted was attention. He didn't want to speak for fear that they would recognize his voice. Davis pointed to his coffee cup and the burger on the menu. She rolled her eyes at him before walking away. He wanted to make sure she didn't interrupt his eavesdropping.

"Johnny, thanks for meeting us here. You're doing the right thing, son," Detective Benson said.

"Man, I don't know why y'all are acting like this meeting was arranged," Johnny said in frustration. "Y'all going to get me murdered. If word gets out that I'm speaking to you—heck if word gets out that I'm back in town, you'll be questioning someone else about my death."

"Sounds like someone wants to keep you quiet," Detective Bower said. "But why? Listen we know you work for Beau and we know he brought some drugs in from Chicago. Help us fill in some blanks. Tell us what you know."

Reaching for his phone, Davis sent Beau a text to let him know what was going on, and within minutes, his cousin replied to let him know it would be handled. He knew it was risky to let Beau know that he had not completed his task of getting Johnny out of sight. Davis knew that tipping Beau off about what was going on would not put him in his cousin's good graces. The alternative of not telling him and getting caught up in whatever tale Johnny was telling, however, was not an option.

"Listen, Johnny. If you tell us what you know, we can protect you. Now if you would prefer to do a written statement, we can bring you down to the station and get this over with," Detective Benson said. "It's only a matter of time before the street starts getting word out that you're in town, and if you don't let us help you, they could find out you spoke to us. I'm sure Beau has several people under his thumb. Don't you want guaranteed security? We can make sure that you're well protected."

There was a moment of pause, and then a female voice came into the conversation. "Johnny! Hey baby," she said leaning down to kiss him on the cheek before sliding into the booth. "Sorry I'm late. Who are your friends?" she asked.

It took everything in Davis not to turn around and see who this voice belonged to, but he didn't dare move an inch. Not until he was certain the detectives had left the restaurant.

"Oh—hey, hey you. What's up?" he asked.

"I see you baby, trying to act hard for the men friends." She paused. "My man has no manners. I'm Veronica and who might you handsome gentlemen be?"

The detectives must have picked up on the same vibe as Davis, "We were just leaving, Veronica. You two enjoy your lunch, and Johnny…we look forward to hearing from you soon."

Davis held his breath as her heard the detectives leaving. He lifted his menu to block his face. He held it in place, peering over the top to watch them walk outside. They stood in front of the restaurant for what felt like forever to him. They need to hurry up and go.

He was so enthralled in what was going on outside, he almost missed the conversation happening behind him.

"Johnny, you really messed up this time. You know that, right?" she asked. "How can you be so careless?"

"How did you even know I was here?" he asked, and then reality struck him like a load of bricks. "Oh snap. Beau knows I'm here, doesn't he?"

"Yep. I'm sorry, Johnny. He's waiting for you back at the club. Go through the back door when you get there. I'm really sorry," she said, her tone solemn.

After Davis saw the dancer from the club through the glass walking to her car, he knew it was time for him to leave, too.

He had no idea that when he walked out of the restaurant, Johnny got up and walked over to the pay phone to make a call. “Detective Benson? It’s Johnny, can you pick me up in back of the Landmark Diner ASAP? He’s gone now and I’m ready to talk.”

Chapter 39

The doctor's office called Ansley on the following Wednesday. Her results came back negative.

She did a praise dance, which consisted of the running man and cabbage patch, right there in the middle of her living room. Followed by uncontrolled laughter and sporadic tears.

When she gathered herself, Ansley got on her computer and logged onto the Don't Date Him Girl site and created an account. She searched and found the entry about Davis and decided to leave her thoughts on this post. Ever since she read this, her mind had been filled with dread thinking she might have a disease. While Ansley knew she probably shouldn't bother, she felt compelled to let it be known. She wrote:

Normally I wouldn't subscribe to participating in something like this, but I thought it was only right to make a comment about this entry. While I don't condone anything that Davis or well Monty has done, I will say that the part about the STD is not true. I went, had my blood tested, and my results came back negative. Please don't think I'm defending him at all because I'm not, but the truth is the truth and a lie is a lie. I think he lied to both of us enough, no need to stoop to his level.

No sooner than Ansley hit enter, she wanted to go back and remove the comment. A part of her felt that the note sounded like it was in defense of Davis, but she did not like the idea of worrying about a non-existent STD. Between him stealing from her and now stressing over her status, she hadn't had the best sleep this month. *What am I doing? This is crazy.*

Just as she went to delete her comment, she saw that there was a response to the post. She clicked on the comment box and was surprised that it came from Bree.

I don't know what your situation was or who you spoke to, but I have no reason to lie. I did contract a STD from him and if you didn't—good for you. However, let me be clear, you don't know my story, so please don't judge me. Everything that I've written about him is true, you just haven't read the last chapter in your story. Every story has a drama twist, hopefully you'll be prepared if that part of his plot strikes you unexpectedly.

As she finished reading the message her phone rang. She deleted her entry and picked up her phone. The caller ID was unknown, but she was betting that it was Bree. She answered, "This is Ansley."

"So I take it that you're the woman who responded to my post on Don't Date Him Girl," she said, "Congrats to your negative status, but I must say it's very presumptuous of you to think that I would make up a thing like that. Why on earth would anyone want to say this is their truth?" she asked.

"You're absolutely right," Ansley responded, "I shouldn't have assumed anything."

"Now that you know my story, perhaps we could help one another. I've been trying to take Monty to court for a while now, but I couldn't locate him. I'm trying to have him served in Atlanta, but haven't had any luck yet. Have you spoken to him since we last talked?"

"I haven't and I would prefer to leave it that way. I really don't want to get involved."

"If you don't assist with bringing him down, he'll continue to prey on unsuspecting women. I guess he must really care for you since you didn't get scammed, but he's no saint and you might be the key to getting him to get his stuff together."

Ansley felt a twinge of guilt about not confessing about recent events in her life with the theft, but it was none of Bree's business.

"Aren't you even curious how I got your number?" Bree asked, breaking into Ansley's thoughts.

She hadn't questioned how Bree was able to contact her. Until now, the thought never crossed her mind. "How did you get my number?"

Bree chuckled. "I have a contact that hooked Davis up with his phone service. Little did I know that he was trying to flirt with her behind my back and tried to run a con on her as well. So she was more than willing to help me do some research. I have his phone records, and I know who he's been in touch with and who has been in touch with him. Your number was the most frequent for incoming and outgoing calls. He thought he was just going to disappear and not have to pay for his actions, but he will see me in court whether it is in Illinois or Georgia," she uttered. Her tone brooked no argument.

Ansley was speechless.

After a moment had passed and Bree never said anything else, Ansley said, "This is all so much to take and I'm feeling overwhelmed. I'm sorry, Bree but I want to move on. Maybe it's time you do the same."

Bree laughed. "He got to you, didn't he? He's always

been a charmer."

"I'm not defending him. Trust me, he wasn't a prince to me either." Ansley threw up her hands. "I'm just over the stress. I have other things to focus on."

"Wait a minute—did he con you, too?" Bree scoffed. "Unbelievable. And, you don't want to go after him… wow."

Ansley didn't try to argue with her. Her mother always got on to her for not sticking up for herself more. She could be very passive at times. Ansley preferred to just cut people out of her life if they disrespected the relationship at this level that Davis had. She didn't think it was necessary to seek vengeance on him, she knew he would get his without her help.

"If you don't tame that devil now, he'll take you for all you're worth. Believe that. You take care."

Ansley had not endured all that Bree had, but she knew that it was time she opened her eyes and made some decisions. Davis could not continue to use women and get away with it. His day of reckoning would soon come.

Chapter 40

Davis arrived at the club in search of Beau. He had called in advance to inform his cousin that he was coming. Beau's discontent was apparent when Davis filled him in over the phone. When Beau told Davis to meet him back at Magic City, his tone was ominous, which left Davis feeling anxious.

From his eavesdropping, he overheard the woman instructing Johnny to go through the back door and figured that's where Beau would be posted up. When Davis arrived, he walked over to one of the bouncers and spoke before going inside.

Davis strolled in, and looked around. The lunch shift was a complete contrast to the way the club partied at night. The strip club during the day just didn't have that same effect on him. There was only one dancer floating around the poles, the club wasn't dark, and the flashing lights weren't as enticing. Overall the energy during the day was more low-key, but Davis felt that today it was eerily dead.

Upon further review, Davis noticed that outside of the dancers and staff, he was the only one there. The thought made him feel antsy.

He took out his phone to call his cousin.

Davis let the phone ring several times before hanging up. Something in his gut told him to get out of there.

He turned to leave and was just about to exit when he

ran into Beau coming through the door.

Davis jumped back, almost dropping his phone. "Man, I was just calling you. What's up?"

Davis was caught off guard when he looked up to see Detectives Benson and Bower walking in behind Beau, whose mouth was set in a deep frown. Detective Benson started to smile while looking around at the place. "Wow… so this is the famous Magic City, huh? I must say it's not too shabby for a strip joint. Is the food pretty good here?"

Davis looked at his cousin and back toward the detectives.

Johnny.

Detective Benson continued, "Since no one wants to make small talk, I guess we can just get to the point of our visit. First, there should be introductions, Beau Cannon meet Davis Montclair. Are you still going with Montclair or has it changed since our last visit?"

The detectives had been hinting around since he first had this displeasure of meeting them that they knew his true identity, but he was getting tired of this guy. "Listen Detectives, you should be contacting my lawyer if you want to speak to me. I've tried to be civil, but I will not continue to be harassed."

Detective Bower finally spoke, "Since we have the two of you together, perhaps you can fill us in on the details of your business transactions that took place in Chicago. Now that we're all caught up on why we're here, why don't the two of you come down to the station? Y'all can catch up on the ride over. Have a little family reunion on us."

Before Davis could respond, Detective Benson chimed in, "This is just great. Montgomery Davis and of course the infamous Beau Cannon…we've been looking forward to spending time with both of you. Y'all have been busy. We have so much to discuss."

"There must be a misunderstanding. We have nothing we need to discuss with you."

Detective Bower guffawed. "Montgomery Davis and Beau Cannon, you're both under arrest for drug trafficking, and kidnapping."

Davis held his hands palm out. "What? Y'all just making up stuff man. This is bogus."As Detective Bower Mirandized them both, a uniformed officer came up behind them and placed handcuffs on their wrist.

On the way out to the waiting patrol car, Davis contemplated the charges placed against them. Johnny must have told them everything. Who knew if they would bring up even more of the dirt Beau had on his hands? Davis would be an accessory to crimes he didn't even know were committed, he just knew they would associate him with everything that Beau was running in Atlanta.

Davis dared not look at his cousin.

"You know this changes everything, right? Beau uttered. "I told you to make sure my name wasn't in the mix—I won't be protecting you in jail. Matter fact, I'm done covering for you. Believe that."

"I haven't said jack, man. From what they just said, you the one been talking loose," Davis said.

Beau's neck snapped in Davis direction. He knew he was pressing, but Davis wasn't about to let his cousin think that he had done him wrong.

"You know better. They setting it up to play us against each other." Beau inhaled. "I swear, you bet not let me find out you snitching. You know what I do to snitches."

Davis couldn't hide his emotions this time. He was

nervous. He was not sure who he feared the most, the detectives or Beau.

Chapter 41

Ansley and Simeon laughed at an old episode of *Martin*—the one where Martin tried to discover who had stolen his new CD player. It didn't matter how many times she saw this episode—it always brought tears to her eyes.

"This show is still just as funny as it was when it first aired. I miss good television like this, don't you?" Simeon asked as she picked up a slice of pizza.

"Yes, girl. *Martin* will always give you a laugh. You want some more soda?" she asked before getting up from the sofa to refill her glass.

"No, I'm good." Simeon got up to follow Ansley into the kitchen during a commercial break. "I'm glad that we are getting to do more than a drive by meet and greet."

"Me, too." She placed the soda back in the refrigerator.

Simeon walked over to the wine rack to retrieve a bottle. "Ansley, I'm sorry about everything you went through with Davis—and me." She carried the wine bottle with her to the living room and sat down.

"Let's not ruin our evening by talking about that jerk... or the past," Ansley uttered as she poured some cherry soda in her glass. "He'll get what's coming to him in due time."

"You're right," Simeon stated. "He's been arrested."

"What?" Ansley walked back in the living room, following her friend's gaze to the screen. Mug shots of Davis and two other men popped up on the television. She rushed over to listen to the news report.

"Criminal solicitation to commit murder, gunrunning, and drug trafficking—what-in-the-world," Ansley murmured.

She wanted to vomit. Who was this man?

"This is crazy. Have you seen this other guy before?" Simeon asked.

"Nah. I don't know who that is. This is just too much." She glanced over at her friend and said, "It's official, I am a horrible judge of character."

Simeon laughed. "I'm right there with you." Simeon took a labored breath. "I don't know about you, but I need a drink."

"Get to pouring. I need something stronger than this soda," Ansley said. She was going to have to go to her boss and inform him of her relationship with Davis before it came out in the news. She prayed that her name would be kept out of this, but the way her luck was going...

"Jason, do you have a minute?" she asked, standing in the doorway of his office. "There's something I think you should know."

He looked up from his Mac, his ice blue eyes beaming. "Sure. What's up?"

Ansley closed the door behind her before taking a seat. "I'm sure you heard about the three men charged with trafficking across state lines from Illinois to Georgia."

She left out the part about soliciting murder, she couldn't form her mouth to say that aloud.

Leaning back in his mesh office chair, he nodded. "Yeah, they made some arrests over the weekend."

"Yeah that's the one. Well, one of the men arrested…I use to date him." Ansley's eyes widened, touching her hand to her heart she said, "But I promise, I had no idea he was leading a double life."

Jason's eyebrows shot up and he leaned forward in his seat. Ansley began crossing and uncrossing her legs.

She could see that hamster wheel of thought racing through his brain.

Jason scratched his head "Whoa. That's—wow, that's some heavy stuff. Have you talked to the police?"

"Yes, well no I haven't. I spoke to them about another incident." She cleared her throat, casting her eyes downward. "My concern is that they will contact me based on his call history. There was a time when we spoke on the regular. Just in case they are trying to find people involved, I just want to be prepared."

"I want you to talk to my attorney, Carlton Rosenberg," Jason said. He reached inside his desk and pulled out a business card and handed it to her "I don't want you talking to anyone without him. Give him a call today."

"Thank you." She grabbed the card and rose form her seat.

He gave her a sympathetic look. "I'm sorry that you're dealing with something like this. You know what, why don't you go ahead and finish the day from home so you can contact Carlton."

Ansley shook her head. "That's not necessary. This will not affect my work," Ansley stated. "Right now, work is what is keeping me sane. I just didn't want you to be blindsided if anything comes out regarding my brief relationship with him."

Jason nodded in understanding. "Thank you for telling me."

Ansley left his office and went to her desk. She checked the Internet to see if there was more information on Davis's arrest.

Nothing new.

Every time her mind was clear of him, something would put him back in her head. Simeon always felt the need to implant him in their conversations and now he was on the afternoon news broadcast and no doubt he would be news at six too.

Then there was Davis, who would call on occasion. He never left a message, but just seeing him in her missed call log was enough of a nuisance. Davis had called her twice over the weekend, but Ansley refused to accept his calls. The arrest was still shocking to her, but considering the life he led, it shouldn't have been a shock at all.

She had rushed into things with Davis, it was clear that she never knew him. The man she thought she knew would've never committed a crime, but the real man was a thief and now a smuggler and a killer. Ansley had fallen for the picture he painted of himself. She supposed she was being too hard on herself, but it was true—she should have been more careful.

Later that evening, Ansley grabbed her mail and headed up to her condo. She was tired and considered going straight to bed, but she needed to get started on her next assignment for school.

She unlocked her door, headed straight to her bedroom and sat down on the edge of her bed, scanning through her mail. Ansley's gaze stopped when she saw the letter addressed from Davis. Her first thought was to throw it in the trash, but curiosity got the better of her.

My sweet Ansley:

I can only imagine what you must be thinking, but I want you to know that this is not what it seems. I never aspired to be a criminal or live the fast life, it just kind of came with the bloodline, I suppose. I may be guilty of many things, but I am innocent of the things they are saying on the news.

Please come to visit me and look into my eyes. There you will see the truth. I know I hurt you, but it was never my intent. I love you and I want to make things right. Please give me the chance to explain myself.

Davis

Ansley threw the letter into the trash. *There you will see the truth? But you signed as Davis? Yeah okay. Boy bye.*

She had an appointment with the attorney in the morning. Ansley didn't want any connection to Davis, although a part of her wanted to have a conversation with him. She wanted to look into his eyes and get some understanding—she needed to know why he chose this lifestyle. Would his eyes really reveal the truth?

Chapter 42

Davis hated the orange jumpsuit, but more than that, he despised being locked up in jail. His bail was denied and his future was dependent on a public defender. Beau was true to his word and refused to have anything to do with him.

He was on his own, and it was a bit traumatic for him. His cousin had always been there to have his back, even over his own brother. Beau was untouchable, and without him, Davis was an easy target.

He had reached out to Ansley a couple of times because he wanted her to hear his side. Since she wouldn't accept his calls, Davis wrote a letter pleading with her to visit him, but she never responded.

Davis believed there was still some part of her that cared for him. Sure, she was hurt, but what she felt for him could not have just been fleeting. Ansley had fallen for him, and while she never said it, he could feel it when she looked at him. She wouldn't abandon him, when he needed her most. He believed this with his entire being.

"You have a visitor," a guard announced.

Davis followed him to the visitation room. He was surprised to see Ansley sitting at one of the tables. She crossed and uncrossed her legs, it was clear that she uncomfortable being there.

"Hey, thank you for coming," he said. Davis reached for her, but she paused him with her hand. He shrugged and sat across from her.

"What do you want?" Ansley asked, getting straight to the point. She had her arms crossed over her chest. He tried to read her expression. She was guarded.

He rubbed his hands across his face. "To tell you the truth."

"I'm listening."

"Yes, I stole from you and I lied to you, but I'm not a career criminal," Davis declared.

Her forehead creased. "Seriously, you were arrested for the solicitation of murder, kidnapping, and trafficking drugs and weapons."

His lower lip trembled. "I-I-I owe my cousin money. He asked me to pick-up a package while I was in Chicago. I didn't ask any questions. No one questions him. I didn't know what I had gotten into."

As her lips twisted up, he could tell she was dissecting everything he said line by line, and from what she'd heard so far she thought he was full of crap. "So your cousin is the brains of the operation and you're just the clown that got caught up in it all. Is that what you're saying?"

Davis glanced around the room. "Why are you asking me that? I've already said way too much."

"I ask because if you know what he's into, why not work out a deal and get yourself off? You brought trouble on yourself. You knew what kind of business your cousin was into, and regardless of what you say, you knew that package contained something illegal."

Davis nodded. "You're right. I do know that he may or may not get involved in some seedy business. But he's family, and he's always been there for me. I told him that I didn't want to get involved in anything that could harm anyone and he assured me that I wouldn't ever have to get involved in anything like this." He looked down at his hands. "It's my fault for not getting all the details, but I owed him money and I did what I thought was just a quick delivery of a package. I trusted that my cousin was taking care of my best interest but this time around, he was just looking out for himself."

Ansley considered his words. "I can't believe I'm about to say this, but I think you're telling me the truth."

"I am," Davis stated. "I'm in a real mess, Ansley. I could go to prison for a long time. I don't have any money and my mom won't help. I have a public defender and like you, he wants me to try to get a deal by ratting out my cousin."

Ansley threw her hands up. "If you're so innocent, then why don't you? Why don't you tell them what happened and what he's involved in? I'm willing to bet it's him that they really want anyway."

"Beau is my cousin, but he is not someone I want to go up against." Davis's eyes filled with water. "I need your help, Ansley."

Her mouth set in a hard straight line. "There's nothing I can do."

Davis's eyes pleaded. "There is something you can do—I need a good attorney."

She shook her head. "Okay, so this is the real reason you wanted me to come see you."

"Ansley…"

She rose to her feet. "I hoped that you wanted to apologize and have a clear conscious, but that's something a mature man would do and not a little boy still living street dreams." Ansley eyed Davis for a moment before saying, "I wish you well."

She started toward the door.

He muttered a curse. "How can you do this to me? I chose you. I could have any woman I want, but I invested my heart in you."

Ansley looked over her shoulder at him. "I guess it turned out to be a bad investment for the both of us. Take care."

She took off her visitors badge and tossed it in the trash on her way out.

"Ansley wait…"

The guard announced, "Visitation is over."

Davis's hope evaporated with every step Ansley took as she walked out of his life.

Chapter 43

Ansley made a pitcher of raspberry, peach sangria. They were gathered at Lanae's house for ladies' night-in. Glancing at the calendar on the refrigerator, Ansley couldn't believe it was September already. This year had not gone like she hoped at all, but she was surviving through all the nonsense—for the most part.

"What's been going on with you, Simeon?" she asked.

Simeon and Lanae were seated on the sectional in Lanae's living room. They were all watching old episodes of *A Different World* on Netflix.

"I've been busy," Simeon replied. She started chewing on her thumb nail and diverting her eyes, which was not missed by Ansley and Lanae.

"Okay…," Ansley uttered. "Is it a secret what's keeping you busy?"

Simeon stopped gnawing on her nail and looked up. "I'm sorry. I've had a lot on my mind lately. Actually, there's something I need to tell you, Ansley. Davis called me last night."

Ansley rolled her eyes. She picked up the pitcher of sangria down and started pouring each of them a glass. "I'm not even surprised. I can only imagine what he wanted."

Simeon grabbed one of the throw pillows and clung to it. "He asked me to get him an attorney."

Ansley laughed. She put the glasses on a tray and carried them over to the group. Shaking her head the entire way. "Unbelievable. Davis asked me the same thing," she scoffed. "I went to see him the other day."

Simeon studied her and asked, "Why did you do that?"

Before Ansley could speak, she interjected, "Please tell me that you are not considering getting back with him. After everything that he's put you through? You can't honestly be entertaining that mess."

Ansley looked over at Lanae, who was covering her mouth to keep from laughing out loud.

"I don't want to be with Davis," Ansley stated. "I needed to hear his story. Understand how we got to this place. It gave me closure."

"What did he say? Do you think he was being truthful?" Lanae questioned.

"Davis owes his cousin money, so when his cousin told him to take care of some business in Chicago, he didn't hesitate and didn't ask any questions. Hence the arrest." Ansley took a sip of her drink. "I believe him."

Simeon shook her head in disbelief. "He's a skilled liar, or have you forgotten that?"

"In this instance, he seemed afraid for his life. I think his cousin intimidates him. If anything, he would've denied any part in the crime. He even admitted to being a liar and a thief."

"It won't do any good to speculate on this. Prayerfully, the truth will come out in the trial," Lanae commented.

Ansley peered over at Simeon. "But what about you? Are you going to help him Simeon?"

Simeon shot Ansley a strange look before she laughed. "Let's talk about something pleasant," Simeon interjected. "I don't want to spend another moment thinking about him or his situation."

Ansley and Lanae exchanged looks.

Simeon finished off her glass and poured another. Clearing her throat she says, "Well okay let's get some music bumping or something." She stood and started popping her fingers and swaying her hips.

As Ansley turned on her iTunes to change the mood in the room, she stole a glance over at Simeon and wondered if she considered helping Davis. And if she did, the question was why would she help him? Did she still have feelings for him? Ansley wanted to ask but decided she wasn't ready for the answer.

Chapter 44

Simeon took a sip of her drink. She was stunned to hear that Ansley went to visit Davis. It made sense why he called her.

When Ansley had refused to help Davis, he decided to contact her—only he threatened to expose her trip to Chicago. The one her friend knew nothing about. Simeon recalled their conversation.

"How do you think Ansley will feel about you if she knew that you went behind her back to seduce me?"

Simeon did not respond.

"If you don't get me a good attorney, I may have to tell Ansley about our little secret."

"There's nothing to tell," she bluffed.

"Don't you think it will matter to her?" Davis inquired. "You two cleared the air and laid everything out there right, except this–you kept this from her and take it from me, she doesn't care for liars.

"I could just tell Ansley myself."

"You could," he agreed, "but you won't because you would have done that by now if you had planned on being honest with her. You have twelve hours to set this up."

Simeon shook away the troubling thoughts. She did what she had to do to preserve her friendship with Ansley. She gave Ansley so much grief for choosing him over her, which she makes no apologies for, but now that they had moved past that she wanted to keep things progressing in their friendship.

Although she secured a lawyer for him, Simeon hoped to see him buried under the jail. She intended to be there when Davis was dragged out of the courtroom.

Simeon intended to celebrate his last day of freedom with glee. Smiling at Ansley, she raised her glass in tribute.

Chapter 45

Ansley was in a moment of reflection; this year had been crazy for her. She'd been fired and then hired at a new publication that she loved, fallen in and out of love, involved in a scandal and had a health scare that shook her core. She couldn't believe the year was about to come to an end. Ansley had become so engrossed in her work it seemed like September came and went without notice, and October seemed to come to a close before it started. Using work as a distraction proved to be effective in more ways than one. Jason took notice of the work she put in and she received glowing reviews from readers. That was one plus that came out of all the madness.

She hadn't heard from Davis since he asked her to get him an attorney back in September. With any luck, she could close out the year with no further interaction with him. She hoped next year would bring more ups than downs, but first she had to make it through this year. Being with her family for the holidays would be a start to closing the year out right.

Ansley went into her closet to grab a pair of tweed dress pants and a hunter green sweater. She was packing an overnight bag. She would be heading to her parent's house to spend the Thanksgiving holiday with them. A part of her family's tradition was to take family photos the day after Thanksgiving. She packed a few outfits to choose from for the photo shoot. Her mother wanted everyone in earth tones.

She drove to her family's home in Alpharetta where she had grown up. She loved coming here, this was exactly what she needed—the love of family. When she spoke to her mother earlier, she said that she had a big surprise waiting for her. She wasn't sure what it could be, but she assumed that her mother had made her favorite dessert.

Simeon was planning to come by later, which she did every year for Thanksgiving. Simeon never spoke much about her family. All Ansley really knew was that Simeon's mother was deceased and she only spoke about her brother. From the pained look on Simeon's face whenever she mentioned her father, Ansley knew her friend had been terribly hurt by him. She never asked and Simeon never told. She just made sure that Simeon always felt welcome to join her family on the holidays.

Ansley pulled into the driveway and grabbed the candied yams and Oreo cheesecake she made for dinner. She walked inside using her key, which she refused to give back once she left the nest for good. The idea of just coming home whenever she wanted to get away from her life, was a perk that she wasn't ready to relinquish.

"Hello family! The favorite is here," she joked, knowing that her sister would have a rebuttal. She walked toward the chatter in the family room and stopped dead in her tracks when she saw Davis sitting with her family looking at an old photo album.

"Well, well—look what we found. Mm-hmm, caught your behind. I can't believe you had a boyfriend all this time and didn't tell anyone. No wonder you've been M.I.A.," her sister Reagan chided.

Reagan was four years younger than Ansley, and a freshman at the University of Georgia, she was in their Dance Program. Her plan was to travel to New York to audition for Julliard next fall, she had just submitted her application and was planning to audition in the spring.

Anslcy signaled for her sister to come closer so they could have some privacy. Walking into the kitchen to put the side dish on the oven and the dessert in the fridge, she turned to her sister and said, “Reagan, how long has he been here?”

She had never introduced him to her family. They had only been dating, officially, for about five months and the first month was rocky. They hadn’t gotten around to any introductions outside of him having dinner with Ansley’s friends. As Ansley began to think about things, she had never met any of his friends. He was always at her place and they frequented her regular spots, but not once had he taken her to some place that he said frequented on the regular.

The only man to ever meet her parents was Ryan. He was the one they all expected her to marry and she didn’t want to bring just anyone home to meet her parents. That man had to be someone special in order for her family to meet him, Davis was special alright, but not in a way that she wanted to expose to her family.

“He’s been here for maybe thirty minutes,” Reagan said and added. “He seems nice enough, but I’ll let you know what I really think once I get to grill him. Mom said I had to wait until you arrived to do a thorough investigation.”

Ansley gritted her teeth, she was beyond furious. He’d gotten her family to befriend him under false terms and had now placed her in an awkward position.

Reagan's eyebrows rose. "Why do you look upset? Did you guys have a little fight or something? He said you probably wouldn't be happy about getting surprised like this, but he knew you were apprehensive about bringing him here and he just couldn't wait anymore. It's kind of sweet—if you like the pushy type," Reagan said with a smirk before walking away.

Ansley took her phone out of her purse and used the Yellow Pages app to find the number to a cab service. "Hello, yes I need a cab at 101 Meadowlark Drive. Would a ten-minute window work for you to be here?"

She was glad she was able to get a taxi secured. Ansley wanted to make sure after she confronted Davis, he had a way to get out of her face fast.

When she returned to the living room, Davis was chatting with her mother.

"Sorry to interrupt this lovely bonding moment, but Davis can I speak to you outside for a moment," said Ansley, as she plastered on a fake smile. Her mother stood, and walked over to give her a hug.

"Honey are you so enthralled with this man that you have forgotten your manners. You haven't given your father and me a hug," said her mother Millicent.

"I apologize," Ansley expressed her regrets. "I should've slowed down to speak to my two favorite people in the world. I wanted to put the food in the kitchen. Daddy I made your favorite."

"Oo-wee, my Oreo cheesecake. I'll just go get a sample to make sure it's right."

He attempted to brush pass Ansley and her mother to make a beeline for the kitchen.

"No Jeff," she fussed, with a slight tug of his arm. "You

can wait until after dinner like the rest of us."

Ansley gave both of her parents a genuine hug and then turned her attention back to Davis. He excused himself and walked outside with Ansley. Once on the front lawn, she wasted no time expressing her anger with him. "You have no right to come here and push yourself on my family. For you to come here and think it's okay—the audacity to even find this acceptable is beyond my level of comprehension. Ansley squeezed her eyes shut and grabbed the center of her nose. She could feel a headache coming. "Please explain to me, why are you here? Shouldn't you be in jail anyway?"

Davis grimaced at the mention of jail. "I got an attorney and I did like you suggested, and gave the police the information they wanted to lock Beau away. I'm on probation and had to pay a fine. Thank you for encour—"

Ansley tapped her foot, her patience was null and void upon the sight of him. She interrupted his little speech. "Davis, I don't care about you ratting out your cousin with your sorry behind. I need you to explain why you're here and do it fast because your ride is on the way."

He put his hands in his pocket, shifting his weight. "Ansley you wouldn't return any of my calls, it's been a couple of months. I had to do something drastic so I could get your attention. Before you ask, you mentioned your family lived in Alpharetta and their names. I was able to look them up and managed to find the Wright family... literally," he said laughing at his own joke.

Ansley's eyebrow shot up. She was not amused and wanted him to get to the point and go away.

When he saw she wasn't laughing he pulled out a rectangular, white gift box with her name on it. It wasn't wrapped, outside of the two pieces of tape holding the box in place. She didn't take it from him. Instead, she stared him down and crossed her arms over her chest.

"What stunt is this? I don't want anything from you. Can't believe you had the gall to show up at my parent's home."

"Ansley please take it. It's what you deserve and more." She took the box from his hands and opened it. The box was full of money. She looked up at him with pure disgust.

Ansley sneered. "What poor, unsuspecting woman did you rob to get this money? Yes, you do owe me money, but I don't want any dirty money. All I want is to enjoy this time with my family, but here you are robbing me of that too."

He clenched and unclenched his fist. "I'm sorry," he pounded his chest with his hands. "I know my apology will never be enough. I deserve all of that anger, and I'm not going to make any excuses about my actions. Just please let me make this right and keep the money," he begged.

Just as Ansley was about to protest, the taxi and Simeon both pulled up to the house. Davis turned and followed Ansley's eyes to see the awaiting car. He turned to leave and headed toward the vehicle.

Ansley watched as Simeon glared at him in passing. She shook her head and continued up the driveway, and stood with her arms crossed over her chest next to Ansley. He locked eyes with Ansley one last time before getting inside the car.

Simeon did a pivot turn towards Ansley. "What was that about?"

Ansley held up the box. "He dropped by unannounced to return the money he stole," she sighed. "Come on girl let's go eat. Nothing like drama to work up an appetite."

Chapter 46

Simeon watched as Davis's car pulled away from the curb. "Ansley, go inside and forget about that jerk."

"Aren't you coming?"

"I forgot something in the car."

"Okay I'll let them know to wait before they bless the food."

Simeon unlocked her car and got inside.

She sat, staring blankly at Ansley's parent's house, before releasing a high pitch scream. Once again, Davis had played her. She had no doubt that the money he used to repay Ansley was pulled from the cash she had given him.

Pulling out her phone, she dialed his number.

He answered on the first ring, but didn't allow Simeon a chance to get out a word. "Don't call me whining. It's done. You gave that money to me to use, and before you even think about saying something, remember I like to talk, too."

Simeon huffed. "You know what tell her whatever you want, as a matter of fact I'll tell her myself. I'm not afraid of what will happen. I'd rather be exposed than be your puppet."

She disconnected the call.

Simeon let out a harsh breath, and then wiped away the tears forming in the corner of her eyes. Pulling down her interior car mirror, she checked her make-up and pushed a stray hair behind her ear.

Looking at her reflection, she felt sad. She turned her head and looked toward the Wright's house. Through the window she could see the family laughing and enjoying each other. *Why can't I have that life?*

She reached into her purse for her medication. Upon pulling out the bottle, she realized it had been a while since she refilled her prescription. She was so tired of hurting, she wanted to dull the pain.

Tossing the bottle back in her purse, she took one last look at the house and backed out of the driveway.

Chapter 47

Ansley checked her phone to see if Simeon had texted her back. Since Thanksgiving, she had managed to disappear again.

That morning, Ansley sent her a text asking if she wanted to go Christmas shopping. When she never heard back that made her certain that something was wrong. Simeon loved shopping and jumped at every opportunity to swipe her credit cards.

After several attempts to connect and getting no response, Ansley got into her truck and drove over to Simeon's house.

She sat in her car parked across the street outside of Simeon's home.

The house was dark and Simeon's car was not in the driveway. She seldom parked in her garage, but Ansley knew there was a chance that her car was parked inside today.

She had been sitting for close to an hour and she was starting to lose hope, when she saw movement in the downstairs window.

She unlocked her door and slid out.

Walking up the driveway, she went over to the window and saw Simeon sitting on the sofa. The television wasn't on and the only light in the house came from the slight opening in the curtains allowing the sun to come inside the house.

Her hair was disheveled, and from what Ansley could see, the house looked like it hadn't been cleaned in a while. Simeon used a cleaning service, which made this unkempt home an oddity. Ansley tapped on the glass, but Simeon didn't acknowledge her presence. Ansley tried tapping harder, this time Simeon's head turned in her direction.

Simeon stared at Ansley before rising from the chair and walking over to the window. They stood eye to eye with only the glass separating them. The crazed look in Simeon's eyes made Ansley back up.

"Uh—can, can you let me in sweetheart?" Ansley asked. "I won't be long, I promise. I just stopped by to say hello."

Simeon turned to head towards the door.

Ansley shivered.

Simeon's eyes were vacant and dark circles had formed under her eyes. She didn't look well.

Once Ansley heard the click from the door being unlocked, she pushed to open it and let herself in.

The odor of the home was pungent, and Ansley had to catch her breath.

With a wave of her hand Simeon explained the mess. "Excuse my place. The cleaning people hadn't been out here, you know with the holidays and all."

"Yeah no problem." Ansley cleared her throat. "You mind if I turn on a light? And crack a window."

Simeon's shoulders hunched and she plopped back down on the sofa. After turning on the lights, Ansley was shocked to see the state of the living room. Taking a look around the room, she saw containers of half eaten Chinese takeout on the coffee table. Moldy cups and plates that had utensils that appeared to be stuck in place. Empty pizza boxes were sitting on the desk in the far right corner of the room.

Ansley walked over to the window, and opened it to allow some air to come into the room. She strolled back over towards Simeon and pushed the magazines that were strayed across the sofa onto the cluttered coffee table.

"Simeon what's—," she started to ask what was wrong, but Simeon had dozed off. Ansley pulled the throw blanket laying on the arm of the sofa and laid it across her. Then she got up and walked into the kitchen, grabbed a couple of garbage bags and began cleaning up.

When Ansley entered the kitchen she frowned. There was a stack of unopened mail sitting on the counter top amid food spills and discarded pizza crust. There were empty wine bottles sitting in the sink, and frying pans caked with grease and grime sitting on the stove top. The floor looked like it hadn't been swept in a while, there were crumbs and dust bunnies in every crevice and corner of the kitchen.

She walked into the laundry room that was adjacent to the kitchen and grabbed a broom and dust pan. Ansley exhaled as she looked around at the task at hand, there was much to be done. She began by collecting the wine bottles and placing them in the recycle bins. She broke down the pizza boxes and placed them in the garbage next. Then she sorted the mail by company so that Simeon could navigate through them with ease. She came across a notebook that was sticking to the counter underneath all the mail.

Ansley cringed at the gunk that was holding the journal hostage on the counter top. The goldish brown liquid resembled syrup. Several pages were ruined, Ansley peered through to see if this was work related before tossing the whole thing away. She flipped through the pages and her breath caught when she saw an entry addressed to her.

Dear Ansley,

Thank you for trying to be a friend to the friendless. You and my brother are all that I have in this world. I thought I had Davis, but you see how that ended. He chose you, and I was jealous. So jealous I even attempted to seduce him on camera so that you could see what you were getting into. Only I didn't have time to set the recorder, and there was no evidence except for the pain I've been wearing behind keeping the secret. Now my discretion is Davis's ammunition to hold me hostage. He threatened to tell you about our tryst and for his silence I had to give him money for an attorney. Money he also used to pay you back. I don't blame you for my pain though, I blame by father for showing me that men aren't worth a crap and they only care about women when they can benefit. My father loves on my brother, and my brother knows that he is loved. But I'm the one that stole his joy, and he'll only ever see me as the reason his wife, my mother isn't here. She died at child birth...it seems I tend to hurt those that care about me the most... All she wanted was to bring life into the world and I took hers. Then there's my wonderful brother, who loves me for me and doesn't judge me for my shortcomings or treat me different because of my bipolar disorder. He loves me for me, but he's hurting too. It's because of me that our family can't get together for holidays. I refused to give my father opportunity to hurt me. I'd rather spend time with your family who doesn't judge me or just be alone. At times I just feel like I don't deserve to be here...it should be me that's gone from this world. Not my mother. I hope to see her soon, and then I'll apologize.

Ansley wiped away a lone tear. She flipped through the

pages and saw entry after entry where Simeon cried out for help. Ansley didn't understand why Simeon didn't think that she could confide in her. Yes they had been through their share of ups and downs, but they were friends. It hurt Ansley to read how alone Simeon felt. These pages explained so much about why Simeon was the way she was with men and why she never discussed her family.

Ansley cleaned the mess on the counter, and replaced the journal as she found it. Looking in the direction of the living room, Ansley was saddened that Simeon was having suicidal thoughts but she was so glad that Simeon only wrote these words and hadn't acted out those sentiments.

Tears began to stream down her face as she considered what it would feel like to only have the memory of death when thinking of one's mother. Even more so when the only parent left, is full of resentment.

An hour later, Ansley walked back into the living room, which was now in a more livable state, than when she first arrived. She positioned herself on the sofa next to Simeon and nudged her to get her to wake up.

"Hey sweetie. Get up." Ansley's eyes glistened as she watched Simeon lay with her eyes closed. The thought of them never opening again was tearing at her heart.

Simeon adjusted her body, but never opened her eyes. "I didn't know you were still here."

"Indeed I am. It's going on five o'clock now. Do you want to go grab something to eat?" Ansley offered.

Simeon opened one eye and then both, scanning the room. "Did you clean up in here?"

Ansley chuckled. "I did for fear that the mold and funk would coat my tresses and clothing. Not trying to take that home with me." Ansley flipped her hair and winked at Simeon.

Simeon smacked her lips. "It was not that bad in here. You're being dramatic."

Ansley's nose crinkled. "Oh really? Smell your clothes so you can be reminded," Ansley teased as she stood up.

Simeon sniffed under her arms and gagged. "I guess I am a little frowsy."

"A little? Now you're not being dramatic enough." Ansley patted her friend on the knee. "You stink. Come on, let's get you freshened up and go grab lunch."

"I'm good right here. I think there's some leftover Chinese in the refrigerator."

Ansley shook her head. "Nah, those leftovers were left over there," Ansley said pointing to the coffee table. "And way over there on that desk, and now they are leftover outside for the department of sanitation to pick up. If you don't hurry to this shower they might pick up your funky behind too."

Simeon guffawed and Ansley joined her, but it was short lived once Simeon's laughter turned to tears.

Ansley scooted over closer and rubbed her back.

"It's going to be alright. I'm here, sweetie. C'mon let's go on upstairs and get you together so we can get some sunshine."

Simeon got up from the sofa without protest.

Ansley reached for her hand and they began to walk towards the back of the house where Simeon's bedroom was located.

"I don't deserve your friendship," Simeon uttered. "I haven't been a good friend at all. There's so much I haven't told you about Davis—or heck even my life."

Ansley held up her hand. "Anything that has to do with

him included some trickery and some foolishness. That chapter is closed and we are good. I don't need you to explain anything to me. I know enough, and I'm not hung up on it. Okay?"

Simeon shook her head. "No I need to tell you everything and clear my conscious."

Ansley held up her finger. "Simeon, I cleaned the kitchen and stumbled upon your journal. I saw what you wrote to me, and friend, if anyone deserves to be on this Earth it's you. Now let's go get you cleaned up, so we can fight another day. You're not alone. I'm always going to be here for you. You're my girl."

Simeon's expression was a combination of shame and relief.

Ansley patted her on the back and started guiding her back towards the bedroom. She hoped her words were enough to make Simeon battle through her depression.

Chapter 48

Ansley could not believe that it was a new year. Christmas with her family had been memorable. Simeon and her brother Richard joined them on Christmas Eve. It was the happiest Ansley had seen Simeon in a while. She was not anticipating her brother being there, it was a surprise and what a beautiful surprise it was.

She was in a good place in her career and she would be graduating in the summer, she was excited for this year. Ansley was in route to Washington, D.C. to interview a couple of faculty members from the Division of Infectious Diseases and Travel Medicine for her column. Ansley parked her car at the Park and Ride Marta station and boarded the train to head to the airport.

Finally arriving at Hartsfield-Jackson International, Ansley walked over to the counter to check her bags, and then prepped her carry-on bag to be screened by the TSA.

She walked through the metal detector.

Received an all clear…and hustled to her terminal.

Ansley arrived just as they were calling her zone to board the plane.

She readjusted her carry-on bag and proceeded down the walkway.

Once seated after placing her bag in the overhead compartment, Ansley pulled out her Kindle Fire and placed it on her lap. It had been a while since she had a chance to read for leisure.

Her phone rang with a number that she didn't recognize. She thought it might be for work and answered.

"This is Ansley," she answered.

"Hello, this is Ruth, Dr. Fadoju's nurse. We are calling with your test results from your most recent pap smear and blood work. You listed on your forms that you were fine with receiving updates over the phone. Is now a good time?" she asked.

"Sure. I'm on a plane and we haven't taken off yet. Please go ahead," she replied, moving the phone from one ear to the other while she fastened her seatbelt. This must be something new they were doing. Normally they sent her results via snail mail.

"We have the results from your labs. Your glucose looks good, cholesterol is down from last year, LDL, HDL, and triglycerides all look great. Dr. Fadoju would like you to come by the office to go over your pap results and she orders some additional testing. Would you be able to come in on Monday?"

"Wait, what? I'm not understanding. Why are there additional test?" she asked.

"You tested positive for HSV-2..."

She knew what that was. Genital herpes.

Ansley felt numb. "I'll be home on Sunday evening. I can be there by nine a.m."

The nurse was talking to her, confirming Monday's appointment and going over more details, but all Ansley could hear was positive. Her heart began to pound and she couldn't breathe. She felt her world stop and her tears start to flow. Ansley looked around the plane, she felt confined as she tried to pull it together.

Disconnecting the call, she stared out the window, looking at nothing in particular. It had taken her months to finally get pass the fear that Davis had given her herpes. Ansley had just gotten to the point where she could move forward in her life without thinking about him period. Now this.

She tested positive.

Davis Montclair… Montgomery Davis.

Ansley hated him with a passion. She regretted that she ever met him. If only she had listened to Simeon and stayed away from him. None of this would be happening. Her head began to ache. She would be considered damaged goods. Who would want her now?

"Can I get you anything?" the flight attendant asked interrupting her thoughts.

Wiping away her tears, she answered, "Yes, could you bring some Kleenex and wine? Lots of wine."

The attendant gave her a sympathetic look and went off to retrieve what she requested.

Ansley couldn't believe this was her life.

The plane landed two hours later.

She departed with the rest of the passengers, marching in a single file line.

Ansley walked to baggage claim in a zombie-like state, thoughts and questions running through her head.

Who would ever take her as a wife?

What would her friends and family think of her?

Her mind was a cloud of confusion.

She had just made it to baggage claim when she heard someone yelling her name in the distance.

Ansley turned around.

"Wait up!" Ryan called out to her.

He was even more handsome than the last time she saw him. Ryan wasted no time embracing her in one of his familiar bear hugs. In his arms, Ansley felt safe, secure and vulnerable. She unloaded all of the hurt on his shoulder.

"Whoa…why are you crying?" he asked, pulling back from her and peering into her eyes.

Ryan comforted her, by rubbing her shoulders. When she didn't respond he placed her head on his chest and allowed her to continue to cry right there in the middle of airport.

She cried for what felt like an eternity.

"Listen Ansley, why don't we split a cab and you can tell me everything. What hotel are you staying at?"

Through her tears, she was able to whisper, "The Madison Hotel at 1177 15th St. NW."

He looked at her with a warm smile and raised his hand to wipe away her tears. Cupping her face in his hands, Ryan told her, "I'm actually staying there, too. Let me grab our bags, and then I'll get us a cab. Whatever is going on with you… we'll get through it together. Okay?"

Ansley nodded. She sniffled, her bottom lip quivering, as she tried to control the tears that would not stop falling.

As Ryan approached with their bags, she shook her head as another dose of reality hit her. He would have never put her in this situation. He was the one that just wanted to love her and give her the world. Even now, he was willing to help her in her weakest moment, willing to stand by her regardless of what she might be facing—she wondered would he still be there once she told him everything.

* * *

After getting checked in, Ryan helped Ansley with taking her bags to her room. Once she was settled in, he told her that he would meet her back in her room in an hour so that they could talk. He was staying on the second floor of the hotel and Ansley was up on the third level.

She hadn't spoken the entire cab ride over and Ryan didn't push her to talk. He remained quiet as well, holding her hand the entire ride to the hotel.

Ansley took a warm shower and slipped on a pair of sweat pants and a tee shirt.

Twenty minutes later, she heard a knock at the door, and walked over to let Ryan inside.

"Hey Ryan, come on in," she advised, moving back to allow him to come inside.

It was funny how life turned out. This man wanted to marry her and she turned him down, leaving herself accessible to the 'Davis Montclairs' of the world. Just thinking about it made her want to cry all over again.

He walked past her and into the suite's living room. "Wow, your room is much nicer than mine," he said. He was staying in the Madison Suite and Ansley was staying in the Hamilton Suite. "Grind House must be doing very well."

She looked at him with a raised brow. "How did you know I was at Grind House?"

"You know I had to follow your career and see how you were doing since you don't keep in touch. Lanae and I keep in contact on Facebook and via email. She keeps me in the loop."

Thank God for friends like Lanae.

"It's really good to see you, Ryan." She looked down at her feet. "Thank you for umm, taking care of me at the airport. I appreciate you being there."

Ryan shrugged. "It's you Ansley. I'll always have your back. No matter what." She could see the love in his eyes. That was a twinkle that she knew quite well.

Feeling her face flush, Ansley sighed. "So are you up here for work or is this a personal trip?" she asked. The last she heard, Ryan was still working as a Financial Analyst for American Express. She never asked about him, or tried to look him up on Facebook because she thought it would be too heartbreaking to find out that he had gotten married or moved on with someone else.

He smiled. "This trip is purely personal for me. My friend and his wife just had a baby, so I'll be visiting them and then I'm touring the White House, the Holocaust museum and Frederick Douglas's house. I'm trying to see all of the sites. I'm on my tourist grind."

"Sounds like fun." Ansley sat down on the sofa, motioning for him to join her. "I know you've always wanted to do all those things. If you're lucky, you might get a glimpse of President Obama."

He sat down next to her, and clasped her hands between his. He looked deep into her eyes before responding, "Aww man. That would be cool."

She bowed her head, trying to avoid his eyes. "So how have you been?" She hoped to distract Ryan from the question she knew he would ask.

He reached across the seat and grabbed her hands. "I've been doing fine, Ansley, but how are you? I can tell that you're hiding something, so tell me, what were all of those tears were about?"

She took a deep breath and moved from the sofa to the large window overlooking the city.

"The short of it is...I was dating an imposter and he stole from me, lied about his identity, and I just found out that he gave me herpes." She turned to face Ryan with tears in her eyes. "I'm damaged goods."

The room fell silent.

Ansley didn't want to look at him anymore—she couldn't. She believed that he wouldn't judge her, but she judged herself and part of her believed she deserved to be in this situation. She lost Ryan because she was selfish. Interrupted her friendship with Simeon because she was selfish. And now she was left to carry karma with her for the rest of her life, because she messed with a man who was selfish.

Ryan rose and walked up behind Ansley. She could feel his breath on her neck as he wrapped his arms around her waist and pulled her into him.

Ansley was humiliated and couldn't face him.

He put his head on her shoulder and she could feel the moisture from his tears. She slowly turned to face him, realizing that he needed to be comforted, too. He shared in her pain, crying his own tears.

They stood there together crying... crying for the damage done, and crying for what should have been.

Chapter 49

Ansley woke up the next morning feeling peaceful. Ryan refused to leave her side and stayed the night, trying to console her. She appreciated having him there.

She glanced down at his hands wrapped around her waist. It felt nice to be in his protective embrace, but she knew it was only temporary and when she flew out on Monday, she would be alone to deal with her emotions.

Ansley eased his arm away and got up. It was a little after six a.m. and she needed to get her mind focused for her interviews today.

She left the bedroom and started a pot of coffee. The aroma awakened Ryan. She looked up to see him walking toward her rubbing the sleep out of his eyes, he joined her for a cup.

"Sorry for waking you," she apologized

He stretched his arms, stifling a yawn. "Nah, you're good. How did you sleep?"

"I slept as well as one can when trying not to have a total melt down."

Ryan walked up to her and took her face in his hands, forcing her to look at him.

As soon as their eyes connected, she began to cry again.

Ryan stroked her hair and kissed her on the forehead. "It's going to be okay, sweetheart."

Ansley wanted to believe him. She wanted to open her

eyes and wake up from this nightmare.

"Why don't you take a shower while I schedule you for a massage?" Ryan suggested.

"I have an interview scheduled in a couple of hours."

"Then you'd better hurry."

He poured a cup of coffee and handed it to her. "You still drink it black?"

She smiled. "Only when I'm working late or studying." Ansley picked up two packets of sugar and cream.

She took her coffee to the bedroom.

When Ansley came out twenty minutes later, Ryan told her, "The masseuse will be here shortly. While she's here, I'm going to my suite to shower and change. Call me when she's done."

"Thank you, Ryan. I really appreciate you being here for me."

"I wouldn't be anywhere else."

Ryan was a good man. Ansley had known this from the moment she met him. She was a fool for breaking off their relationship. The truth was that Ryan was the only man she ever really loved.

While she had been fond of Davis, Ansley was never in love with him. Ryan had always been the one, but now it was too late.

After her massage, Ansley dressed and called Ryan on his cellphone.

"Hey. Thank you for arranging that for me. I really needed that."

"Let me know once you get back. I'll order lunch for us."

Ansley bit her bottom lip. "Ryan, you've already done beyond enough. You don't have to babysit."

Ryan huffed. "I told you. This is where I want to be and lunch with you is what I want to do today. I'll go check out a few exhibits and meet you back here. What time do you think you'll be done?"

"I'm interviewing them together at ten a.m., I should be done by noon."

"Bet. I'll see you then."

Two hours later, Ansley headed back to her suite, peeling her clothes off to grab a shower. As the water hit her body, she reflected on her interview. She thought the interview went well, but it didn't take much to distract her considering her article was on HPV and cervical cancer.

She knew the doctors would test her again, checking her for HPV. The thought of that scared her, having HPV would increase her chance of cervical cancer. Each year, there were over twelve thousand cases of women being diagnosed in this country with cervical cancer. The way her luck was set up, she felt overwhelmed with that possibility.

Stepping out of the shower, she wiped the steam away from the mirror and looked at her reflection. She put her hands through her damp hair. *You'll get through this.*

She wrote articles on sexually transmitted diseases. Had conducted countless interviews with doctors and people who are living with the disease. Those people lived normal lives. She knew that to be the case, but what Ansley wanted to know was when she would feel normal again.

The phone in her room rang, and she walked over, sat on the bed, and answered it. "Hello."

"Hey Ans, glad you're back. Come down to my suite. Lunch is ready."

Ansley held her breath, then let it out slow. "I'll be right there."

Ansley left her suite and took the elevator down to his floor. She searched the wall for room number two nineteen.

He left the door propped open for her to enter.

Walking into Ryan's suite, she was greeted by the familiar sound of Jodeci's song, *Come and Talk to Me*, playing in the background.

"Huh? What you do think? Did your boy come through or what? I got all of your favorites on deck." Ryan stood in a b-boy stance with his legs parted and his arms crossed.

The counter in the kitchenette was full of her favorite late-night college cram foods. He knew she loved brownies, and he somehow managed to get every kind of combination there was from caramel walnut brownies to cheesecake brownies. There were grapes, cherries, sliced pears and mangos. He had a blanket laying across the floor and created a place setting so they could enjoy a pepperoni pizza and some lemon pepper wings.

She put her hands over her mouth. "Wow. This is too much."

Ryan took her hands into his, locking their fingers together. "Nothing is too much when you love someone. When you love someone there are no conditions in place. All I have ever wanted to do was be with you."

"Ryan, no—please stop. I messed that up. You deserve more. You deserve better. I have this disease now and—."

He released her hand. "And what Ansley? Things happen Ansley. No one is perfect, but you're my well-constructed, God-sent, image of perfection. You're the one I compared others too. You're the perfect person for me and I'm not letting another moment pass without us working this out. Now are you ready to stop running?"

Ansley knew that Ryan loved her, she felt that every

time he looked at her. But she wanted to be certain that he could be strong enough to go through this with her.

She nodded. "I do want this, but—," she paused and Ryan groaned.

"But what Ansley," he questioned.

"I have a doctor's appointment on Monday at nine a.m. I want to wait to get retested and have the doctor check me for everything before starting a relationship. Some people say they are okay with dating someone with a disease, but it's not only going to affect my life, it would be a change for you as well."

Ryan's head bobbed. "I understand, but I'm not going anywhere. We're a couple and that's that."

Ansley's eyes widened. "Now you know that is not how this works. A girl needs to be courted."

Ryan pointed at the pizza box. "Consider yourself courted. Now stop playing and give your man a kiss."

Ansley reached up and put her arms around his neck, and planted her lips on his.

He was willing to be patient with her while she figured everything out, and this time she would stick around to let him love her like she deserved.

"Now that's what I'm talking about." He patted her on the behind. "Now text me the address, I'll be at the appointment with you on Monday." He crossed his arms over his chest. "Now enough of this pity party, woman go over there and fix us some pizza."

Ansley giggled. "Whatever chile."

Chapter 50

Ansley managed to enjoy her time in D.C. thanks to Ryan. She could have never imagined on the day that she got some of the worse news of her life, she would have a second chance to correct the worse decision of her life.

Once she landed back in Atlanta, she was surprised to see that Simeon sent her a text about a dinner party on Monday night—she even invited Lanae. Ansley was grateful for Simeon's dinner invitation—it provided a much-needed distraction from thinking about everything the doctor told her.

Ansley walked into the doctor's office at eight a.m., she was an emotional wreck. She tried to talk Ryan out of coming with her, but he was sitting in the lobby waiting for her.

"Due to the abnormal cells we found on your pap smear, I have ordered a colposcopy. We can do that here on site today."

Ansley swallowed hard. "What is that? Is it painful?"

"The procedure will allow me to exam the vagina and cervix for abnormal cells using a lighted magnifying instrument called a colposcope." Dr. Fadoju explained. "You will experience some discomfort, but most compare the pain to a menstrual cramp. This is an outpatient procedure that will take about ten minutes and no anesthetic will be used. So you would be able to drive yourself home."

Ansley looked over at Ryan with trepidation. Ryan gave

her an assuring look and squeezed her hand.

Dr. Fadoju stood from her desk. "If there are no further questions, shall we can go ahead and get started?"

Ansley nodded and rose from her seat.

"Do you want me to come back with you?" Ryan offered.

"No. You can wait for me in the waiting room. I'll see you after."

Ansley followed Dr. Fadoju down the hall to one of the testing rooms. Ruth, Dr. Fadoju's nurse, was waiting to give her instructions.

"Okay sweetie. Please remove your clothes from the waist down including your undergarments. Once undressed I want you to lay back on the table and place your feet in the stirrups. There's a sheet that you can use to cover yourself. Any questions?"

Ansley shook her head. As the nurse exited, she did as she was told and prepared for the test.

Dr. Fadoju reentered the room, and pulled her tray of instruments closer to Ansley. "I'm about to insert the speculum, you'll feel a slight discomfort," Dr. Fadoju informed her.

Ansley wished she were under anesthesia, she didn't want to have to think and remember why she was here in the first place.

Hours later, she was still rubbing her lower abdomen. The discomfort she felt was stronger than what her menstrual cramps felt like. Then there was the shame of it all, it was all a lot to deal with in one day. Ryan had been supportive, he offered to drive her home but she didn't want to inconvenience him any further. Of course he didn't mind, but she told him that she would call him later and sent him home.

Now she sat in her car, parked outside of Simeon's home, trying to muster up the strength to put on a brave face. This was one secret that she didn't plan to share with her girlfriends.

Her phone began to vibrate.

Ansley glanced down to see Simeon's face on the screen. She wiped away her tears and answered, "Hey lady. I just pulled up."

She disconnected the call and looked up to see both of her friends standing in front of the house watching her, concern etched across their faces.

Ansley burst into tears. *So much for trying to fake it.*

Lanae was the first to speak once they got Ansley inside of the house. "Simeon and I are going to finish getting the food together, and when you're ready, we are going to talk. No judgment, just love and understanding."

Wiping her face with the back of her hands, Ansley walked across the room to the oversized recliner, and sat down.

Simeon went back to the kitchen to brew a pot of herbal tea. While Lanae fixed Ansley something to eat.

"Ansley, Simeon made that delicious gumbo you love. Here, why don't you try to eat some?"

She sat up straight and took a few small bites of the soup because she knew her friends wouldn't be satisfied until she put something in her stomach. Ansley took a sip of the tea and cleared her throat. "Thank you both for doing this."

Lanae lowered herself on the arm of the chair where Ansley was sitting. "I'm not sure what had you crying in the car, but we want you to know that we're here for you."

"I know that," Ansley stated. "I just wished I'd listened to Simeon and stayed as far away from Davis as I could."

"I'm confused. Did he do something else? I thought he'd finally left you alone," Simeon questioned.

"He left me alone, but not without leaving a parting gift," Ansley responded. "I have herpes." She glanced over at Simeon. "If you haven't done so, I urge you to get checked."

"I don't understand. Why are you just now finding out? Have you had symptoms?"

Ansley hugged herself. "Not that I was aware of, but you know most people have the disease and aren't aware that they have it. But I don't think that was the case for Davis, when I heard from his ex, Bree, she mentioned in her post on the site Don't Date Him Girl that he gave her a STD. I got tested after reading her post, but I was told that I was negative. So imagine my surprise when I went for a routine check and heard otherwise."

Lanae spread her hands, the words not forming right away. "What are you going to do now? Is there anything we can do?"

Ansley lifted her chin. "You can both pray for me. Because I'm going to need it once I have him served. I'm going to sue his trifling behind."

Chapter 51

Davis was pretending to read a magazine while he watched the beautiful blonde at the counter talking with the barista. She came here every morning and ordered a tall, chai tea latte and a piece of fruit. He decided that it was time he started trying women outside of his race. He didn't want to discriminate, after all, money was green regardless of who was carrying it.

They had been playing the staring game the past few times he came here. Today he would take action. This cat and mouse act was not helping his financial aspirations. He walked over to the counter to grab a napkin. Before he had a chance to speak, she flirted with him, "It's about time that you came and spoke to me. I'm Charlotte Bradley, and who might you be?"

He extended his hand to her, "Everyone calls me Monty. It's short for Montgomery."

She accepted his hand. "Monty, it's a pleasure to meet you, but my daddy told me to never trust a man that didn't give his last name."

She definitely had game. She was caressing his fingers and trying to get his guard down.

It was working.

He grinned. "You got me. It's Montgomery Davis. Promise not to Google me?" he half joked.

She squinted her eyes, assessing his statement and then chuckled.

As they continued their banter, he looked up and noticed a Hispanic guy in a steel gray suit staring him down. Annoyed, he decided to call him out. "Excuse me, can I do something for you or do you two know each other?"

The man got closer, "My bad. I couldn't help, but over hear you. Did you say that your name is Montgomery Davis?"

The beautiful blonde sat there oblivious to the way Davis began to fidget, his hands drumming the table. He started to ask the guy who the heck he was, when Charlotte interjected, "Hello—Monty... anyone home up there? Well, since the cat has his tongue, I'll answer for him. Yes, that's his name and I'm Charlotte. Who are you?"

Davis wanted to reach across the table and mush her in the face. He didn't know this person and wasn't enthused about her giving out his information.

Smirking the gentleman said, "That's what I thought you said. Cool, I'll just hand you this and be on my way," he placed the envelope in Davis's open palm and said, "Consider yourself served. Have a great rest of the afternoon," he said before walking away.

Davis was fuming. Had he not been flirting with her and paying attention to his surroundings, he wouldn't have put his name out there for this guy to corner him.

Charlotte, reached across and took the envelope from his hands. "Did he just say you had been served? Wow, what did you do?" she asked.

Snatching the envelope from her hands, he scowled at her. He opened the service, and read it to himself. His eyes widened when he realized it was Ansley filing a suit against him. Personal injury? He never hit her. He had the inclination to show up at her place and confront her, but he knew that wouldn't be smart considering that Barney Fife would be waiting and willing to call the police on him.

Davis spewed curses as he got up and stormed out of the café.

Charlotte walked out behind him and yelled, "Wait. Don't you want to give me your number?"

Chapter 52

Today was the day.

Ansley was going to have her day in court with Davis. She planned to fight and Lord willing win. After speaking with an attorney, she was advised that she did have a case and they recommended she file a personal injury tort claim against Davis. Ansley wasn't as concerned about being compensated, she knew he didn't have any money anyway. Her concern was to teach him a lesson and hold him accountable for his actions. She was too lenient with him, that was her fault, but now she wanted to take action.

All of her friends came today to support her. She smoothed out her navy pant suit as she walked toward the door. After talking with Bree, she even managed to get her to come to testify against Davis.

"Are you ready for this?" Lanae inquired.

Ansley pushed her shoulders back and turned to Lanae. "I'm pumped to be honest with you. This makes me feel in control of the situation. When I first got that call, I felt weak and hopeless but this lets me take back some power. Whether I win or lose, this moment is—major for me and who I've become as woman."

"Go head then. That's what I'm talking about. God's got you on this one honey. He takes care of his kids."

"Amen to that," Ryan said. "Okay, baby girl, let's go ahead and get inside. Besides, Davis keeps eyeing you and

I'm two-seconds from introducing myself."

She patted him on the back. "Stand down Kevin Costner, I don't need a body guard today. I don't want anything to keep him from hearing the judge fine his behind."

Ansley turned to say something to Simeon, but she was no longer standing with them. Before Ansley could ask if anyone saw where she went, she heard her friend's voice.

"Drugs? Gunrunning? STDs? How do you sleep at night? Nothing and no one matters to you—you don't care about anyone but yourself. You date women, sleep with them, steal from them, and then they are disposable to you. You're a loser. You deserve whatever punishment you have coming to you."

"That's enough. Please exit to the right, ma'am," one of the deputies interjected.

Davis looked at his attorney and burst into laughter. "Don't you think you're just a little jealous, Simeon? You practically threw yourself at me, but I didn't want you. You even tried to seduce me after your girl and I were dating. You think men just fall over themselves for you, but you're not as attractive as you might think. You're nothing special. Your father doesn't even like you. You're pathetic."

"What did you just say?" Simeon hissed. "Look at me and tell me that to my face."

"Come on Davis, that's enough," his attorney, Grant Marshall stated, trying to push Davis toward the courtroom.

Davis shook his head in disgust. "Look at you— just pitiful. I've met crack heads with more pride than you. Go take your meds and get out my face? You unstable heifer."

With a quickness, Simeon grabbed the ink pen from Grant's front coat pocket, and plunged it into the side of

Davis's neck, as she pushed him down to the floor, she slapped his face over and over.

Grant reacted by grabbing Simeon from behind.

The deputies followed, struggling to restrain her.

Simeon looked up to see Ansley, Lanae, and Ryan looking at her in complete shock. "What's happening…get off of me. What is your problem? What happened?"

"Ma'am, you're under arrest," the police officer said. "You have the right to remain silent. Anything you say or do may be used against you in a court of law…"

"I didn't do anything. What's going on? Ansley… Ansley… call my brother… what's going—oh my gosh."

Ansley glanced around in disbelief, her mind racing.

"Ansley, tell them… tell them it wasn't me," Simeon pleaded.

Everything was in slow motion at that moment. She saw the District Attorney holding Bree, attempting to calm her down. Lanae was staring at the scene before her in disbelief.

Ansley allowed the darkness to overtake her.

Epilogue

Simeon sat in a holding cell, awaiting her bail hearing. After she attacked Davis, she was booked, photographed, and fingerprinted. All of her belongings, along with her blood-stained clothes, were now the temporary property of the State of Georgia. The first phone call she made was to her brother, Richard. The sound of his tears pierced her heart. Of all the people that mattered to her, her brother was number one on her list and she never wanted to hurt him.

When it was time, she was escorted into the courtroom.

Tears streamed down her face as her gaze landed on her brother. He winked at her, showing his support. Beside him sat her father, Samuel Harris. He didn't try to hide his disappointment, but that's what Simeon expected out of him. Even when she was on her best behavior, he was never there to offer a kind word. She was an embarrassment to him, once again—she could never make him proud.

Ansley was there along with Ryan and Lanae. Simeon couldn't believe how supportive Lanae had been. She just knew that Lanae would judge her, but it had been the opposite. Simeon was never strong in faith, but if she ever needed God in her life—she hoped He would have mercy on her now.

"Ms. Harris, do you understand the charges against you?" the judge asked.

"I do, your Honor," Simeon responded.

"Do you have an attorney available to you?"

"I do, your Honor."

Her attorney requested that she be released to her family and under doctor's care to get her medication and counseling for her bipolar disorder.

"Do the People object to this request?"

"The People do not have any reservations about this request."

"I'll allow it. Bail is set at $100,000 and trial will be set for 350 calendar days from today. Court is adjourned."

As Simeon turned around to face her friends and family, she sighed heavily when she saw her father vanish into the hallway.

Richard pulled her close and whispered in her ear. "You know how he is, Simeon. Don't let that get to you. Right now, you just need to think about your future."

"Easier said than done, Richie. I just wish he would speak to me," Simeon revealed.

"You have a long journey ahead of you, but you don't have to walk it alone."

"That's right. I'm here for you too, and will be here for you," Ansley said as she joined them.

"Yes, we will," Lanae stated.

Simeon burst into tears. For all of the rude things she had said to Lanae, and the pain that she had brought into Ansley's life—there she stood here by her side. The road ahead would not be easy, but she hoped that she would be able to make it out of this a better person. Only time would tell what lay ahead for her.

* * *

One year later....

Ansley couldn't believe a year had gone by since Simeon attacked Davis. Sometimes when she closed her eyes, the scene would replay in her head without warning. Simeon's father retained The Fairell Firm, to represent Simeon when she went to trial. They were among the best attorneys in Atlanta. Ansley knew a few colleagues who used their services and they recommended them to all of their friends and family.

Out of everything that Simeon and Ansley had gone through together, neither ever thought they would add a murder trial to that list.

She couldn't believe that Simeon had stopped taking her medication months before the incident. It explained so much about the sporadic behavior Simeon had been exhibiting. Then with Davis toying with her emotions—it turned out to be a deadly trigger.

If only she would have shared what she was going through, Ansley could have been there to help her through the dark times.

They would soon know Simeon's fate, and Ansley hoped if given a second chance, Simeon would get the help she needed before allowing herself to get out of control again.

Ansley had become more accepting of her situation, but when it came to other people knowing about her status, she was always worried what they would say about her.

Ansley was finishing her review of an article she wrote on bipolar disorder. She wanted to get it over to the copy editor before the weekend. Just as she was logging off of the computer, her phone rang. Her heart swelled when she saw that it as Ryan calling.

"Hey baby," she greeted. "I was just about to leave to meet you at the restaurant. What's up?"

"I'm glad I caught you before you left then because I need to stop by my place for a minute. Do you mind meeting me there and then we can ride together?" he asked.

"No, that's fine. Actually, that would be perfect. I have a change of clothes in the car and want to freshen up anyway," she replied.

"Sounds good, babe. See you in a little bit."

Thirty minutes later, Ansley was pulling her car into the driveway of Ryan's ranch-style home. She was enamored with his place. When he told her that he was in the market to purchase a home, she introduced him to the agent that helped her purchase her condo.

Before she could even knock, Ryan opened the door. "It took you long enough, slow poke."

"Oh hush," she said. "After submitting my article, I got caught up talking to the copy editor ."

"I put a towel and washcloth in the guest bathroom. Feel free to go ahead and freshen up."

"Thank you, babe. I promise not to take long."

"Take all the time you need," he said before walking into the living room.

As Ansley walked up the stairs, she could not help but think of the feminine flourishes she would add to this place. The walls could use a pop of color—maybe a few pieces of art or family photos.

She laughed out loud when she saw that he had left the buzzer to the Taboo game in the bathroom. Just like a man to have stuff all over the house.

Once Ansley got out of the shower, she was going to put a challenge on the table. She had not played Taboo in a long time. It was about to go down.

Ansley walked down the stairs fifteen minutes later to find Ryan asleep on the sofa.

She understood his pain because she was tired, too. It had been a long, but productive day. Ansley took the throw from the back of the sofa and laid it across Ryan.

Walking into the kitchen, she picked up one of the take-out menus and ordered Sesame chicken for Ryan and General Tso's chicken for her. After finalizing the order, Ansley walked back upstairs and grabbed some comfortable clothes out of Ryan's dresser drawer.

She put on what she knew was his favorite collegiate t-shirt and a pair of his boxers.

Ryan was awake when she returned downstairs.

"Is that what you're wearing to dinner?" he asked, while stretching out his body.

"You were sleeping so I ordered Chinese food. You don't have to change, but you do have to play me in a round of Taboo."

"Taboo, what made you want to play that?" he asked with a goofy grin on his face.

"Well, someone apparently likes to take the buzzer with him to the bathroom. I don't even want to know why it was in there," she said turning up her nose. "But it was laying on the sink, and I brought it back downstairs so I can show you how a champ does it."

Ryan broke into a grin. "Is that right? Go ahead, miss mouth all-mighty, grab the box from the top of the closet, and set it up on the table." He watched her as she walked to the hall closet to get the game out.

Taking the box over to the kitchen table, Ansley opened the lid and stood there in shock. In the spot where the buzzer should go was a ring box. She turned to look at Ryan and he was down on one knee.

"There's not a day that goes by that I don't thank God for bringing you back into my life. When we were younger, I thought I was doing the right thing by letting you spread your wings, but I should have fought harder to make you stay. I never want to go another day without seeing your face. I had you help me pick out this home because I wanted you to choose where we would live. You have always had my heart and there is no one else that I would rather share my life with. You are my other half. Ansley Wright, I am certain that I'm meant to be your husband and you are meant to be my wife. Will you marry me?"

She opened the box and saw the engagement ring that he had given her in college. He added more diamonds to the ring, but she could tell it was her original ring. Her heart overflowed with joy. Ryan took the ring and placed it on her finger. She looked into his eyes. "Of course, I'll marry you. There's no one else that I would rather devote my heart to than you."

He stood and pulled her into him, giving her one of those Hollywood kisses. "Ansley Bennett, I like the sound of that," he said, lifting her up off the ground.

"Wait a minute, wait a minute—this was your plan all along? The Taboo buzzer in the bathroom and the ring sitting in the box?"

"Ding, ding! One point for you, my love," he said with a laugh. "I knew once you saw that buzzer you were going to challenge me to a game."

"I'm glad I won," she said kissing him on the lips.

"Actually baby, this was a tie. There were definitely no losers in this game," he said.

Ansley agreed. Everything was coming full circle for her—life was good.

CPSIA information can be obtained
at www.ICGtesting.com
Printed in the USA
LVHW01s2307131117
556123LV00001B/191/P